# SHE HAD TO HAVE GAS

# SHE HAD TO HAVE GAS

by

## Rupert Penny

RAMBLE HOUSE

ISBN 13: 978-1-60543-383-7

ISBN 10: 1-60543-383-7


Cover Art: Gavin L. O'Keefe
Preparation: Fender Tucker

# SHE HAD TO HAVE GAS

# I

ON THURSDAY OCTOBER 20TH, AT 6.45 P.M., Mrs. Agatha Topley was standing on the corner of Marine Drive, Craybourne, waiting for her bus. It was a wet evening, and she perceived without surprise that her umbrella had yet another hole in it: she could half feel and half hear the filtered raindrops intermittently landing on her black straw hat.

"I really must get it mended' she thought. 'Really must. Three and sixpence at Baldwins', round by the buck of the hippodrome.'

Yet she knew perfectly well that without the least difficulty she could find half a dozen ways of spending the three and sixpence. The soles of her second-best pair of winter shoes badly needed attention, the insurance man would be round again on the twenty-fifth of the month, she was behind with her contributions to the Christmas Club, and she wanted if possible to get in a quarter of a ton of coal before the price went up. She already had nearly ten shillings saved towards that; but how long would it remain intact, she wondered? How long before she was compelled to use it for something else?

"Money's tight, that's what,' she muttered inwardly. 'And all along of that dratted girl. I could just do with the three pound she owes me, that I could. I wish I knew what to do. I daren't hardly ask Alf to have a word with her—she'd be out of the house at the very sight of a policeman on the doorstep, I'll be bound, and me not a penny the better off. I wish I knew what to do.'

At that moment her bus came in sight, and for a spell she gave up worrying at the problem which had been tormenting her the last few weeks; but all the way home it remained just below the surface of her mind, ready to inflict itself upon her at the slightest opportunity.

Mrs. Topley's trouble was concerned with her lodger, Alice Carter: at least, that was the name she gave, though doubts were possible about its correctness. Alice was a well-built girl of about twenty-four, fair-haired, blue-eyed, and pretty in a rather dissipated careless sort of way. Mrs. Topley had summed her up almost instantly as no lady, and had never seen cause to take back her judgement.

The girl had rung the bell of 14 Weatherall Road about midday on Wednesday August 31st, and after due bargaining had secured the use of Mrs. Topley's first-floor front for twenty-seven shillings and sixpence a week, breakfast and one bath included as well as electric light.

"And cheap at the price, Miss," Alice had been told more than once since then. "Why, I could have asked thirty-five, it being in the season. Craybourne's a growing town, you know. In ten years it'll be one of the selectest watering-places on the south coast."

But Alice Carter had not been impressed.

"Then why didn't you ask thirty-five?" she had queried in her high and somewhat common voice; and Mrs. Topley had preferred to say no more. The full answer would have taken too long. It would have needed to include the odd fact that, somehow, Craybourne in her lifetime had always been just about ten years short of popularity; that Weatherall Road was a good three-quarters of a mile from the sea by any conceivable route; and that the only service it could offer was the making of beds and the not very skilful cooking of bacon and beef sausages.

In short, as she well knew, Mrs. Topley was never cut out for a seaside landlady, in Craybourne or anywhere else. She had too much softness in her nature; her bark was mostly an apologetic cough, and her bite almost nonexistent. In her husband's day she had overlooked her own deficiencies: he possessed enough force of character for half a dozen, and she had been content to sit back and allow him to run her life for her in his spare time. But the wing of a lorry caught him just below the left hip one wet evening two years ago, and sent him slithering helplessly under a corporation tram: one minute he had been crossing the road within reach of her hand, and the next he was a huddle of blood and rags, unfamiliar, obscene, not to be approached without loathing.

From various sources she received close on four hundred pounds in compensation, and of this she still had almost a third left, but it had taken her eighteen months to understand that when it was gone she would be in line for the workhouse unless she could shift for herself. In a panic she set about preparing for the only occupation which seemed at all suitable—that of running a small boarding-house in the holiday season. Unfortunately, visitors to Craybourne had been fewer this year, which explained her price of twenty-seven shillings and sixpence to Alice Carter, her first lodger.

She believed to begin with that her venture would be a success. The girl gave no trouble, paid her rent promptly the following Wednesday, was economical with the electric light, and rarely stayed out after half past ten at night. In that initial week her behaviour was exemplary, even if she remained something of a mystery. It occurred to Mrs. Topley, cleaning the steps one morning, that she knew scarcely anything about her lodger except what she had managed to pick up casually.

The girl was no holiday-maker—that was certain. She neither looked nor acted the part. Young women on holiday with any pretentions to beauty do not spend a great part of the morning pottering about their bedrooms their dressing-gowns and slippers, brewing innumerable pots of tea on the ring attached to the gas-fire and reading twopenny magazines. Yet it was equally clear to Mrs. Topley that Alice Carter did not belong to Craybourne. She had admitted one day that she knew nobody in the neighbourhood, and considered the town a dreary hole; but she said nothing about going, for which the older woman—then—had been grateful.

As a general rule Alice talked very little, especially about her own affairs, so Mrs. Topley got no help there. In the end, to satisfy her curiosity, she invented the theory that the girl was a pro, probably in the chorus; and that for some reason at present unknown she was 'resting'. It was too unsatisfactory to be at all credible for more than twenty-four hours, however. Chorus girls out of a job spend at least part of their time in looking for a new one; unless they are in poor health, which Alice certainly was not. Again, no right-minded person would choose Craybourne for such a purpose: particularly one who showed openly that she thought little or nothing of the place. It beat Mrs. Topley altogether; but after all, she consoled herself, it was really none of her business, and money is money.

It was in the second week of her lodger's stay that things began to go wrong. Alice Carter's cousin turned up, and a more suspicious-looking man she had never seen. Not that he was anything but polite to her, in a gruff off-handed way; but she always felt that he was ready to snarl if she gave him the excuse. Perhaps it was that which made her from the beginning acquiesce in his behaviour: bottling himself up with the girl in her room for hours on end, doing heaven only knew what, and never so much as a word to ask if she minded. Or perhaps it was the fear that by opening her mouth she might lose twenty-seven and six a week.

He was a short stocky man, habitually dressed in a long blue trench coat tightly buttoned at the neck, a check cap, and dark-green horn-rimmed spectacles; he rode a motor-cycle, which he left outside the house, and his movements were somehow stealthy. He never stood under the light in the hall, where a respectable person could get a look at him, and if he were asked a question—"A nice day, isn't it?" or "Can you oblige me with the time before you go?"—he was apt to answer with his head half turned away.

He had a temper, too: several times Mrs. Topley heard his voice raised as she passed near the first-floor front on her way to the bathroom, and occasionally she detected Alice's shriller retort. She never managed to catch any distinguishable words, though: the house was too well built for that. At other times there would be silence, which provoked her curiosity even more. She was convinced that the man in the blue coat was no more Alice Carter's cousin than he was a prince in disguise. She was similarly convinced that her lodger's room was the scene of goings-on which, if known locally, would soon lower the reputation of 14 Weatherall Road. Yet what could she do, she had asked herself? Complain, and risk losing her only source of income? Turn a blind eye, and let herself be patently put upon? Or climb a chair, and look through the glass partition between the first-floor front and the passage to the bathroom?

That this could be done she had felt sure. In the course of years the frosted paper on the glass had peeled away in places, and although the bed was out of sight directly underneath, there might still be sufficient evidence in the way of discarded clothes or bare legs. The girl was untidy enough with her things, heaven knew. But both times that she allowed inquisitiveness to triumph over principle she was unlucky. On each occasion the man had his back to her; his cap and spectacles were off, but not his coat. Once the two of them were playing cards, and once chatting by the fire, and it was a real mercy she hadn't been seen, so quickly did the girl glance up. In fact, she half believed in her heart that Alice *had* noticed, only nothing was ever said. She would have tried the key-hole too, but that she had heard somewhere of a woman permanently blinded as the result of such an activity. The suspicious inmate of the room in question had loaded a fountain-pen filler with pepper, and discharged it neatly at an opportune moment.

She finally resolved to do nothing unless her hand were forced, whether by outside gossip or by a too blatant infringement of her rights as the lady of the house. This was an easy decision as far as the first part went, for, strictly speaking, Mrs. Topley had no immediate neighbours. No. 14 stood between a small tin chapel which had been gutted by fire in 1931 and left derelict, and a builders' yard, beyond which was the street corner; and opposite was only the brick wall which hid the gas-works. In fact, the house was oddly out of place: it belonged at the other end of the road, a good fifty yards away. She had vaguely considered the idea of selling it, but had been reluctant to approach the agents. It had belonged to her husband's father, and she felt that nowhere else could be a real home to her, after thirty-one years. She knew every corner intimately, every creak on the stairs, every cracked window-pane. The mottled linoleum on the hall floor she had bought the year the war ended, and she had a great affection for its worn and shiny homeliness. It would never fit in another house, nor the blue flowered carpet in the parlour; no other gas-stove would ever provide the same intensely individual service as the one in the scullery; and what bath, even if free from pits in the enamel, would ever feel the same at ten o'clock on a Saturday night? If she had to take in lodgers in order to exist, she would exact her own price from life, and insist on doing it in the home she knew and loved. The name of Alice Carter's visitor was Ellis, and he first came to Mrs. Topley's on the afternoon of Saturday September 10th. The following Wednesday the girl was half a crown short with her rent, but promised to make up the deficiency the week after. When the day came she did in fact do so, but at the same time complained that she was tired of straining her eyes with a 40-watt bulb, and it was bad for her cousin's eyes too, which were naturally weak, as Mrs. Topley might very well have guessed for herself, and would she please obtain one of a higher power without delay? On September 28th Alice Carter made no attempt to pay anything, but after a tactful reminder produced fifteen shillings the next morning. From then onwards her landlady began to feel uncomfortable as the middle of the week drew near. One Wednesday it would be "I'm sorry, but you'll have to let me owe you ten bob this week. My sister's just had another baby, and I had to help her." The next week the excuse differed but the result was the same, and subsequently worse, and at midday on October 19th Alice Carter's debt to her landlady stood at three pounds four shillings.

This state of affairs, whether reasonably or not, Mrs. Topley attributed at least in part to the man Ellis. Until his appearance there had been no trouble over the rent: after he came, there seemed to her to have been little else. And, when she began to reckon things up, she realized that she knew even less about him than about the girl: not as much as his Christian name. Where he lived, or where he worked, or what was in truth the precise nature of his relation to her lodger, she had no notion.

His visits were irregular, and might last any time between twenty minutes and two or three hours, though he hardly ever stayed after six o'clock in the evening. Sometimes the girl went off with him, perched on the end of his motor-cycle and seeming not to care how much of her well-turned legs she showed the world: sometimes he departed alone. His manner of arrival and his appearance were always the same, though. He rode up in the long blue coat and the check cap, below which he peered through the tinted glasses which masked his face, he accelerated the engine of his machine before switching it off, he invariably came when Alice Carter was indoors, and he always rang the bell smartly three times, ting-ting-ting. At this signal the girl would issue from her bedroom so speedily that she might have been waiting up there poised, and she would come clattering down the stairs to let the man in. As if, Mrs. Topley had often thought bitterly, she herself had no say about who might and who might not traverse her threadbare doormat.

The day before yesterday, Tuesday, he had called in the middle of the afternoon to take the girl out, and he had called again today, just after 2.00. Alice Carter had spent the morning in bed with a headache: yet the common little thing hadn't scrupled to open the front door to him in her dressing-gown and slippers. Mrs. Topley, watching from a chink in the dining-room hinge, had somehow resented deeply the sight of her lodger so assuredly crossing her own hall like that. A decent girl, she thought, would have blushed scarlet to be seen by anyone, man, woman or child, cousin or no cousin, with a hole in the seam of her shiny stocking-calf twice the size of an egg, and little underneath her gaping gown but a slip which barely hid her gaudy garters. Admittedly she had pulled the wrap round her tight before actually opening the door, and kept it so while re-crossing the hall, but small enough credit that was to her. Who could tell what happened to it in the privacy of the room upstairs? Or to the green petticoat?

'No breeding,' she had informed herself. 'No wonder she don't pay her rent.'

Mrs. Topley had felt indecisively uncomfortable about leaving them together like that. In a way it seemed to her that by going put she would be condoning not only their probable misbehaviour, but also their shabby financial treatment of herself. Yet every Thursday afternoon without fail she went to visit the widow of her husband's step-brother, an old woman of seventy-nine who lived alone at the other end of the town and was pitiably glad of someone to talk to for a couple of hours a week. She had been going since long before Arthur died, and it was hard for her to break established habits.

She chose, after consideration, to go; but—with unusual initiative—to make some sort of gesture first. Accordingly she got out her pad and wrote a short letter.

*Dear Mr. Ellis* she said, *I am not the one to make trouble, far from it, but as a friend of Miss Carter my lodger perhaps you will be good enough to have a word with her about the back rent she owes me, three pounds four shillings it is, and has been acumulating almost since your first visit to her here. Yrs faithfully, Agatha Topley.*

"And if that does no good,' she told herself, feeling extraordinarily courageous as she licked the flap of the envelope, 'then I really will fetch Alf round to see if he can't frighten her or something.'

For she had always that card up her sleeve, if she dared play it. Alf Turner was station-sergeant in the local police-force, and he had been her husband's best friend. Secretly she had never thought much of him in the way of brains, but there was no denying that he had the majestic presence and ponderous tread of the old-style policeman, and also the thick drooping moustache. She felt sure that to oblige her he would come round in uniform one evening instead of in plain clothes; and if that didn't scare Alice Carter into settling her just debts, then Mrs. Topley would have to sacrifice the money and bundle the girl out. Casually she had mentioned Alf's existence several times already, though apparently without rousing her lodger's interest: there were none so slow to take a hint as them that didn't want to. But things might not come to that; in fact, it hardly seemed possible that they could. Her note to Ellis would settle matters, and no hard words on either side.

So, at any rate, she had viewed things for the next few hours; but now, getting out of the bus and manipulating her sodden umbrella for the short walk home, she began to be the prey of doubts. Suppose she entered the house, to be met by defiance? Or suppose she found the place deserted? She could scarcely tell which she would prefer, but in her present mood either seemed more likely than what she would choose for herself if she had the power: a contrite Alice Carter, properly dressed, waiting at the head of the stairs with an envelope containing not only the three pounds four, but a month's rent in advance as well.

'Pah!' said Mrs. Topley, not quite under her breath. 'Daydreaming again! Must be Aunt Ada's port-wine—I shouldn't have taken the third glass. Yet real nice port-wine it is—you can tell she was a lady when she was young. Oh dear, I do hope things will be all right, but I've a funny feeling they won't be—a funny sort of a feeling . . .'

At all events, the motor-cycle was no longer there, but her lodger was presumably still in her room, since light could be seen through the drawn blinds. And, somewhere, was the sound of music: as if, thought Mrs. Topley, the municipal orchestra were playing out of doors two streets away. She mounted the steps, put down her umbrella, shook it, and then fumbled for her key: the time was scarcely five minutes past seven when she entered the cold stuffy hall of 14 Weatherall Road.

Immediately she became aware that the music had grown louder: that it was not even one street away, but here in her own house, abnormally loud and yet in some way muffled, or perhaps distorted. It came from upstairs, from somewhere among the shadows of the first landing, and she grasped without hesitation what had happened. Alice Carter, the brazen little slut, had borrowed her battery wireless set without permission from the corner table in the dining-room; the set her husband had given her only three weeks before he met his tragic death under the corporation tram. Mrs. Topley, standing listening in the hall, realized suddenly that the hand which held her wet umbrella shook: that she had lost her temper for the first time since the butcher's boy had been unexpectedly sick at the back door last Christmas Eve.

"The hussy!" she said aloud in a sharp malevolent hiss. "The wicked little hussy—I'll teach her!"

Towards the stairs she went, her shoes clicking purposefully on the worn linoleum; up to the landing she marched with the step of an executioner, turned to the right, and a second later was facing the stout brown door of the first-floor front.

"Stop it!" she cried. "How dare you! How *dare* you!"

But the noise persisted.

She banged upon the door with her umbrella till a large flake of paint fell off; she tried the handle furiously, and found as she had expected that it was locked; and still the din went on inside, a blatant medley of strings and wind and brass, an impertinent cacophony.

It was beyond bearing, and she screwed up her eyes a little and shut her mouth tight. It was too much. She would trap the reptile somehow—push chairs against the door if need be and then fetch Alfred Turner, and have her taken away and whipped.

And then, with her mouth firmly closed, she drew in a deep breath through her nose: and her fury faded like a dream. She was left icy cold down her back, as if she had been stripped naked by an explosion, and as panic-stricken. She had smelt gas.

There was no possibility of mistaking it, once noticed. The landing was poisoned, and of the air within the room she dared not think. As the realization of what must have happened came to her she stood quite still, trying to control her wits, fighting the impulse to run away—no matter where, provided she escaped the nauseating smell and the shrill defiant death-music.

To her credit, common sense defeated her incipient terror, and without needing to ponder details she knew what she must do: fetch the chair from the bathroom, look through the glass partition again, and find out if the girl were still alive. If so, then at all costs the door must be broken down at once and the poor wretch rescued: if not, then she must pursue her original intention of fetching the police, though now for a grimly different reason.

She went to get the chair, noting a second time as she hurried down the passage that the light was on inside the room. Back again with her burden, she placed it against the wall, got on to the seat, put her fingertips on the grimy ledge below the glass, and with difficulty managed to raise her eyes an inch or two higher. Then she screamed.

Many times in the days that followed was Mrs. Topley compelled to relate exactly what it was she had seen through the decaying paper pattern, but her story never varied in essentials. From where she stood only the far half of the room came within her vision: in the middle of the rose-decked wall facing her was the gas-fire, and In front of it a blanketed still form. Of the girl's body

only the legs were visible, apart from the general outline: first
there was the striped edge of the blanket, then a bit of the pink
dressing-gown, then a rumple of green which was her petticoat,
and then her shapely legs drawn up. From their position it was
clear that Alice lay on her right side, her back obliquely towards
the bed, and to Mrs. Topley it was equally clear that the girl had
not been out in her absence, since she was wearing the same gaudy
garters and the same old blue slippers, and the upper leg was enclosed in the same torn stocking.

There could be no doubt that the figure in the blanket was void
of life. She was certain of that by the absolute absence of any motion such as breathing would cause, and the presence of an evil-
looking curve of red rubber tubing that disappeared into the blanket by the head. That was how the poor thing had done it: turned
herself from living flesh into a hooded suicide, an object to be
peered at through torn paper and dirty glass; into a mere stiff pair
of legs which were oblivious alike of the watching eyes and the
blaring wireless set.

Mrs. Topley screamed, and screamed again, deliberately: it
somehow relieved her stomach to do so. Then she got trembling
off the chair and dashed unsteadily down the stairs, out of the
house with a slam of the door, and wildly along the rain-swept
pavement towards the police-station two hundred yards away in
Blenheim Street. She must see Alf Turner: she must tell him.

It was still pelting, and she found it hard to keen her footing.
She saw no one until, her breath gone and her heart beating fit to
crack, she blundered through the swing door into the arms of a
uniformed figure coming out of the charge room.

A full two minutes passed before she could speak coherently.
Then, in a torrent of words, she reported her discovery. Her late
husband's friend listened with his normal air of bovine compla-
cency, but thereafter surprised her by the briskness of his orders.
Within five minutes more she was being conveyed back to I4
Weatherall Road in a police car, accompanied by two constables
and another sergeant.

To her mind the odour on the landing was perhaps just the least
bit worse, but everything else seemed the same: the door locked,
the wireless strident, the light still on, the bathroom chair where
she had left it. The sergeant looked at the latter, tried the creaking
seat with his hand, marvelled that it had stood even an old
woman's weight, and sent its owner below. Then he and his com-
panions broke open the door, their damped handkerchiefs tied

round their mouths. Five minutes later the three of them marched importantly downstairs again frowning. Full of gas the room might be, they allowed, reluctantly, or undoubtedly had been before they opened the window to let it out, but as for a body, dead or otherwise, perhaps Mrs. Topley would explain what she meant by playing practical jokes on the police at her time of life?

She went up with them, in tears, when it was deemed safe, and saw for herself that there was indeed no body, nor any rubber tubing, nor any sign of Alice Carter's suitcase or clothes or personal possessions. The blanket was back on the bed, jumbled in a heap, one corner pressed down by the wireless set which the sergeant had switched off. In spite of the gaping window, through which could be seen thin sheets of silver rain, there still lingered about the room the unmistakable smell of coal-gas. All these things Mrs. Topley perceived in duff stupefaction, not ceasing to weep: less because Alice Carter had committed suicide, and then impossibly vanished, as because the policemen so plainly disbelieved her when she gave them her solemn oath that just after five past seven there had been a blanketed body visible through the glass partition.

# II

e xtracts from the report by Inspector Creevy to Colonel John Bagshaw, M.C., O.B.E., Chief-constable of the local police-force: compiled in the early hours of Friday October 21st, and presented at 10.30 A.M.)

*14 Weatherall Road.*

The single-fronted red-brick house is situated between Messrs Ribleys' builders' yard on the west side and a derelict chapel on the east side, and has ten rooms. It faces the gas-works. It is the property of the resident, Mrs. Agatha Topley, widow of the late Arthur Topley, a clerk employed by the town council, and extends to three storeys, the top one not being in use. The first floor contains four rooms, namely: Mrs. Topley's bedroom, a furnished spare room, a bathroom-lavatory, and the large bed-sitting-room which was rented by the deceased, Miss Alice Carter (see below) for twenty-seven shillings and sixpence a week, breakfast included. Mrs. Topley states that this was the room formerly occupied by her husband and herself, but that since his accidental death two years ago she has preferred to use a smaller back one, where she would not be so continually reminded of her loss.

The house is supplied with gas, there being fittings in every room, in the hall, and on the landings. All these are workable, but mostly not used except when the local electric service fails. The house was wired for current (220v. A.C.) in 1928, at the same time as the chapel next door. Mrs. Topley rents two gas-fires from the supplying company. One is in the dining-room downstairs, and the other in the first-floor front room. The latter has also its own gas-meter, installed in May of this year for the convenience of anticipated occupants.

*Mrs. Agatha Topley.*

As already noted, above is a widow: her age is 61, and she has no surviving children. Her late husband . . . was an intimate personal friend of Station-sergeant Turner. In the neighbourhood Mrs.

Topley has the reputation of being a quiet respectable woman, inclined to be easy-going and perhaps a little lacking in self-reliance. She owes no money locally except for 3/6 to a Christmas Club, and the tradesmen with whom she deals speak well of her. She has fewer friends than might be expected, which may be due to her somewhat negative character. Every Thursday afternoon for the last five and a half years, however, she has visited Mrs. Ada Wright, the widow of her late husband's step-brother, except when prevented by illness, which has not happened this year. She leaves 14 Weatherall Road soon after half past three, catches the 3.40 bus from the corner of Arundel Street and Causeway Gardens, and takes a twopenny fare to Marine Drive, at the other end of the town. With equal punctuality she returns by the 6.48 bus from Marine Drive, reaching Arundel Street at 7.00. She is home between four and five minutes past seven, unless the bus has been delayed.

Until Alice Carter's arrival (see below) Mrs. Topley lived entirely alone since her husband's death, keeping no servant, and she says that it would be most unusual for anyone to call on her on a Thursday evening before 8.00, all her friends and acquaintances being aware of her regular outing to visit Mrs. Wright.

*Miss Alice Carter.*

The only information at present available about this young woman is that supplied by Mrs. Topley. Her age is given as about 23 or 24, and her height approximately 5 ft 4 ins. She is a blonde, possibly natural, of average build with a good figure, and is described as being pretty in a rather hard way. Her teeth are stated to be in apparently excellent condition, and her hands fairly well kept, except that she had a habit of biting her thumb-nails. Mrs. Topley does not remember noticing what her bare feet were like. Her voice was inclined to be high-pitched and she spoke with what was taken for a London accent.

She first appeared at 14 Weatherall Road about midday on Wednesday August 31st last, and inquired about the card in the front downstairs window advertising apartments to let. The two parties soon came to the terms previously mentioned, the rent being payable in arrears. Alice Carter was vague about the length of her stay, but said it would not be shorter than a fortnight, and might be prolonged. Mrs. Topley concluded that the girl was not on holiday. Not being used to matters of business, she omitted to raise the question of notice to terminate the tenancy, and also to secure any payment in advance.

Apparently Alice Carter was a model lodger for the first two weeks or so, apart from considerable and habitual untidiness, but then began to fall behind with her rent. . . . By October 19th she was in debt to the extent of £3.4.0, having in fact over a period of four weeks paid only £2.6.0 out of £5.10.0. Various explanations of the weekly deficiencies were offered, none very convincing . . .

In Mrs. Topley's opinion Alice Carter was definitely not a native of Craybourne or district, and in all probability a Londoner. She spoke little of herself, but mentioned Piccadilly and the Strand on two separate occasions, and Kennington Oval once. She also stated (see excuse for non-payment preceding) that she had a sister, residence unknown, who had recently had a baby. Whenever she was asked questions concerning her plans or past, however indirectly, she became evasive. There may or may not be some truth in Mrs. Topley's idea that the girl was at one time on the stage. There was no indication that she was married, but a certain amount of negative evidence to show that her moral character was not wholly above suspicion (see below).

On Saturday September 10th Alice Carter was visited by a man who called himself Ellis, and was alleged to be the girl's cousin . . . Mrs. Topley never remembers seeing him without his coat, cap, and coloured spectacles, and doubts if she would recognize him differently dressed, though she is of the opinion that she might possible know his voice again. His age seemed to be about 35, and he always arrived by motor-cycle, make and index no. unknown. He came thereafter at irregular intervals, and on subsequent occasions was invariably admitted by Alice Carter herself. When they were both in the house they shut themselves in the girl's room, and Mrs. Topley believes they quarrelled violently at times. She is not sure if they locked the door. She was never asked to supply food apart from breakfast, or service but for bed-making, and so had no cause to disturb them.

During the whole of Alice Carter's stay she received only one letter, in the first week, post-mark indecipherable, handwriting small, and had no other callers but the man Ellis.

Mrs. Topley was asked for as complete a list as possible of her lodger's clothes and personal possessions. She recalls the following items:—

*Clothes (outer).*
1 pale-blue linen frock, white buttons, white leatherette belt, V-neck, somewhat soiled.

1 dark-green woollen frock, high neck, brown leather belt:
   cleaned while at 14 W. Rd.
1 grey flannel coat & skirt, new.
2 blouses, one ornate pink silk, one plain white.
1 woollen jumper, pillar-box red.
1 dark-grey tweed coat, fur-trimmed collar.
1 fawn raincoat, new.

*Underclothes etc.*
2 three-piece sets (vest, petticoat or slip, french knickers), one in
   white art. silk, new, one in medium green (see below).
1 pr black lace cami-knickers.
1 cotton vest, worn.
1 pr light-blue silk knickers, directoire pattern, darned.
1 pink suspender-belt.
4 (or 5) prs stockings, cheap, usual flesh colour.
1 pr multi-coloured garters.

*(Note:* It is stated that Alice Carter wore these only indoors.
   When she went out she left them hanging on the bed-post.
   The visible presence of these on the body, as seen by Mrs.
   Topley through the glass partition, makes her fancy that the
   girl did not leave the house between her own departure at
   approx 3.30 P.M. and her return shortly after 7.00. This may
   be considered open to question. Mrs. Topley last saw the girl
   alive from the dining-room doorway when she (A.C.) went
   across the hall to let in Ellis about 2.00 P.M. She was then
   wearing her dressing-gown (see below), the green petticoat
   from the three-piece set (and presumably accessories), slippers (see below), and stockings the left calf of which had a
   large hole in the back seam; also the garters. The body wore
   the same stockings.)

*Night-clothes.*
2 prs cotton mixture pyjamas, cream with red and blue edgings
   respectively.
1 pink woollen dressing-gown, cord belt, very soiled.

*Shoes etc.*
1 pr brown, court pattern, fairly new.
1 pr nigger suede, brogue pattern, worn.
1 pr dark-blue leather.

1 pr slippers, blue trimmed with white fur, very worn.

*Hats.*
1 dark-blue felt with white feather, smart.
1 brown straw, shabby.
1 close-fitting woollen cap, matching red jumper.

*Sundries.*
1 silk scarf, white with large red spots.
2 prs gloves, one brown suede, one chamois. About a dozen
   handkerchiefs, various.

*Personal belongings.*
1 stubby umbrella, dark blue, handle head of dog in white.
1 brown handbag, imitation crocodile.
1 black handbag, chromium fittings.
1 large brown fibre suitcase, expanding type.
1 smaller ditto.
1 wrist watch, gold(?) case, moiré strap.
Various toilet accessories, shoe-cleaning apparatus etc., none
   outstanding.

*Jewellery.*
2 necklaces, one coral, one small brown translucent beads (am-
   ber?).
1 large enamel ring, blue and white, clearly valueless, worn on
   middle finger of right hand.
Sundry cheap dress clips, brooches, ear-rings, etc.
1 travelling clock, brown leather case, glass cracked.
1 coloured china ornament, 8" high, figure of nude girl balancing on sundial. (A.C. said to value this: assured Mrs. Topley
   it was worth £4.10.0.)

*Investigation.*
   The enquiry into the disappearance of Alice Carter's presumably dead body from the first-floor front room of No. 14 Weatherall
Road on the evening of the 20th inst. is proceeding, but so far with
little definite result. The following theories may be considered
tenable:—
   (1) That Alice Carter committed suicide, for reasons unknown,
during a temporary absence of the man Ellis; and that he returned
(having borrowed A.C.'s keys) a moment or so after Mrs. Top-

ley's departure to notify the police. It is estimated reliably that a period of approximately nine minutes elapsed between the time she left the house (say 7.12) and the arrival of Sergeant Osgood and two constables at 7.21. In this interval Ellis must somehow have disposed of the body and all clothes etc., conveying same to some place unknown. The difficulty of carrying out such a proceeding without the most thorough preliminary preparations will be manifest. This tends to invalidate the theory in my view. It would also have been necessary for there to be very little gas in the room as a whole until *after* Ellis's departure; i.e., upon Ellis's entry Alice Carter, her head in the blanket, had absorbed only just sufficient gas to cause death. He would have shut off the supply while he collected together the clothes etc., and upon leaving finally have turned on the tap again, perhaps to delay investigation. This would presumably mean that Alice Carter was actually alive when seen by Mrs. Topley. The only convincing point in favour of suicide seems to me to be the presence of the wireless set, tuned in to a foreign station believed to be German. There have been a number of cases reported recently of suicides electing to die to music. A point of interest is that the bedroom key was found on the mantelpiece: but the one from the spare room fits the lock. The girl Carter was given a key to the front-door on the day of her arrival.

(2) That Alice Carter was murdered by Ellis after a quarrel. Possibly he stunned her, became frightened, and finished her off by gas. His subsequent actions would be as above, except that his absence while Mrs. Topley was in the house, 7.04 to 7.12 say, would almost certainly be connected with arrangements for the disposal of the body.

(3) Alice Carter was murdered by Ellis, but the murder wholly premeditated and all plans laid beforehand. Only, where was Ellis between 7.04 and 7.12?

*General remarks.*

It has not yet been possible to find anyone who had the house under even casual observation between 6.00 P.M. and the arrival of Sergeant Osgood at 7.21, but enquiries are being prosecuted. No useful lead as to the identity or whereabouts of the man Ellis has been discovered. The conjunction of non-removal of cap, buttoning of long coat to neck, and wearing of coloured spectacles, strongly suggests a disguise, in which case all we have to go on are his undisguisable physical features and the motor-cycle, possibly not his. Mrs. Topley estimates Ellis's height as 5 ft 5 ins, and says he was sturdily built. His voice was gruff and he was clean-shaven.

The body was undoubtedly removed from 14 Weatherall Road between 7.12 and 7.21 last night, together with clothes, suitcases etc. I say this after due consideration. I have twice interviewed Mrs. Topley, and am convinced not only that she honestly believes the truth of her story, but that she could not possibly have been mistaken in supposing she saw a body in the room. The legs, torn stocking, petticoat, and coloured garters rule that out. Her eyesight appears reasonably good for a woman of her age.

She denies ever having had any red rubber tubing in the house. This would seem to make it either a case of suicide, tubing procured for that purpose by Alice Carter, or of premeditated murder, tubing specially obtained by Ellis. As already mentioned, the gas supply in the room is controlled by a penny-in-the-slot meter in a cupboard. There is still between three and four pennyworth of gas paid for but not consumed.

The few fingerprints in the room have been carefully preserved or photographed. There are several sets, some superimposed on others, on the tooth-glass in the bathroom which was set apart for Alice Carter's exclusive use, and these in my opinion may safely be taken as hers. Copies of Mrs. Topley's fingerprints have been secured, and it is intended to compare them with those found in the room and on the tooth-glass. The handles of both the front and bedroom doors have been examined, but without success. All but the inside bedroom handle bear a multiplicity of irrelevant prints (e.g., Mrs. Topley's, the sergeant's, those of the two constables): but it has none. The same is true of the wireless set, which was obviously wiped clean.

Mrs. Topley does not recollect if the key-hole in the bedroom door was blocked in any way when she banged with her umbrella. She says she is practically sure that the china statuette was in its usual place on the mantel-piece above the gas-fire, or she would have noted its absence, but does not recall seeing any other of Alice Carter's personal possessions—e.g. the toilet things on the dressing-table in front of the window on the left-hand side. The far end of this would have been visible to her, but she says— understandably—that the whole of her attention was centred on the body.

To return to the removal of the latter: for want of evidence to the contrary, I am assuming that this was effected by Ellis. It seems certain that he must have used a car of some sort; the motor-cycle would be useless. Enquiries are being made about whether any person answering to his description has hired or attempted to hire a suitable vehicle recently in Craybourne or district, or alternatively whether one has been stolen.

The roadway outside No. 14 is badly illuminated. Thursday evening was dark and wet, and there were probably few pedestrians about in the vicinity. P.c. Hodson, who patrolled the road at 5.50, does not remember meeting anyone between Nos. 1 and 92 (Arundel Street and Thomas Street). It may therefore have been possible, though risky, for Ellis to have carried the body out to a waiting car unobserved: more particularly as there are no houses opposite.

*Addendum to above.*

Before her departure to visit Mrs. Wright, Mrs. Topley wrote a short note (copy appended, exact wording as far as she can recall) to the man Ellis about the rent owing to her, and put it in a prominent position on the hall table, addressed *Mr. Ellis.* She came down to the police-station half an hour ago to report this, having forgotten to do so earlier. She says that the note has gone, and she assumes that Ellis took it. Obviously Alice Carter's debt might conceivably have provided her with a motive for suicide, and it strikes me as being just within the bounds of possibility that the knowledge of her money difficulties may have afforded Ellis a reason for murdering her. For example, she was blackmailing him into providing accommodation for her; he lost his temper and killed her when he learnt that she was mis-spending his money. But (1) can a person murder another in a fit of temper by gas-poisoning? (2) What about the length of rubber tubing? Did he go straight out to get it as soon as he had read Mrs. Topley's note? Then not in Craybourne, it being early-closing day; but how many men habitually carry rubber tubing about with them?

# III

C HARLES DIGBY HARRINGTON looked worried. He sat in a favourite arm-chair before his study fire, leaning forward a little with his hands supported on his podgy knees, and he stared fiercely at his slippered feet. Then with an abrupt movement he extended his left arm, glanced at the gold watch on his wrist, and saw that the time was two o'clock all but a minute. Then he pressed the button of the bell to the right of the carved oak mantelpiece.

The next minute he spent in gazing round the small book-lined room, and, as always, he found it pleasant; not with the vague contentedness of familiarity, but with a genuinely sharp appreciation of its comforts. There were bronze chrysanthemums in a crystal vase on the oak desk, and above them a delicate water-colour study of a negro girl asleep under a tree. He had bought that in Paris ten years ago, he remembered, and had never to this day been able to discover the artist's name. The signature was illegible, and the dealer from whom he acquired it an old man with a poor memory.

His gaze passed to the radio-gramophone in the corner, and the neighbouring cabinet which housed his records: Beethoven and Bach and Mozart mostly, with a little Schubert and Brahms, and all either orchestral or instrumental. The sound of the organ reproduced badly, in his opinion, and he disliked the human voice upraised in song almost as much as he disliked what his niece Philippa called 'swing' music.

" 'Swing' indeed!" he had growled at her more than once. "People responsible for animal noises like that ought to. I'll make my next victim a swinger—you see: cut off his slimy head in the middle of his waulings. *Murder for Art's Sake*—not a bad title."

For Charles Harrington was a writer of murder mysteries, and the books and the desk and the records and the sleeping negro girl had all been earned for him by his productively imaginative pen. To date he had contrived twenty-three such works, and the plot for the twenty-fourth was in course of construction. His sales averaged thirty thousand copies per book, including the United States and editions down to half a crown, and as well there were at least five magazines of repute which would take a short story whenever he cared to offer one, and send him by return a cheque for round about forty guineas. It may readily be estimated that his income was considerable, yet as far as capital went he was not a rich man. Nine-tenths of what he earnt he spent, and got—he believed— good value for seven-tenths of it. He had a pleasant house set in pleasant gardens, and no one could deny that Belling Sands seemed safe enough for a bit from the tripper and the jerry-builder. He had a good car, and servants, and every year he invariably passed one month in Scotland and one on the Continent: and all those things cost money.

If Philippa had had an atom of sense she would have realized that, he mused, and seen the impossibility of expecting him to produce a cheque for £5000 with the same ease as he produced her allowance of £20 on the first of every month. But that had always been the trouble with Philippa, or one of them: she was bone self-ish, and wanted too much. Admittedly this particular matter of the £5000 was exceptional, but all the same—

A neat vacant-faced maid answered his ring.

"No, sir," she said, in reply to his query, "Miss Philippa hasn't come back yet, nor rung up."

He frowned again, dismissed the girl, and went across to the telephone by the window. Three-quarters of an hour later a car drew up outside, and Colonel Bagshaw was shown in.

Harrington was a small stout man with penetrating brown eyes, a gentle voice, and an engaging ready smile. Bagshaw was tall and thin, looking as if he had been somehow starved for six months, and the severity of his expression in repose often deceived strang-ers into thinking that he must be a bore at the very least, if not also a taskmaster and tyrant. Actually he was none of these, though his position as Chief-constable of the local police might have afforded him every chance to be.

He sat down now a little stiffly, and Harrington saw that his face was strained and tired.

"You're not looking too fit, John," he remarked. "Busy?"

"Up most of the night," was the reply. "A devil of a business over at Craybourne—disappearing bodies, and mysterious strang-ers in tinted glasses, and the lord knows what all else. You'd better watch out, or life'll be catching up with you."

"Sounds interesting," agreed the novelist. "But why didn't you tell me on the phone? I wouldn't have bothered you."

"Oh, no bother: a change of problem'll do me good."

"Problem?"

"Well, you said you wanted my advice, so I presume you're in the usual mess with your current plot, and want the usual dose of common sense applied. Not that I've got much left, I don't doubt, but I'll try. I never could sleep in the day-time, anyway. Come on, get going: anything to forget the vanishing lodger and the stupefying Creevy. You never saw a man like him, Charles—there never was one. Listen: a girl's corpse is lying in a gas-filled room one minute, and gone the next, and nobody knows how or why. Creevy investigates, and turns in a thousand-page report of what's supposed to have happened and what he's been doing about it, and he devotes about half to saying 'See below', and copying out the condition of the corpse's vests and pants as described by the corpse's landlady."

"The feminine of pants is pantees," observed Harrington. "*The Clue of the Knitted Knicker*—*not* a bad title."

"Yes—I'll recommend it to Creevy. I dare say I'm exaggerating, but he does get me rattled at times. He's so finicky—he worships details. But let's stop talking about all that. What's your trouble? Something a bit more serious than I reckoned, perhaps?"

"Or I'd be taking more interest in yours? You're right, John. This time it's a real-life problem."

Harrington had become wholly serious. He put his hand for a moment on the arm of his friend's chair, and spoke even more softly than usual.

"You won't mind if I ask you to treat it in confidence?" he murmured.

"Of course not—I'm off duty, ain't I?"

"Thanks: then it's about Philippa, and it's rather a long story. At least, it would be if I knew all the facts. To begin with, as far back as last spring I noticed she wasn't her usual bright self, and mildly wondered what was wrong without suspecting anything very terrible. It went on for so long, though, that in the end I got a bit anxious, but she showed no signs of saying anything, and I didn't like to ask questions. And then one night about the middle of May, without a shadow of warning, she came in here late one night and asked me to lend her £5000. Just like that—as cool as you please, and not a word about why she wanted it, except for something 'very special'.

"As it happened, I was feeling a bit liverish that day, and wasn't quite as sympathetic as I might have been. I told her frankly that I thought I already did my fair share for her in the money line, and that she was about due to get a few sensible ideas into her head. That life wasn't just a question of having good times, and seeing how many cocktails you could drink in an evening, and grumbling if there weren't a dance to go to five times a week, and somebody to pay for you, and so on. I expect I laid it on a bit thick, but not before it was my turn, I think."

"No fear," agreed Bagshaw. "I always wondered why you were so patient, as a matter of fact."

"Did you? Because I was fond of her mother, of course. You never knew her, so you won't appreciate that, but you can take it from me that it's a good reason. All the same, there are limits, especially when the daughter takes after the father."

"A bad lot?" queried Bagshaw gruffly.

"Well, it's not my place to crab the man: after all, he *was* my half-brother, and she *did* prefer him to me. He was nowhere near up to her mark, though. But leaving all that aside, I honestly consider I've treated Philippa fairly."

"Just a moment," interrupted the other. "Forgive me for being curious, but how do you treat her? In the way of money, I mean?"

Harrington coloured a little.

"And you're the man who hates details!" he murmured. "However, if you really want to know, I make her an allowance of £20 a month, and pay for the upkeep of her little car."

"Which you gave her in the first place."

"Yes—but that was a Christmas present."

"Oh, quite. I'll come around Boxing Day and see what's going. Carry on."

"Well, you can imagine that Philippa didn't much care for the lecture. We had an argument, and she went off in a huff, and from the way I heard her cursing Mary I gathered she was in a pretty bad temper."

"Mary? Sorry if I'm slow today."

"Mary Adams, her maid."

"Oh, I know—Best's girl friend."

"That's the one. Incidentally, why in the world doesn't he marry her?"

Colonel Bagshaw shrugged his lean shoulders.

"How the devil should I know?" he queried. "I'm not responsible for whether my common-or-garden coppers marry or whether they don't. Even my favourite coppers," he added with a smile. "Best's a good lad, though—he won't go getting her into trouble or anything."

"Oh, I know that: and I don't think Mary would let him if he wanted to. You know, John, maybe it's a rotten thing to say, but I've looked at the two of them together, Mary and Philippa, and wished it was Mary who'd been Julia's child. Still, you never knew Julia, as I said just now, so it's not much good going on with that.

"The next morning Philippa came in here again, and very nicely apologized for the previous evening. Whether she was pretending or not I can't say, but she seemed genuine enough. She then told me what she wanted the £5000 for, and I never had such a shock in my life."

He paused at that for some seconds, as if undecided at the last moment whether to go on with his story or to remain silent. Bagshaw appeared to understand, for he made no attempt to force his friend's confidence: he continued to lean back in his chair with his eyes closed, and only the periodic puffs of smoke from his pipe showed that he was still awake.

"Ever meet Robert Oakes?" enquired Harrington at last.

"What, the actor fellow? Got a bungalow down on the sands and all that?"

"Exactly—especially the 'all that'. You see, Philippa was part of it."

The colonel sat up with a jerk, really startled.

"Good God!" he exclaimed, and then sank back. "Sorry," he murmured. "Carry on."

"But before I do, tell me what you know about Oakes, will you? It may save my breath."

"Forty," said the colonel, his eyes again closed. "Forty and famous. At present playing lead in *Thy Name is Legion* at the New Gaiety. Done a lot of films, toured the States, made his name in Shakespeare . . ."

"I meant his character, not his career," interposed Harrington mildly.

"Oh, sorry. Forty and famous, and a bad hat. Married three or four times, I forget which: divorced roughly same number. Paints, I believe—preferably his girlfriends in their birthday suits, or thereabouts. Has week-end parties on the sands in the summer when he's in England. Self and partner, and dumb handyman to air the bed; or else half a dozen Bloomsbury horrors in the most putrid clothes, men like skeletons and girls like sausage balloons, all as loud as a brass band in a crypt and in no possible sort of taste whatever. His bungalow's very slick and shiny inside, I hear, and one room's fitted up as a studio. I also heard they make tea with gin instead of water, but that mayn't be true."

"Did you ever meet the man himself?"

"Once: at least, we were at the same bun-fight. Quite the dashing hero, full of charm and what-not, but a bit too suave for my taste. I must say he wasn't quite as vicious-looking as I'd expected, though. That do?"

"Admirably. I met him once, too, and not down here at all, strangely enough, but at some scribbler's club I belong to in town. He published a couple of murder stories some time back, and then got tired or something. They were good, too, as far as the mechanism of the plot went—one of 'em left me standing. A man was found dead in a—But I'd better not start on that now.

"Well, you can probably guess what kind of a shock Philippa handed out. For some time—six months or so—she's been head over heels in love with the brute: roughly, from last September to March of this year. Then—so she says—she suddenly woke up and realized what a loathsome creature he really was, and quit. I don't fancy that's quite the whole truth, though: I think Colin Dennison came into the picture about that time.

"You have met Colin, so you'll hardly need telling that it would be a job to imagine a bigger contrast to Oakes. Colin's younger, scarcely thirty, and he might strike some people as being a bit of a prig. At all events, he's the essence of correctness, and Philippa, by some whim of fate—sorry, that's jargon—fell for him about five times as heavily as she'd previously fallen for Oakes."

The colonel grunted unintelligibly. He well remembered Dennison, described by people who ought to know as a rising young man in the Foreign Office, and had secretly always considered him more of a machine than a human being. His appearance and behaviour were almost self-consciously unexceptionable, and the idea that he could flutter the heart of a high-spirited minx like Philippa seemed to Bagshaw laughable. Yet, accepting that as possible, he began to see dimly where the £5000 came in.

"Carry on," he muttered. "Letters?"

Harrington's tufted eyebrows lifted in momentary surprise, but he kept it from his voice, knowing the colonel too well to pay him indirect compliments.

"Partly," he agreed. "The girl must have been mad, of course, but there you are: when the heart's in the head's out. Yes, there were twenty-five letters, and the sweep wanted £100 apiece for them."

Bagshaw whistled softly.

"And the balance of the £5000?" he asked, opening his eyes for a second. "Surely she wasn't daft enough to pose for him in the nude?"

"All but: as *Salome,* she says, with only one veil left. And the threat behind the demand, of course, was a complete and utter absence of marriage bells."

"Eh? Don't jump too many fences at once. You haven't said anything about Colin's falling for Philippa to that extent."

"My dear ass, was it necessary? It would take a man of steel to hold out against her if she really set to work to charm him."

"Then why the fluster? Afraid she couldn't hold him?"

"Yes, more or less, Dennison being the kind of man he is: temperamentally incapable of accepting damaged goods, shall we say? In any struggle between his career and his puritan standards on the one side, and a rather off-white Philippa on the other, however attractive, however maddeningly desirable—and she could be that, you know, just as her mother was—there isn't much doubt which side would win. And to give her credit, she had enough gumption to realize it. She decided that it all costs she must get the letters and the portrait back, so that Oakes could never flourish them under Colin's nose."

"Just a moment: had Oakes any other motive but money? I mean, did he still want Philippa for himself?"

"Oh no: that was all over and done with. He knew she'd never come back to him on any terms, and so his policy was to make her departure as profitable as he could. He actually told her as much."

"So she went to you."

"Yes: and asked—very humbly—that if I couldn't let her have the money I'd at least advise her what to do. Well, I didn't beat about the bush. I said that the only way I could lay my hands on £5000 in cash would be by borrowing £4000 of it, and that my sympathies didn't go that deep. All the same, if the odd thousand was any good, then she could have it and welcome. Not in cash, of course, but I promised I'd meet any bills that Oakes cared to send in up to that amount, and it would be her job to get as much for it as she could."

"Ah: and I bet that was more than she really expected."

"Maybe. As for advice, I was generosity itself there. In the first place, I said, the portrait wasn't nearly so important as the letters. Pictures can be painted from snapshots, and once she had the letters back—it was specifically mentioned in them—then she could afford to put her tongue out. Her story then would be that the whole thing was a frame-up: that Oakes was trying to blackmail her with a full-length of some model's body and her head on it, not worth a damn as evidence of her moral character, but quite useful for showing up his. Naturally she must be careful not to let him suspect her intentions, but as a first step she must concentrate on the letters. And in any event, I said, £100 apiece was a fantastic price for him to expect her to pay whatever they had in them, and if she played her cards right she ought to get the lot back for the thousand I was ready to let her have. How she was to prevent him from making photostatic copies before he handed them over, of course, I didn't pretend to know.

"Well, John, what do you think so far? Ought I to have borrowed and settled the business at once?"

Bagshaw shook his head without hesitation.

"The idea of paying blackmail goes against all my principles," he said. "Seven times out of ten the devil's only bluffing, and the other three times it hurts less to face things out than let yourself be bled. All the same I can quite understand that it wouldn't have been so easy in this case. To do the courageous and sensible thing, and blow the whistle for me, would have been quite as effective in stopping the wedding bells as anything Oakes could manage. I imagine it would cause a sight too much scandal and publicity for young Dennison's liking, however little of the truth came out. Incidentally, I hope you made it clear that if she couldn't get all the letters back, then it wasn't worth getting any?"

"Yes, I did. But don't shirk: what would you have done in my place?"

"Ah. It's a bit difficult to say, off-hand. I think, if I'd still been me, I wouldn't have upset myself too much. If things went absolutely wrong, and Dennison dropped Philippa because of something she'd done in the past, then I'd be prepared to comfort myself—and her, if need be—with the reflection that she was well rid of him. Maybe I'm old-fashioned, but there aren't many things I hate worse than fair-weather friends, and a fair-weather husband sounds perfectly vile.

"Again, suppose he did drop her: is it at all likely that she wouldn't get over it? After all, Philippa obviously isn't a one-man girl, and if she could change direction once, why not twice? That may sound cynical, but I can't help it: I've been up practically all night. From what I know of the young lady I should imagine that a man's something of a necessity to her: how else do you explain her infatuation for Oakes? It seems to show she can't be so very particular. Yet I fancy that what she told you about suddenly waking up and seeing him as he really was rings true. She realized about six months too late what she'd got herself tied up with, and chucked him the same minute, and on the rebound fell even harder for the exactly opposite type, the puritan."

Harrington nodded slowly.

"Yes, I dare say you're right—I hadn't looked at it quite like that. And I'm glad you don't think I behaved too badly. Well, that was the position four or five months ago. She wasn't able to do much about it then, though, because soon afterwards Oakes cleared off to America in preparation for another Broadway triumph. Only, by some miscalculation, it didn't quite come off, and in the middle of August he was back again making arrangements for his present show. He wrote to her, but I don't know if she answered, because we were due for a month in Scotland in a couple of weeks."

"With the Dennisons," put in Bagshaw.

"Precisely—with the Dennisons. As you may know, Colin had been granted three months' leave of absence because of a poisoned arm. We went up there with him and his father and sister, and I can honestly say I've never seen Philippa happier. In fact, she was so bright and cheerful that I couldn't help asking her point-blank one day if Oakes had relented, and returned the letters for nothing. She clouded over a bit at that, and said he hadn't, but added that somehow she felt things were going to be all right. I assured her I hoped they would be, and left her up there for an extra fortnight. Colin was due to report at Whitehall on Wednesday, and I thought I'd let them have as much time alone together as I could. If he proposed, and she accepted him, there was a fair chance he might think he'd lose more face by letting her down than by standing by her. If there was trouble from Oakes, I mean."

"But why should your presence interfere with proposals and acceptances?" asked Bagshaw.

"Oh, it might easily have done. Old man Dennison is paralysed, and spends all day every day playing interminable games of chess with his daughter, and used to insist on packing me off with Colin and Philippa, deerstalking and playing golf and what-not, and some of the time I had to go. Anyway, I came back here on the 5th, and Philippa and Mary returned yesterday. They came by car, starting on Tuesday and taking it easy, Colin went direct to London by train.

"Well, Philippa turned up about half past three yesterday, and almost the first thing she said was that there hadn't been a proper proposal."

"Ah, bad luck!" murmured the colonel.

"Not quite: she went on to tell me that she'd deliberately choked Colin off from proposing. Two days after I went she'd had a letter from Oakes, forwarded from here. He said he was thinking of exhibiting the *Salome* portrait in town, and would insist on sending her and Colin tickets for the private view: unless, of course, she preferred to buy the thing herself. Would she please let him know one way or the other by the end of the month?

"She told me she simply hadn't known what to do. She wouldn't willingly give up a moment with Colin, yet she didn't dare let him ask her to marry him."

"Why on earth not?" asked the colonel sharply.

"Because she daren't bank on his future support if she couldn't buy Oakes off."

"And once he'd let her go, even if she could manage to make him believe he'd been wrong, he'd be a sight too proud to get up on his hind legs and beg."

"Yes," agreed Harrington. "If she still wanted him to. I think that was what worried her most: the idea of falling out of love with Colin. So every time he started proposing she changed the subject, and tried to imply that he'd do best if he didn't rush things too much. The minute she got back here she came straight to me for more advice.

"Now we'd decided that the portrait was dangerous only if Oakes still had the letters, so I suggested that she tackled him about them at once. Then she gave me another shock. She said she'd practically got them all for nothing already, but that the person she'd persuaded to act for her had run up against something even worse."

"Wait a bit: who was this intermediary?"

"I don't know—she wouldn't tell me. I've half an idea it was a private detective."

"And what do you mean by saying she'd practically got them all back? That she had twenty-four out of twenty-five, or that the whole lot were in the post?"

"Again, I'm not sure. I rather fancy she meant that the go-between had them."

"Huh! That might be *de fumo adflammam*—educated for a copper, don't you think? And what was Oakes's ace of trumps?"

"Half a dozen camera studies of Philippa posing for the *Salome* thing: two of them without veils. And now comes the problem, or part of it. Here in this room yesterday Philippa solemnly assured me that never in her life had she been photographed in less than a bathing costume, by Oakes or anyone else. What's the answer, John? Can you see a sensible one?"

"Can you?" countered Bagshaw quickly, and Harrington's plump face became still graver.

"I've found an answer all right," he replied: "only I don't know if it's sensible or not. Let's hear what you've got to say."

The colonel stroked his chin with the bowl of his empty pipe, and once more shut his eyes.

"Either the fellow's bluffing or he isn't" he declared heavily. "Can't see much sense in supposing he is—therefore suppose he isn't. The answer then boils down to three words. Philippa was never photographed stark in her life—*to her knowledge.*"

Harrington nodded gloomily.

"I was afraid you'd say that" he observed. "It's feasible, presumably?"

"Oh yes. She was doped. Or she went to sleep. Or she was snapped from a distance by the dumb servant while she was genuinely posing. You can do all sorts of long-range stuff with a good telescopic lens, I believe: enlarge your image from a mere nothing to post-card size at least, and still keep it sharp and detailed. If Oakes has got a set of photos—and I can't see why in the world he should say he has if he hasn't—then you can rely on their being genuine. He wouldn't play about with them as you suggested he might do with the portrait. His ultimate proof will be the negatives, which is why I rather suspect that some of them aren't confined to Philippa in the nude. Oakes is probably there too, actually arranging her pose, but looking exactly as if he's just persuaded her to tear her last covering off and let him put it in his pocket. Where did he paint her—at the bungalow?"

"Yes."

"And you can't even guess at the intermediary?"

"No—I wish I could. I can't help wondering what she expected him to be able to do that I couldn't have done."

"Give the fellow a good thrashing, perhaps—you're hardly his size. And what's the position at the moment? Incidentally, I take it that this ambassador chap must have told her about the photographs after her return here yesterday?"

"I don't know—why?"

"Well, you said that what worried the girl in Scotland was Oakes's threat to put the picture on view; but that scarcely counts compared to the threat, implied if not stated, to send Colin Dennison a post-card of Philippa as a veilless *Salome*. Since she wasn't worrying about that in Scotland, I assumed she didn't know till she got back here. Or maybe she had been told, but for some reason didn't wholly believe it till she returned. Anyway, I'd risk sixpence I know who it is, but I'm not going to tell you, so don't bother to ask."

Harrington smiled.

"I'm not terribly bothered about it," he said. "And I can think that way too—with a pen in my hand. At all events, that's how things are now, with this difference. Last night about 11.00 Philippa told me she was going out 'on business'. She didn't say where, and she didn't take her car—just wandered off with a handbag and an umbrella: and so far she hasn't come back, John."

The Chief-constable frowned.

"Nor telephoned? I see—sounds queer. Has she ever gone off like that before?"

"Never without ringing me up first thing the next morning to say where she was."

"Ah. And you're worried."

It was more of a statement than a question, and the novelist said nothing for a moment, staring at the fire. Then he smiled nervously.

"I'm damned if I'm sure why, quite," he told Bagshaw, "but if you really want to know, I'm as worried as hell."

# IV

C OLONEL BAGSHAW walked into Craybourne police-station at quarter to four.

"Any news?" he asked.

"Yes sir," answered Inspector Creevy, his thin face wearing its usual look of deep abstraction. He had a lofty forehead, and he tried consciously to live up to it.

"You remember that in my report I made mention of Messrs Ribleys' yard, next door to Mrs. Topley's place? It appears that for the last six months a grocer by the name of Deacon has been in the habit of garaging his van there. It's a small Morris Commercial, index number XW 5037, with the ordinary double doors at the back and shelves inside, and he pays half a crown for the use of a shed. Twenty minutes ago the van was reported missing."

"Ah, was it now?" said the colonel. "Carry on."

"Deacon discovered the loss himself, sir, just after three o'clock, and came round to report it."

"What's the fellow like? Know anything about him?"

"Almost everything, sir," replied Creevy, in a matter-of-fact voice.

"Good—let's have it. Only be fairly relevant—no darned pants, I mean."

The Inspector sighed: not so much because he minded his Chief-constable's teasing as because he feared that Bagshaw would never realize the responsibilities of his position. Slap-dash methods might do well enough for the army—he neither knew nor cared: but he felt that nothing could be too trivial for a policeman's notice. 'Trifles make perfection' he was wont to say, quoting from a childhood precept whose source he mistakenly believed to be Napoleon, 'but perfection is no trifle.'

"I knew Alfred Deacon's father," he said now: "the family used to live over at Tilgate. The son is twenty-five years old, unmarried, and resides with his mother over their shop at 54 Arundel Street. He only opened it last March, but has managed to build up quite a good business in a small way. Right from the beginning he set out to get what local custom he could away from the bigger stores, and he's always made a point of free delivery within a two-mile radius—hence the van. He never takes it out till about 4.00 except on Thursdays, early-closing day, when he's usually finished and put it away by 2.00. He did yesterday, and naturally thought it would still be there when he went along this afternoon. When he found it wasn't he questioned the men working in the yard, who knew nothing, and then came straight here—no one has any authority to touch the van."

"I see. But why go for it at 3.00, if he wasn't going to use the thing till 4.00?"

"He says he wanted to change a tyre, sir."

"And the people in the builders' yard couldn't help?"

"No sir, except that they're dead sure it wasn't taken out today, and not before they knocked off at 5.00 yesterday. The shed Deacon uses wasn't locked, but none of them had had occasion to go inside."

"What's the van like?"

"Definitely second-hand and quite inconspicuous: no name on it."

"No? I should have thought he'd be just the chap for a snappy slogan. *A. Deacon—Orders Taken Daily.*"

Creevy smiled dutifully.

"Perhaps he thinks the van's too shabby to be worth it," he suggested. "He says he's on the look-out for something a bit smarter, now he's got his business going."

"Anything else to report?"

"No sir—not in the way of facts."

"But you're bursting to unfold a brilliant theory about how Ellis surreptitiously bundled Alice Carter's gas-filled body into Alfred Deacon's plain van, and delivered same free somewhere within two miles. Is Deacon above suspicion?"

"Oh yes, sir."

"Why? Because you knew his father?"

"Not entirely, sir. Ellis is described as being on the short side, but Deacon stands about five foot ten."

"And tall men never help short ones to get away with murder. Sorry if I'm being frivolous, but I've been up six or seven hours too long, and it takes me that way. What're you doing about it?"

"The van's being watched out for, sir. I've just instituted enquiries, here and all over the county."

"Good—but better cast your net a bit wider. Nothing to stop him delivering in Kent or Surrey, since he's not Deacon: or even in Scotland if it comes to that, like Dr. Thingummy. By the way, ever hear of Charles Harrington?"

"The man who writes those crime books, sir?"

"Yes—how eloquent is the word 'those'! He also lives at Belling."

"Does he now?" said Creevy, surprised. "I didn't know that."

"Then I score for once. Well, he's a friend of mine, and he's got a niece, and she hasn't been seen or heard of since about eleven o'clock last night. I'll give you a description, and then you can institute more enquiries." He regarded Creevy's spotless desk thoughtfully, selected a blank sheet of paper, pretended to blow dust from it, and took out his fountain pen.

*Philippa Frances Saunderson* he wrote, *aged 22, height 5 ft 3½ ins, hair flaxen and bobbed, features considered pretty. Is probably wearing brown tweed coat and skirt, fawn cashmere jumper, brown brogue shoes, fawn raincoat. May also have brown felt hat, umbrella, and pigskin handbag. Recently returned by car from Scotland, reaching her home (Cairngorm, Belling Sands) at approx. 3.30 P.M. Thursday the 20th. Last seen indoors about 11.00 P.M. same day: is believed to have gone out on foot soon afterwards, destination unknown. Present whereabouts sought.*

"That do?" he asked Creevy, who puzzled for some moments over the Chief-constable's untidy writing.

"Yes sir, as a start. Had she any money with her?"

"Don't know—forgot to ask. You'd better ring up Harrington and find out. Meanwhile I think I'll have a word with Deacon. If you've heard nothing of me by the first of next month, take it I've disappeared too, and notify the police in the usual way."

Five minutes of Deacon's company in the stuffy living-room behind the grocer's shop was enough to convince Bagshaw that the owner was no murderer's accomplice: merely a sleek and slim and faintly objectionable young man with prominent ears.

'The devil of a fellow with a bag of raisins, I bet,' thought the colonel unamiably. 'He can deliver himself two miles out to sea as soon as he likes, for my taste.'

"So anybody could have stolen the thing after the builders' men stopped work on Thursday?" he said aloud. "Just walked into the yard and wrestled with it?"

"Well, yes sir," agreed Deacon. "That's about what it comes to, right enough. Anybody who knew it was there, that is"—with a smirk at his own smartness.

"And how many people do know—a lot?"

"No, not so many. You see, I haven't been in Craybourne but eight months, and what with setting up in business, and putting things ship-shape, and book-keeping, and Mother's bad knee, I haven't hardly had time to make a lot of friends. There's Mother knows, of course, and the men at Ribleys', and my young lady, but I can't say as I can think of any more at the moment."

"Insurance company and licensing authorities, I suppose?"

"Oh yes sir—I was forgetting them."

"And the young lady? You've been here long enough for that?"

Deacon smoothed his faultless hair and smiled complacently.

"I goes to chapel Sunday mornings" he confided. "Chapel's more friendly-like than church, don't you think? I hadn't been here but six weeks when I met Miss O'Hara there, and I count my time well spent, I can tell you."

"Splendid," murmured Bagshaw despondently: he felt certain he would loathe Miss O'Hara. "Engaged?"

"In a manner of speaking, sir, thank you. We'll be taking a look in the jewellers' windows pretty soon, I wouldn't wonder."

The Chief-constable grunted at this information, and remained silent for a full minute. So far nothing had got into the papers about the disappearance of Alice Carter's body, but the matter could not be kept quiet much longer. That being beyond doubt, he felt justified in mentioning it in some detail to Alfred Deacon, standing now before the fire and smiling rather vaguely. He was plainly puzzled that the theft of a mere tradesman's van should be dealt with by the Chief-constable himself, and as plainly gratified to be entertaining so important an official in his own home. Every time the sharp sound of the shop bell echoed through the thin glass door between he frowned a little, as if ashamed that his method of obtaining a livelihood should be so audible to his visitor.

"D'you happen to know Mrs. Topley, of 14 Weatherall Road?" asked Bagshaw presently, looking up.

"Topley? No sir—she doesn't deal with us."

"Her loss, I dare say. Now, you're wondering why I should bother about your van, aren't you?"

"Well—er—I'm sure it's very kind of you," murmured Deacon lamely.

"Nonsense," contradicted the colonel, with his severest expression. "I haven't time to go round being kind to people. I'm here because it so happens that I'm particularly interested in vans and things like that, Mr. Deacon."

"Yes?" said the other, with obvious lack of understanding.

"Yes, and I'll tell you why, only you must keep it to yourself."

"Oh yes sir, of course—you can rely on me."

"I hope so. Ever read detective stories?"

"Detective stories? Why, yes. It's funny you should ask that—it's about all I ever do read in the way of a book."

"Then you won't need telling that one of the hardest parts about committing a murder is getting rid of the body."

"Eh? Murder?" Deacon's mouth fell open a little, and he stared at Bagshaw with an intentness that seemed almost suspicious.

"Well, possibly murder, possibly suicide," said the colonel. "It's like this. About 7.12 last night, in a certain house in a certain road, in a certain room, there was a dead body. Between 7.12 and 7.21 the house was left vacant while the owner notified the police of her discovery. When they broke into the room, however, there wasn't a body any longer."

"You don't tell me!" exclaimed Deacon raptly. "Well I never did!"

"Nor me—nor any of us. That's why we're interested in your van: the house in question is only a stone's throw from Ribleys' yard."

The grocer's brown eyes suddenly brightened.

"14 Weatherall Road!" he said. "Next door! The yard's 10 and 12—says so on the gate. But what sort of a body, sir? Man or woman?"

"It's immaterial," was the disappointing answer. "And please remember you're not to pass any of this on. The point is, would it be possible to carry a fair-sized box in your van? A box containing a human body?"

Deacon nodded eagerly.

"It's plenty big enough—I've had a couple of tea-chests in her many a time."

"No difficulty in opening the door at the back?"

"No fear—turn the handle and there you are. I say, fancy somebody using my van to get rid of a dead 'un! But what would he do with it? Where'd he go?"

"If I knew," the colonel told him acidly, "I wouldn't be wasting *your* time. Now, Mr. Deacon, having explained things so far, I shall have to ask a few more questions. To begin with, when do you generally use the van? Every day?"

"Bar Sundays. I take her out round about 4.00, and I put her back between 6.00 and 7.00. It depends on how much stuff I've got to deliver, and where I've got to take it to. I was early today, as I told them at the police-station, because I wanted to put the spare on at the back."

"Had you a puncture, then?"

"Oh no, but the tread was a bit bad."

"And before I forget, how much petrol was there on board?"

"Best part of two gallons."

"Thank you. And once you've put it away for the day you don't use it again till about 4.00 the next day?"

"Oh—well: now and again I do, like."

Bagshaw nodded, pleased.

"I thought you might, somehow," he observed. "Miss O'Hara appreciates a little run round now and again, I don't doubt?"

"That's it," said Deacon readily. "Only not so much lately, now it's getting towards winter. In the summer we used to go out two nights a week regular."

"Which two nights?" pursued the Chief-constable relentlessly.

"Tuesdays and Saturdays."

"Not Thursdays?"

"No sir. You see, Peggy—Miss O'Hara—works in a tea-shop, and Thursday's one of their best days."

"Really? I never have tea out, so I wouldn't know. What? No, it doesn't matter. Oh well, perhaps just a cup—thank you."

The conversation was suspended for some minutes, while Mrs. Deacon boiled a kettle and asthmatically cut bread and butter. Then Bagshaw resumed his questioning.

"D'you ever go out on Sundays?" he asked.

"Well, no: Sunday's Mother's day off, like. Once I'm back from chapel in the morning I carry on till we close at 6.00, and then Peggy and I usually go to the pictures."

"So much for trading regulations!' thought the colonel, but said nothing.

"Ah—I dare say it makes a nice change from chapel. Still, I mustn't wander. When was the last time you took the van out in the evening? This week at all?"

"Yes, sir, as a matter of fact: Tuesday, it being so fine."

"And where did you go?"

"Oh, nowhere special: just for a run along the coast road."

"Which way—towards Tilgate?"

"No, towards Belling. We generally do, somehow."

"Because it's quieter, perhaps," suggested the colonel, as if with sudden inspiration: but in reality he had had the germ of an idea in his head for some time. "You pull up by and by, and—and discuss the rosy future with Miss O'Hara?"

Deacon smirked again, but not so complacently.

"Ay, we do pull up once in a while," he agreed, though with little enthusiasm. It seemed clear that he preferred not to go into details about his evening trips with his young lady.

"Ah. Sorry to be such a nuisance, asking all these questions," remarked Bagshaw cheerfully. "You see what I'm driving at, of course?"

"Well, no sir, 'fraid I don't."

"No?"—with false surprise. "I was hoping you would. Look at it this way, Mr. Deacon"—becoming several degrees more confidential. "If your van had anything to do with my disappearing body, then it would appear probable that whoever stole it studied your movements first. Found out where you kept the thing, I mean, and when it'd be safe for him to pinch it. Now, it strikes me as just possible that he might have gone even further than that, if he was thorough: he might have taken the trouble to find out as well where you usually went on your evening runs round."

"But what on earth for?" asked Deacon.

"Why, so that he'd know where it'd be safe to leave it, of course. He takes the van in order to get rid of the body; but when he's done that, he's still got the van on his hands. It wouldn't be very safe to return it to the yard—its loss might have been discovered. Again, he probably wouldn't want to attract attention by leaving it somewhere that people aren't accustomed to seeing it, especially if he's keen on a few hours' start. But suppose he knew that you were in the habit of parking in the same place two nights a week, then the presence of the van there wouldn't be so likely to worry even inquisitive people like policemen. Anyway, not for a bit."

"Oh, now I see!" exclaimed Deacon. "And what with being on the coast road, there's the deep blue sea all nice and handy, as you might say."

"Just so: wait till the tide's going out, dump the body in, and there you are. It'll get washed up somewhere sooner or later, but it won't be in too good a shape. Now tell me: *have* you been using any special place for parking?"

"Yes sir," answered the grocer at once, no longer at all secretive. "We generally draw up in a little bit of a lane about a mile and a half or two miles this side of Belling. I can't tell you its name, but it's a sort of short cut through to the new by-pass."

"I know the one," said Bagshaw. "Thanks very much—I'll probably have a look there on my way home."

He rose to go, and then remembered another point for query.

"Ever seen a policeman about there?" he asked.

"Yes sir, once or twice. They came up to see we were all right, to begin with, but they don't bother us now."

"I see. One was tall and dark, and not bad-looking, and the other was a sergeant with a moustache?"

"That's them. The tall one's that chap who got his name in the papers a couple of months ago. He stopped—But I dare say you know all about that, sir."

"I ought to," agreed Bagshaw, now in a good humour. "I'm his boss, ain't I?"

By the time he got away it was quarter to six, and quite dark. He drove towards the sea-front through Craybourne's narrow shop-lit streets; when he came to the fork which offered a choice between the old coast road and the connecting-link to the comparatively new by-pass, he chose the former, switching on his head-lights and proceeding cautiously. The surface of the road was bad, and he prided himself upon his careful driving.

To his left, beyond shadowy sand-dunes, stretched the unquiet sea; to his right lay rough fields. The soil hereabouts was harsh and gritty, and little grew within quarter of a mile of the water's edge but reeds and coarse grass. Once, it was reputed, the sea had been at least that much nearer to the gently swelling downs, and in receding seemed to have left its ineradicable mark upon the land. In daylight the surroundings were desolate, and the colonel believed that this fact alone would prevent Craybourne from ever becoming really popular. The town might stretch a little in the other direction, perhaps, towards Tilgate fifteen miles away, but it would never expand appreciably. Its permanent population would remain about fourteen thousand, and in the height of a fine summer it would never hold more than twice that number.

The side road about which Deacon had told him was five miles by the speedometer from Craybourne, and a bare two miles farther on lay Belling Sands, part village, part town. Almost every acre of it belonged to the eccentric Lord Belling, and while he lived it would continue in its present seclusion. The number of munificent offers he had already refused from speculative builders was said to reach double figures, and their total value approximated to a million pounds.

Colonel Bagshaw was not at all sure, as he drove along, whether he really expected to find the missing van or not. Had anyone asked him direct, he would probably have denied being so optimistic; yet when presently his headlights picked it up he realized that somehow he was not greatly surprised.

'That's it—must be,' he thought. 'A couple of hundred yards from the coast road, about.'

He pulled up not quite opposite, and sat for a moment staring.

'That's it all right—XW5037. Not worth fooling about with no torch—I'd better run back and tell Creevy, I suppose. Wonder if the body's inside? Shouldn't think so—else why bother to take it away at all? Unless he's bashed it about. But that's be risky—they patrol as far as this every night since those burglaries at the bathing chalets. Shall I have a look? He said all you have to do is turn the handle. But there might be fingerprints and things, and poor old Creevy'd sulk for a month. And there won't be anything inside, anyway—not a hope.

'And yet, why not?' he asked himself later, returning to Craybourne. 'How much hope was there I'd find the blessed thing at all? An utter fluke. Ah well, better be lucky than handsome in my job. Wonder if Philippa's turned up yet? It's a pity Charles didn't keep a better tab on her comings and goings. I bet no girl of mine would ever run round with a swine like Oakes in nothing but a veil. But she's rather inclined to be that sort, with all due respect to the late beloved Julia. You can see it in her lips, and the way she walks, and that slow rather intense smile, and the impudent fit of her clothes. Queer she should go and disappear the same day as Alice Carter. And I wonder what Ellis did with *her*—if it was Ellis. The sea, probably—the currents are tricky about here. That old German who got out of his depth the summer before last fetched up at Hillchurch: only fifty miles, but it took him ten days, and nobody would have known it was him at all if he hadn't had his innards all sewn together with silver wire. Ha! Wonder if it was German silver? And who *is* Ellis? Where in the world do I start looking for him? Or previous tracks of Alice Carter, for that matter. Maybe I ought to call in Scotland Yard—I'll have to get in touch with them about the prints on that tooth-glass. Dear Sirs, Kindly loan me the services of one bona-fide detective at your own expense. Same not to behave like the last specimen sent, who thought he was a general inspecting recruits, and knew little or nothing about the use of the pocket handkerchief. God, how that man sniffed!'

# V

A T NINE O'CLOCK THAT EVENING, after having consulted Inspector Creevy and received his rather grudging congratulations, Colonel Bagshaw drew up outside Yew-Tree Cottage, Belling. In answer to his knock the door was opened by a plumply attractive girl of sixteen: Polly Tukes, only daughter of Sergeant Samuel Tukes.

"Hullo Polly!" said Bagshaw. "Father in?"

"No sir, I'm afraid he isn't. He was off to my aunt's an hour ago, but he'll be back soon—he's on at 10.00. Would you come in and wait?"

The Chief-constable put his head round the cottage door and sniffed the air of the cosy living-room.

"Is that coffee?" he enquired.

"Well sir, it's meant to be," said Polly with a giggle. "For their supper. Do come in, sir—there'll be enough if you'd like some, and John's upstairs."

"All right, thanks," he agreed; and thus it was that when, five minutes later, Police-constable John Best came down to eat before going on night-duty he found the colonel comfortably settled in front of a log fire, playing with Polly's ginger kitten.

"Oh, good evening sir," said Best, whose dark good looks justified Baghsaw's passing description of him to the grocer.

"Evening, John. Mind if I have a bite with you?"

"Of course not, sir. Ah!"—as the kitten made a violent spring for the colonel's knee, and hung there desperately for a moment before slipping down. "You be minding his claws, sir—they're like needles."

"Pretty little beggar, though. Oh no you don't, my lad! I'll need that finger tomorrow. Besides, it'd be too tough for you."

Within another five minutes the two men were seated one each side of the small table by the curtained window. Between them stood an oil lamp, and on the far side was a vacant place for Polly's father. Polly herself had withdrawn to the kitchen to look after the coffee, the kitten was suddenly and soundly asleep in the chair from which Bagshaw had just risen, and for some moments they ate their stew in silence. Then Best looked up with a pleasant smile.

"Any news, sir?" he asked.

"News, John? What sort of news?"

"Well, sir, about that body they're all talking about. It really did disappear?"

"Absolutely—when did you hear about it?"

"At the station, sir, when I came off duty at 6.00 this morning."

"Ah. You weren't along the coast road, by any chance?"

"Yes sir, a good bit of the time."

"Between what time and when?"

Best's handsome face took on a slightly puzzled expression, as if he failed to follow the trend of the colonel's thoughts.

"I was down there on and off from 10.45 till the best part of 3.00, sir."

This information was received with so stern a frown that the young policeman asked anxiously if anything were wrong.

"I wouldn't wonder," said Bagshaw, and then smiled: Best's face was so very worried. He sat with his knife and fork poised over his almost empty plate, and stared at his superior fixedly.

"Eat your stew," recommended the latter. "Too good to waste. Who cooked it—Polly?"

"Yes sir—I dare say."

"Ah. Go on, eat up—nothing's as wrong as all that. Only you rather missed a chance last night, I fancy."

"A chance of what, sir? A cop? I mean, an arrest?"

"Cop's good enough. I don't know—maybe. What I meant was a chance of promotion, though,"—and he winked.

The younger man made no comment, but waited patiently with an air of bewilderment.

"Ever heard of Alfred Deacon?" continued Bagshaw presently. "Ah, here's the Sergeant. Evening, Tukes—if you're sorry to see me, blame Polly. I cadged for coffee, and got stew as well—mind?"

"Not a bit, sir," replied Sergeant Tukes with a genial smile. "Any news?"

"Might be," said the Chief-constable, with another wink at Best. He refused to say more until Tukes had started his meal, and then, between sips of the steaming coffee which Polly had brought in, he repeated his question, addressing both men.

"Ever heard of Alfred Deacon?"

Tukes was about forty-five, burly and thick-set, with a round cropped head and a carefully tended moustache. Usually Bagshaw found him silent and alert in manner, if at times a little dull, and he had never been quite able to get on friendly terms with the man. Tonight, however, he seemed amiable enough: perhaps because he was at ease in his own home, and the Chief-constable his guest.

He contented himself now with a shake of the head for answer, but Best openly expressed his ignorance.

"No sir, never—should I have?"

The colonel shrugged his shoulders.

"Chap's a grocer in Craybourne," he informed them. "Fairly tall, slim, dark, fond of himself, has a young lady by the name of Peggy O'Hara. Also has a van, index number XW 5037."

But still his subordinates showed no signs of comprehension.

"The number means nothing to you?" he asked, remembering that neither had been on duty since Deacon's discovery of his loss.

"No sir," they chorused.

"Then it bally well ought to—you've both seen it. However, let that go. In connection with the body you were kindly enquiring about, certain developments have taken place."

"Ah!" murmured Tukes, dissecting a dumpling.

"The house from which it vanished," continued Bagshaw "stands next to a builders' yard, which is visible from the bathroom window and contains a shed, which in turn contains Alfred Deacon's van. Or used to, till it was stolen some time between five o'clock yesterday afternoon and three o'clock today. At least, you can put it earlier than that—9.00, I dare say."

"What kind of a van, sir?" asked Best, with considerable interest.

"The kind you could put a big box in, and nobody'd see it," was the answer.

"Eh? A big box?" exclaimed the Sergeant. "And inside that?"

"The body!" said Best suddenly. "That's what you mean, sir, isn't it? And the van's a ramshackle dirty-looking thing, and Peggy What's-her-name's a fat girl with red hair and a face like a full moon, and I ought to be kicked all the way to—to—"

"To the place you last saw said van," finished the Chief-constable gently. "Ah well, you're beginning to wake up. Your turn, Sergeant: any details to add to Peggy's appearance?"

"He ought to have," declared Best with a grin: but Tukes's apparently slower wits were unequal to the question.

"I'm all at sea," he confessed.

"Then you'd better keep a look-out for Alice Carter," suggested the colonel. "I don't doubt she's there too—what's left of her."

"Smuggler's Lane" prompted Best, as Tukes still stared. "That's where the van was last night. Don't you remember telling me about it back in the summer—the young chap and his girl, and how she tried to pretend she'd only taken her blouse off because she'd come over faint?"

"Oh, them!" said the sergeant, as Bagshaw began to laugh. "There last night, were they? Then—?"

He glanced enquiringly at the colonel, who shook his head.

"The van was: the usual occupants weren't."

He went on to give a summary of the position at the moment, describing how a preliminary search by Inspector Creevy and himself, with the help of a Craybourne sergeant, had proved that the van was empty, and how it was now in Creevy's charge, being rigorously examined for clues. He then looked at his watch, and bade Tukes telephone the police-station to say that he and Best would be late on duty. When the sergeant returned he waited till Polly had cleared the supper things away, dutifully kissed her father, smiled upon Best and himself, and gone upstairs to bed, and then he settled down to business.

"Now John," he said, filling his pipe, "tell me everything you know about Alfred Deacon and his van."

"Well sir, it isn't much. I first noticed it parked in Smuggler's Lane round about the middle of last May. Near eleven o'clock it was, as far as I remember, and I walked up to see what was going on—his lights were out. Well, he and the girl were inside, and not too pleased to see me, but the chap was quite civil—said he didn't think he was in anybody's way and all that. And of course he wasn't, really, so I told him he'd be all right so long as he either put his lights on, or pulled off the actual road. Then about a week later the Sergeant here spotted 'em too."

"And dispensed a similar blessing?" asked Bagshaw mildly.

"In a manner of speaking, sir" answered Tukes: "provided they didn't make a nuisance of themselves."

"I see. Can't say I altogether approve, but maybe that's because I never had either a van or a red-haired moon-face. And anyway, nobody ever uses Smuggler's Lane—the surface is practically criminal. How often were they there after that, John?"

"Most weeks, sir, only of course we didn't patrol as far as that every night then. I only went near once, when my torch gave out, so as I could see to mend it—he put his lights on for me."

"Remember seeing them on any special nights?"

Best thought for a moment.

"Mostly Saturdays," he said. "And Tuesdays too. They may have come other times as well, but those were what you might call their regular turns, sir."

"Would you swear they never came on a Thursday?"

"Well, no, I wouldn't swear to it."

"And last night?"

"I noticed him there about half past eleven, but only because somehow I always glance up the Lane."

"And you weren't surprised because it was a Thursday?"

"No sir—never thought about it."

"And you didn't see it go?"

"No sir, but I didn't walk right down to the lane again, as a matter of fact, so it might have been there all the time. I'm sorry."

"So am I, but it can't be helped. Presumably there was nothing to attract your attention? No voices, rattling or banging of any kind?"

"Nothing like that, sir."

"And you, Sergeant?" asked Bagshaw, turning to Tukes. "Were you round that way last night?"

"Yes sir, but I didn't go as far as Smuggler's Lane, and I'm afraid I can't tell you much. I met Best at 1.30 about a couple of hundred yards short of the old Martello Tower, and had a word with him, but he never said anything about the van."

"Very well. Now, John, answer this one carefully. Did you notice anything in the slightest degree out of the ordinary anywhere at any time last night?"

"Yes sir," replied Best without hesitation.

"Good man!" exclaimed Bagshaw, surprised. "Carry on."

"Well sir, since those reported burglaries down at the bathing chalets last month, we've been instructed not to go too far away from them. Round about midnight last night I thought I heard someone moving about near there, sir, so I got down on the beach and went as close as I could. I waited a bit, and then explored, but I didn't hear anything else or see anyone, so I reckoned I must have made a mistake. Well, not far short of 1.15 I started towards Belling, where I was due to meet Sergeant Tukes at half past. When I got to the Martello Tower I was surprised to see a man standing on the sheltered side. He had his collar turned up and his hat pulled down, and he looked pretty cold and wretched. I went up and asked if he was all right, and what he was supposed to be doing. He said he'd arranged to meet a friend there at midnight, but the chap hadn't arrived. I suggested it was a queer sort of place to arrange a meeting on a night like that, and he said his friend was a queer sort of person. And he wasn't being smart or anything, sir, I don't think. He said it more as if he was thinking aloud than talking to me. And then he said good-night all of a sudden and cleared off this way, walking fast."

"Without saying anything else?" demanded Baghsaw, intensely interested.

"Nothing that I could catch clearly, sir, but he did mumble something under his breath. About somebody making a damned fool of him, it sounded like."

The colonel leant back thoughtfully, trying to decide if the encounter could have any possible connection with the business in hand.

"Describe the man," he said.

"He was medium tall, and he had a black overcoat on and an Anthony-Eden hat—I didn't notice his feet. He spoke in a soft sort of voice, and I'd say he was a gentleman. And quite sober," he added.

"Carrying anything? Bag, stick, brolly?"

"He picked up a small suit-case when he went off, sir."

"Gloves?"

"I don't know, sir—he kept his hands in his pocket, and I didn't notice when he reached for his bag."

"And his face?"

"Well, I didn't get much of a look at it. He was clean shaven, and didn't wear glasses, but that's all I can be sure of. I believe I'd recognize his voice again, though."

"You're certain he was wearing an overcoat? It couldn't have been a long dark-blue trench coat?"

"Oh no sir: it was black all right—double-breasted and pretty smart."

"And he went on ahead of you?"

"Yes sir: but the Sergeant here didn't see him, so I guess he must have turned off before he got to Belling itself."

"Odd," said Bagshaw—"confoundedly odd. Anything else?"

Best smiled and nodded.

"But not about him, sir, and maybe nothing at all—I don't know. About quarter past two I was walking down towards the coast road again from going round by Mr. Harrington's place, and

I suddenly heard a car start up a good way along towards Cray-bourne."

"Aha!" exclaimed the colonel. "Why on earth didn't you mention that before?"

"Well sir—because it wasn't the van."

"Not?"

"No sir. I've heard that old thing, and it makes a terrible row, but this was a real car: a sort of high-pitched whirr, and then the engine running nice and quiet, even when it drove off. The funniest part is that he couldn't have had any lights on: I only heard him, I didn't see a thing."

"Which way did he go?"

"Away from me, sir, and pretty fast, I think."

"And that was at quarter past two?"

"Or just after."

"And about how far was this car from where you were standing, by the sound of it?"

Best wrinkled his forehead while Bagshaw watched him, also frowning: only Sergeant Tukes, placidly fingering his moustache, seemed undisturbed by present disclosures.

"It's darned hard to say," declared the constable at last. "At a guess, a good quarter of a mile. It'd stopped raining by then, and there wasn't anything of a wind either, and I've got pretty good hearing, so it might even have been farther."

The colonel nodded, got up, took from his inside pocket a large-scale map of the district, knelt down, and spread it out on the worn black rug before the fire. At a gesture Best brought the lamp nearer, and indicated approximately where he had been when he heard the car. The sergeant swivelled his chair round, but remained seated. Presently Bagshaw grunted, folded the map, and rose stiffly. His pale blue eyes stared fixedly in Best's direction, but without seeing him. They were not focused upon material things; inwardly they contemplated the ghost of a possibility.

"Seen Mary or Miss Saunderson since they came back?" he asked suddenly, life returning to his face.

"Mary?" echoed the young policeman in surprise. "No sir, neither of them. I—I dare say I'll slip along in the morning. I rang her up at tea-time today, though."

'Quarrelled or something?' wondered Bagshaw.

"Did she tell you about Miss Saunderson?" he asked, aloud.

"Yes sir: she said Mr. Harrington was a bit worried."

"Yes, I heard that too. Wonder you didn't have supper with her," he added obliquely, his curiosity getting the better of him.

"She goes over to Tilgate Friday evenings," was the answer.

"Tilgate? What in the world for?"

Best looked even more surprised, and perhaps a little resentful, and Bagshaw realized afresh that Mary Adams, Philippa Saunderson's maid, was undoubtedly the chief interest of the young man's life. He also recalled Charles Harrington's query about when they were going to get married.

"Oh, sorry," he murmured—"none of my business."

He paused in some embarrassment, and glared fiercely at the silent Tukes.

"Seen Mr. Oakes about the place lately?" he asked.

"No sir, not for some little time. He doesn't come much in the winter."

"Not likely to be at home if we called?"

"I wouldn't think so, sir."

"Good!" said the Chief-constable approvingly. "I ought to be in bed, but I dare say I can stay awake just a bit longer. You boys do your buttons up pretty, and then we'll just have a peep through Mr. Oakes's windows."

"Why, sir?" enquired the sergeant stolidly.

"Oh, no particular reason. To make *sure* there's no one at home—put it that way."

# VI

COLONEL BAGSHAW APPROACHED THE BUNGALOW with a caution for which he could not have given any rational explanation. He did this by the simple method of accelerating up to seventy-five miles an hour, and then shutting off his engine. The slight slope of the road made it possible for the car to run on thereafter a good five hundred yards.

The building lay midway between the coast road and the seaweed-strewn highwater line. Leading up to it across the grassy dunes was a narrow gravel path about twice the length of a cricket pitch, and before he ventured along this the Chief-constable stood for a moment trying to catch the outline of the roof against the starry sky. The moon was not yet up, and the night fine but cold, with a noticeable breeze from the murmuring sea. High tide would not be reached for another hour.

"Come on," he said at last, in a low voice. "Darned if I can make anything out."

The others followed him in silence, finding their steps by the light of his electric torch: those which formed part of their equipment for night-duty were Still at the police-station, since they had not yet officially paraded. When a minute later all three stood on the wooden veranda which surrounded the bungalow, Bagshaw leant against the rail listening; but there was no sound of human activity inside, nor any hint of light.

"Nobody here, sir," remarked Tukes, with an inflexion in his whisper which was clearly meant as a reminder that he had prophesied as much before they set out.

"Maybe—maybe not" said his superior shortly. "Stay here for a bit, both of you."

First he examined the back entrance, which was locked. He then walked heavily round to the front, at the seaward side of the squat building, and knocked on the door with his gloved fist.

"Anybody in?" he called in a penetrating voice: but there was no reply. He tried the handle, and finally turned his torch on the windows, but all were heavily curtained, and all impossible to see through. Bagshaw grunted, returned to the back of the bungalow, and addressed the dark blur which was Tukes.

"Know anything about opening windows, Sergeant?"

"Beg pardon, sir? Opening windows? Well, I dare say I might have a try."

"What with? How d'you go about it?"

"Depends on how they're fastened," replied Tukes solemnly: yet from his tone the colonel fancied that he would very much have liked to ask questions.

"Well, I've got a trick pocket-knife, if that's any good. Full of gadgets—corkscrews and scissors and things for getting flies out of horses' eyes and so on. See what you can do—I just feel like a nice bit of burglary. And don't make a mess."

"No sir," agreed the sergeant. "Could I have a lend of your torch, sir, please?"

The colonel passed it across, and moved to where Best was standing patiently by.

"Any idea what we're looking for, John?" he queried significantly. For a full half-minute the young policeman made no answer, and then he cleared his throat in the dark.

"Miss Philippa, sir, I think" he muttered, almost under his breath.

"Ah. Been doing a bit of work for her in your spare time, haven't you? Private ambassador, and what-not?"

"Yes sir"—very quietly. "Who told you, sir—Mr. Oakes?"

"Oakes? Never spoken to the man in my life. What over makes you ask that?"

"Oh, I don't know, sir—I thought maybe he might have done."

"Too big a handicap," declared the colonel abruptly. "Hate talking to people when I can't see their faces. We'll settle that business later, John."

"Yes sir" said Best: and Bagshaw, listening intently, believed he detected relief in the other's voice.

'So I *was* right!' he mused. 'Two flukes in one day—not bad going. But dammit, they're supposed to come in threes, aren't they? Or is that accidents? I wonder if there'll be anything inside. Hope there isn't—hope to God there isn't. All the same, I've a funny kind of a feeling . . .'

"Got one of the windows open, sir," came Tukes's voice through the blackness. Bagshaw started from his reverie: for the moment he had forgotten the sergeant's task.

"Been dashed quiet about things," he said. "Which room is it? Let's look."

The window in question was of the ordinary sash variety, and this might have surprised him if he had not known that the bungalow dated from before the war. He now took his torch back from the sergeant and shone it inside the room, holding the double velvet curtains aside with his left hand.

"Bedroom," he announced. "All very smart and fancy, by the look of it—and damned uncomfortable too, I wouldn't wonder. At least, perhaps not—perhaps not. Never slept in a chromium bed myself, but if it suits Mr. Oakes, I dare say it could be a lot worse."

Then, allowing the beam from his torch to travel upwards to the ceiling, he uttered an exclamation of mild astonishment.

"Electric light! How's that? Fellow got his own plant or something?"

It was Best who answered.

"No sir, off the main. It cost him three-fifty, so I heard."

"Well, well! But I suppose it would, come to think of it: must be a good half mile from the next place that's got it. Wonder the chap didn't go the whole hog and have limelight installed. Now, who's going through this window? Seeing it's my idea, I probably ought to do it myself, but what with not going to bed much, and all that stew . . ."

"I think I can manage it, sir," said Best confidently. "What do you want done when I'm inside?"

"First switch on the light in this room. Then go and open the front door."

"And if there isn't any light, sir?"

"Eh? Oh, there's bound to be. Anybody who could afford that much to have it put in wouldn't bother with having it cut off when he ain't at home—that'd be mean. Still,"—as he remembered Oakes's price to Philippa for the letters and portrait, "you may be right—better take the torch. Get along in, and mind your head. Manage without taking your coat off? Good."

The colonel's surmise was correct: half a minute later he and Tukes were almost blinded as Best reached the switch.

"Limelight's about the mark!" muttered the sergeant. "I bet that's a 120-watt lamp."

"Really? You one of those blokes who know all about amps and ohms and therms and things? Then maybe you can tell me what 220v. A.C. means? Inspector Creevy obviously expected me to grasp it, and I simply daren't let on I—Hey! What the devil's up?"

He had every reason for asking: from the inside of the bungalow had come a hoarse shout, and then a moment of tense silence, and then the clatter of feet as Best panted towards them.

"What's the matter, man?" demanded Bagshaw sharply, catching him by the arm. "Where's the torch—I can't see a thing. Good God, he's going to faint! Here, take hold of him, Tukes."

"It's all right" came Best's voice weakly. "Sorry. You'd best go inside, sir. There's—there's something pretty horrible. Ugh! Horrible! Body—girl—got no feet."

The colonel swore unrepeatably under his breath and started towards the door from which Best had just come running. It now stood wide open, black against the pale shaft of light from within. Then he halted, regaining control of his wits.

"No good flustering," he said aloud. "You chaps got gloves? Then put 'em on, and don't touch more than you need, and mind your feet. Better stay outside, John, on second thoughts—doesn't sound the sort of thing you'd want to see twice."

"It's awful, sir—horrible."

"Who is it? Not—not anyone you recognized?"

"Don't know, sir—it's got a sort of bag over the head. And hardly no clothes on, and no feet—"

His voice died away, and in the light from the door Bagshaw could see that he was white and shaken. He had taken his helmet off, and Tukes, still supporting him, had already undone his greatcoat and was fiddling with the top buttons of his uniform. The colonel felt more anxious than ever to get inside and view this appalling discovery for himself, yet he waited a moment longer. Taking off his gloves he fumbled at an inner pocket, and brought out a silver flask.

"Brandy," he said, removing the stopper. "Take a swig."

Best did so, and declared that he felt better.

"Good—we'll have ours in a minute, Sergeant. Which room?"—leading the way indoors.

"To the left," came the constable's voice from behind. "I didn't put the light on—saw it by the torch."

"Which you promptly dropped," said Bagshaw, as he trod on it. "And smashed," he added, a moment later. "There's an open door here—is that the one? Right."

He moved across to it, blocking most of the light from the bedroom obliquely opposite; he could make out nothing distinctly but his own distorted shadow merging into the farther blackness, and he braced his mind for a shock.

'It'll give you a turn' he warned himself, as his left hand moved up the inner wall, 'but it'll be dead, and it can't move or anything, and it won't be as bad as it was for John—you do know more or less what's coming. And let's hope to heaven it isn't Philippa—I'll never be able to tell Charles. Don't see who else it can be, though.'

And then he found the switch, and the darkness gave way instantaneously to a white blaze, and a second later his eyes were tightly closed in revulsion.

The room was square, and scarcely furnished at all: by the easel in the far left-hand corner, and the dozen canvases leaning face to the wall, it was plainly Oakes's studio. In the middle of the polished wooden floor was a Persian rug in rich shades of claret and blue, and upon this was stretched the most gruesome object Colonel Bagshaw had ever seen or imagined. It was the body of a girl, and he knew that he would carry an exact memory of it in his mind till the day he died.

She lay awkwardly on her right side, facing the door and whoever should enter it, and she was clad only in underclothes. Round her waist was a screwed-up green petticoat, bespattered with curiously bright blood: above was a vest of similar material, awry and barely concealing her bosom, and below extended her thighs, bare to about six inches from the knee, where two garish garters clasped the tops of her stockings.

But that could all be regarded without flinching: all between forearm and neck, neck and ankle, however still the flesh, however distasteful the red-pink trickle of blood running out of sight between her dead breasts. It was the extremities of her body whose appearance inspired nausea. Bagshaw was never afterwards certain which had revolted him the more: the stumps of her legs, where her feet had been chopped off, stocking ends and all, or her wrists and neck, alike encased grotesquely in yellow oilskin tennis-racket covers. What they hid could hardly be worse than what was visible below her shins: yet, imperceived, there was a suggested possibility of greater vileness. 'It *must* be worse' prompted the depths of his consciousness. 'The devil didn't mind showing the legs, but he couldn't bear not to cover the neck and wrists . . .'

That was how the colonel analysed his own feelings afterwards. At the time, his eyes shut fast, he had room only for one definite thought. 'It's Alice Carter—it isn't Philippa at all. Point to

Creevy—if he hadn't gone into all those details about her clothes, I wouldn't know.'

Fortified by the realization, he allowed himself another and longer glance, and then turned his head: to discover that he was the only living person in the room. A moment later, from outside, came the sound of movements, and then of someone being sick.

They were on the veranda again, with Sergeant Tukes obstinately apologetic.

"Don't know what came over me, sir," he said. "I was all through the war, and saw plenty worse. All the same, I never dreamt it'd look like that."

"Ghastly," agreed Bagshaw, and found to his annoyance that he was trembling a little. "Now look here: someone's got to stay here and see nobody interferes, and someone's got to get busy on a telephone. This'll be a Scotland-Yard job."

"I'll stay, sir," volunteered Tukes. "Yes, I'd rather. You take young John with you and pack him off to bed, sir—I'll be all right."

"Sure? You needn't go inside again—no sense in trying your nerves too far. Stop in the fresh air and smoke—here's some cigarettes. I'll be back as soon as I can."

# VII

AT 1.00 A.M. ON SATURDAY OCTOBER 22ND Chief-Inspector Edward Beale was awakened by the ringing of the telephone at his bedside. He sat up rubbing his grey eyes and frowning: a rather plain man of forty-three whose brown hair was just perceptibly beginning to grow thin at the temples. His face and features, as he was always the first to admit, were undistinguished: a casual glance might have placed him as a lawyer or a bank-manager, or even a doctor, but rarely as a member of the C.I.D. At the moment the most striking thing about him was the design of his pyjamas: yellow and purple stripes on a dark-green background. They were a present—unsolicited—from a twice-convicted house-breaker for whom he had found a good word in the witness-box; but he wore them more because of their warmth in cold weather than because their appearance appealed to him.

For ten minutes he listened in silence to Superintendent Vinney's metallic voice from Scotland Yard, hung up with a sigh, and reached for his alarm clock. With some feeling of displeasure he set the third hand for six o'clock instead of half past seven, and then turned to the telephone again. He had a standing arrangement with his friend Anthony Purdon—somewhat taller, definitely uglier and the assistant editor of *The Stockbroker*—to inform him whenever there was a case on hand which promised to be interesting.

That these cases were usually concerned with murder was less an indication of Tony's tastes than of Beale's aptitude for solving murder puzzles. He had now at least half a dozen such solutions to his credit, and knew without any special degree of self-congratulation that in the estimation of his superiors he was becoming something of a star man. This fact was not wholly without its drawbacks, though, for often enough it meant that at a minute's notice he would be expected to drop whatever enquiry engaged his attention, and apply himself to more lethal matters: in the present instance, to abandon a particularly intricate case of robbery without violence for this business of a mutilated corpse at Belling Sands.

Nevertheless, it certainly sounded anything but dull. He knew Robert Oakes by sight, and he could imagine that the actor might prove the sort of man to appreciate unexpected publicity, even if brought about by the finding of a headless half-undressed female body in his seaside bungalow. And not only headless: it appeared that both hands and feet had also been removed. 'Which doesn't happen every day' he told himself tritely as he waited for his number to reply. 'Nor in conjunction with presumed carbon-monoxide poisoning. And why take her dress off? Because it could have helped to identify her, perhaps. But it's not a scrap of good getting preconceived ideas into my head, especially when she's supposed to have been seen by the landlady in her dressing-gown.'

Tony at first seemed sleepily resentful at being disturbed so late, but at the mention of Beale's reason for ringing up he brightened.

"Oh, that's different," he said: "I'm always willing to help a lame dog into the ditch. Belling, is it? Near a hovel called Craybourne, I fancy, and if so I only hope it's better. Craybourne's the sort of place you go in to bathe once at, and spend the rest of the time getting rid of the fishy smell. So a chap told me, anyway. What train do we catch?"

"Train?" repeated his friend. "Train? Why do you suppose I'm wasting part of my precious sleep like this—to hear twaddle about trains? Be outside with the Bentley at ten to seven if you want a cup of tea before we start, and ten past if you don't."

"Oh, all right: half a crown a furlong and immunity from prosecution—they're my terms. Is 'Horsey' Matthews coming?"

"Yes—we'll pick him up on the way. Good-night."

In fact, however, there was a fourth passenger the next morning. Just as they were leaving Beale's rooms near Marble Arch they heard a noise which Tony likened to a faulty road-drill, and a motor-cycle swept perilously round the corner.

"Good work—just in time," observed its owner, dismounting. "Think I can leave this here?"

"Not outside anywhere I live," declared Beale firmly. "The proper place for that thing is South Kensington. Whatever department deals with the origins of mechanical transport would do nicely."

"Pity," said Richard Donovan, crime correspondent of the *Evening Sentinel*. He frowned thoughtfully, and brushed back his tousled hair with an oily hand.

"I couldn't pop it down an area, could I?" he suggested. "Ah, behold: one genuine copper approaches. Good-morning, Sergeant."

"Good-morning, sir," returned the constable heavily. "Oh, good-morning Inspector!"—catching a sight of Beale.

"Hullo, Tom. Could you do anything about that smoking ruin by the curb, do you think? Lose it somewhere?"

"Yes sir, certainly—if it's safe to move."

Half a crown changed hands, and the motor-cycle was left in the charge of P.c. Hanbury: who, after regarding it dubiously, became presently so interested in Dickie's home-made carburettor that he was several minutes late in meeting his sergeant farther along the beat, and so received a reprimand which he felt to be altogether unfair.

They reached Belling Sands at quarter past nine and were directed from the police-station to Colonel Bagshaw's house, where they were glad to find breakfast waiting. As noon as they had finished the Chief-constable began to explain the position, starting with Mrs. Topley's discovery noon after 7.00 on Thursday evening.

"Nasty," murmured Tony, when the finding of the body had been described. Then he took out a note-book, and gravely made an entry.

"Solved it?" asked Bagshaw with a smile: he was feeling better after four hours' sleep, and Tony's standing had already been made clear to him.

"Pretty nearly," was the answer. "Anyway, I fancy I've made a start, provided you're fairly sure that the butchery was done on the premises?"

"You shall see for yourself—in the kitchen, if it helps. Most of the actual blood had been washed up, but the place must have looked like a slaughter-house, which points to the fact that she hadn't been dead very long, poor wretch, so the doctor tells me. For heaven's sake! There's another,"—as Matthews too produced writing materials. Dickie had been scribbling shorthand from the beginning. "Do all you people do this? Ought I to?"

Beale smiled: he felt he would get on well with the colonel, whose speech and manner contrasted so strongly with his lean gloomy appearance.

"It isn't absolutely essential, sir," he said. "Tony's probably bluffing, and Matthews remembered a birthday or something."

But the detective-sergeant, small and equine, denied the charge with a twinkling grin.

"No sir, quite genuine," he assured them. *"I* can't afford to remember people's birthdays. It needn't be a secret, though: if you look at the place from the road, can you tell it's got electric light inside? Not much fun chopping a corpse about in the dark."

"Yes, there's a cable quite visible," Bagshaw told him. "Provided you know what it is, of course. I always thought it was something to do with a telephone myself—they gave me all the wrong books at school, I'm afraid.

"Well, after that Best and I went along to the station, and I duly sent him off to bed. I rang up Inspector Creevy—the one whose report I've just read you, and Superintendent Walters, who's down with 'flu, and we all agreed we'd better have you fellows down here at once. After that I got hold of a camera and a doctor and so on, and went back. We made a thorough search of the whole place, and photographed everything, and eventually the body was taken away for examination. Dr. Duncan's on it now, as a matter of fact, and he promised he'd be along as near 10.30 as he could.

"As for the Craybourne end of the business, unfortunately there isn't very much to tell you. All the fingerprints in the room from which the girl disappeared have been compared with the landlady's, and the ones Creevy mentions on the tooth-glass. Yes?"— to Matthews, who had cleared his throat.

The detective-sergeant made no apology for interrupting: the subject was his speciality.

"What were the ones on the glass like, sir?" he asked. "A left-hand set and a few odd ones? Or two clear sets?"

"Sorry, don't remember," said Bagshaw. "Does it matter much?"

"I couldn't say till I've seen the glass myself, sir, but it might. Tooth-glasses are funny things. One used by a right-handed person nearly always shows seventy-five per cent of left-hand prints, and back foremost. Which was the girl?"

The colonel stared at Matthews with more respect.

"Size no criterion," he observed. "In short, you've got the painstaking Inspector Creevy on the run. With all his love of detail he never said a word about it, and the old woman's bound to know. But I don't follow all that right and left stuff."

"Well sir, if you're right-handed you keep that one free for the brush—most people do."

"Ah, I suppose so—not bad. To go on: the prints have been compared. Now, the main point of interest is that there were very very few in the bedroom: almost everything seemed to have been wiped clean. What we did find have been identified either as Mrs. Topley's or as corresponding with those on the glass, except for two on one of the wooden bed-posts: two fingers, so they tell me, though how they know they're not thumbs I can't imagine. And please don't ask which hand, Sergeant, because I haven't the slightest idea: but—if it's of any interest—they were on the post usually used by Alice Carter for hanging up her garters on. Provisionally we're supposing those prints to belong to the man Ellis, though of course they may still be the girl's own.

"So much for 14 Weatherall Road. In respect of the van, all the prints there were made either by Deacon or his girl. We routed 'em both out of bed last night and made them give us their impressions."

"Did they mind?" asked Beale.

"No, they didn't seem to—it wasn't the same bed they were in. As well, Inspector Creevy found one clue, as he calls it. On the floor of the van there's a nail sticking up an eighth of an inch, and on the head was a wisp of some brown fibrous material—I'll show it to you over at Craybourne presently. And now you all know as much as I do, and I hope you can make something more of it. At least, I'm afraid that isn't strictly true: but you know as much as I can tell you at the moment."

As he said this the colonel looked a trifle uncomfortable: he was thinking of Charles Harrington, and wondering how far friendship might be allowed to interfere with duty. Beale, unintentionally, showed his surprise by his raised eyebrows, but said nothing. He judged that it would be better not to ask the exact meaning of the Chief-constable's last remark in front of so many witnesses. Dickie Donovan was less tactful, however.

"How long is a moment?" he enquired amiably.

"Time it!" was Bagshaw's tart retort. "It's just 10.25 now."

The reporter grinned.

" 'The police will be obliged if the press will remember its place'," he said. "Well, I suppose I can't grumble. May one ask how far this bungalow is from Smuggler's Lane?"

"Of course. I'm not trying to diddle you, only I don't feel I can pass on other people's very private information till I at least know if it's relevant. The distance is about three-quarters of a mile, and the bungalow's this side, and the road isn't the right kind to take tyre prints, worse luck. Not that the van would have left any if it were," he added. "The tyres are all smooth."

"And there's a point or two I'd like to raise, please," put in Beale.

"Splendid. It's your case now, you know—that's what you've been dragged down here for."

"Thank you, sir. Then first, is the bungalow provided with gas?"

"No: the nearest supply is nearly a mile off!"

"I see. Secondly, what was the method of entering the place? Not yours, but that of whoever put the body there."

The Chief-constable accompanied his answer with an unhappy frown.

"We don't know," he said. "The only window that looks as if it's been tampered with is the one Sergeant Tukes tackled, and the door obviously hasn't been forced. Tukes wasn't on the watch to see if he was the first there, but I don't much care about the idea that he picked just the one window the other johnny had messed about with. He says there was no particular reason why he chose it, except that it was the one he happened to be standing by."

Bagshaw paused, appearing even more embarrassed. He must clearly give this man Beale what help he could with regard to Oakes, yet he wanted if possible to keep Philippa Saunderson's name out of things. If only the little wretch would turn up, he thought: then Charles would drop his fantastic theory that in spite of the underclothing and garters, the headless body might be that of his missing niece. His difficulties were resolved almost immediately, however. There came a knock at the door, and Harrington himself was shown in, accompanied by the young police-surgeon.

To the colonel's mind the novelist seemed to have aged ten years since the previous afternoon. His plump face was a pasty white, save for the dark circles under his eyes, and his clothes were carelessly put-on. After the necessary introductions had been made, Bagshaw turned to his friend enquiringly.

"Want a word with me alone?" he suggested; but—to his surprise—Harrington shook his head, and faced Beale.

"I've heard of you," he said in his gentle voice.

"And I of you."

"Yes? Then I dare say I could get away with my presence here by pretending professional curiosity, but I'd rather not. My interest is purely personal, Inspector, and I propose to tell you why. On one condition, that is: that all of you will give me your promise not to repeat a word of what I say without first consulting Colonel Bagshaw. That particularly applies to you, sir,"—to Donovan.

"More spinosity, *alias* murk," remarked the reporter with a cheerful smile. "Due to the same cause, I wonder?"

"The same," answered the Chief-constable. "I don't think you need worry—you won't be asked to suppress any information that concerns the Alice-Carter affair. Mr. Harrington merely wants to make sure that certain family secrets don't become public property."

"All right, that sounds fair enough."

Everyone duly promised what the novelist required, and he thanked them quietly.

"I'm sorry for all this mystery," hc said, turning again to Beale. "I know it's my trade, but I hope that when I've finished you'll understand. Incidentally, you needn't be afraid that I shall waste your time."

He then proceeded to tell them what he had told the colonel the day before.

"Well, that's how the situation stood last night" he observed. "This morning, early, Colonel Bagshaw knocked me up and informed me about the discovery at Oakes's bungalow, and I immediately began to wonder if the body mightn't really be Philippa's. Perhaps you'll think that idea ridiculous, in view of the clothing, but I can't help it. In my job you get used to swapping bodies and cutting off heads and all the rest of it: a murder hardly counts unless there's some such trick in it. One day somebody'll write a simple straightforward one and have everybody guessing: the dagger in the back really was the weapon used, the suspicious stranger really did deserve to be suspected, and really was a stranger. *Death on the Level*—not a bad title. I might do worse myself, but till then I stick to convention.

"At all events, I insisted on being allowed to look at what they found last night, and I have looked, God help me, and all I can say for certain is that I saw nothing to indicate definitely it *was* Philippa. On the other hand, I didn't see enough against the idea to make me drop it. What indications there were mostly pointed to Alice Carter, I agree: it's simply that they didn't do that positively enough to satisfy me.

"After all, consider the matter from my standpoint. My niece gets herself stupidly involved with a bounder to the extent of blackmail. Next she goes out 'on business', as I said, and doesn't return, and finally the body of a young girl of approximately the same size and colouring is found in the bounder's studio—the very room in which the portrait was painted which partially involved her. And what a body! The doctor here will give you the details, but I'm sure he won't mind my saying that every attempt seems to have been made to prevent identification. Can you wonder I'm not entirely convinced I'm wrong, even by the cause of death."

"Which *was* carbon-monoxide poisoning?" asked Beale quickly.

"Yes."

"Inhaled through the agency of coal gas, in my opinion," put in Dr. Duncan quietly. He was about thirty, and to judge by his expression and bearing a pleasant young man. Beale somehow fancied that he had not officially dealt with death in such violent guise before.

"Yes, Doctor, I know" agreed Harrington rather sharply. "But it isn't conclusive—coal gas isn't all that rare, leaving aside any possibility of your being wrong. Still, you shall have your say in a minute; just let me point out one more significant aspect of the affair, and I've finished. If the body in the bungalow is Alice Carter's, Inspector, then it was presumably placed there by Ellis, the fellow in coloured glasses. Anyway, that seems to me to be the natural presumption to make. If you accept it, you immediately come up against the question of how Ellis gained access to the bungalow, in view of what the colonel says about the door and windows. My answer to that conundrum is—for once—the simple one: the person who entered used a key, which rules out Ellis and rules in the one person likely to have a key—the owner."

He paused, surveying them all with a faint smile.

"And once Ellis is out," he said, "then so is Alice Carter, for there can't be any possible connection between her and Oakes."

"Why not?" queried Beale gently. "Surely your powers of invention wouldn't be beaten by that. In one of your novels, I mean," he added hastily, as Harrington stared at him coldly.

"He was just tackling me about the method of entry when you came in, Charles," said Bagshaw. "It's a puzzle, all right."

"But owners of houses sometimes lend or give a key to close friends," continued Beale. "What about Miss Saunderson in that capacity?"

"Honestly, I don't know," replied the novelist. "She never said anything about having one, but I must admit I never raised the point."

"I see: and thank you for being so frank. I appreciate your position, and I won't lose sight of the possibility that your niece's disappearance may be connected with last night's discovery, much as I hope it isn't. Now, Doctor, do you mind telling us what you learnt from your examination of the body?"

"Preliminary examination," amended Duncan, rising with a quick smile. "I haven't done a full autopsy yet, of course, but I can give you quite a lot of information."

He studied some notes for half a minute, and then addressed the room in general.

"The remains in question are those of a young woman between twenty and thirty years of age, in quite good condition physically. She was fair-haired, and I estimate her probable height as between sixty-four and sixty-five inches: naturally the absence of the head and feet makes it difficult to be at all exact. Death was due to carbon-monoxide poisoning, as Mr. Harrington just said, and in case you aren't familiar with the subject, perhaps I'd better go into a few details.

"Carbon monoxide, CO, is a colourless odourless gas generated whenever incomplete combustion of carbon takes place. The commonest source is household gas, where its proportion may vary from as little as 4% to as much as 30%. It is also contained in the exhaust gases of cars, the rate of production being roughly one cubic foot per minute per twenty horse-power.

"CO is what is called an irrespirable gas. When breathed in it combines with the haemoglobin in the blood—the colouring matter of the red corpuscles—about three hundred times as readily as oxygen, with the result that it has a cumulative asphyxiating action. As little as 1% in the air of a room will cause unconsciousness in from fifteen to twenty minutes. A concentration in the blood of 30% gives rise to headaches, and the symptoms grow progressively worse up to 70% or so, when the victim becomes unconscious—if that hasn't happened already—and dies very soon afterwards through lack of oxygen.

"To give you some idea of the rapidity with which the gas takes effect I will instance the presumed circumstances of the present case. If Alice Carter covered her head with a blanket, and had near her mouth or nose a tube connected with an active gas supply, she would be insensible within thirty seconds and dead almost immediately after. It so happens that I know something of the nature of the gas distributed in Craybourne: it contains usually about 24% of CO."

"Which is quite a lot" suggested Tony.

"Well, certainly above the average. You see, the kind of gas needed nowadays is one with high heating properties rather than luminosity. That necessitates a high hydrogen content, the cheapest way of producing which is by passing steam over hot charcoal. Unfortunately the result also contains a high proportion of CO, about 40%, and it's not a commercial proposition to eliminate this. Obviously, the cheaper the cost of producing household gas, the better the consumer can be treated as regards price, and consequently the general tendency is to increase the percentage of water-gas used. Equally obviously, in my view, the greater the CO content, the higher will be the suicide rate. Putting your head in an oven isn't like shooting yourself or swallowing a bottleful of hydrocyanic acid: you *can* take your head out again if you change your mind quick enough, but the more toxic the atmosphere inside the oven the less chance you'll have. Sorry if I've bored you."

"Not a bit," said Beale: "your last point seems very sound."

"Thank you. In my opinion, the girl was subjected to a high concentration of CO," continued Duncan, "and died very rapidly. That would make me think the source was household gas rather than the exhaust of a car, even if I didn't know the circumstances. All the same, I won't be absolutely definite on the point, and I feel I ought to advise you to have the body examined by the Home-Office pathologist."

Harrington nodded two or three times at this suggestion, which Beale received with a smile.

"Well, that's handsome enough," he remarked. "I've met a lot of police-surgeons who take it as the ultimate insult if you even mention the man's existence. Can you give us some idea of when death took place?"

"Not a very precise one, I'm afraid. The circumstances are rather against precision, you know: in particular, the fact that within a comparatively short time of death, not more than two hours I should say, the head and hands and feet were removed. If it's of any use, you can rely on death having occurred between six o'clock last night—I mean Thursday night—and three o'clock on Friday morning. And I don't mind admitting," he went on, with a frown "that if I didn't know she was supposed to have died about 7.00 I'd have put the probable time as nearer midnight."

"Ah!" exclaimed Harrington softly, and stared pointedly first at Bagshaw and then at Beale. "Kindly note the possible significance of that, Inspector."

"I will," was the quiet answer. "And how were the extremities removed, Doctor?"

"By sheer force—no question of anatomical knowledge. I should expect the instrument used to have been a sharp cleaver or butcher's chopper: something pretty heavy, and for preference with a straight edge to the blade. The feet were severed just above the ankle, the hands at the wrist, and the head just under the chin. In each case the dismemberment was effected with one clean blow, which suggests the exercise of considerable strength. The person responsible was probably a man rather than a woman."

"A big man?" asked Tony.

"Not necessarily: his muscular development would count more than his size. Other things being equal, though, you'd have been likely to make a better job of it than the sergeant."

"So he ought to have," said 'Horsey' Matthews. "He's double my weight, and anyway I'd be a bit more subtle."

"I wouldn't be too sure about that," observed Harrington unexpectedly and judicially. "In my opinion, the state of the murderer's mind is likely to be a good deal more important than either his size or his muscular development. There must have been—to him—some terrifically urgent reason for rendering the body unidentifiable, as near as he could: fear of the possible consequences if he didn't, and fear can lend even a feeble man the most astounding strength."

"You're speaking from your own point of view, that the body is your niece's?" asked Dickie curiously.

"Yes—why?"

"Oh, nothing: only Oakes was a big hefty fellow last time I saw him."

The novelist said nothing to that, and the doctor resumed.

"The beheading and so on was certainly the work of a determined man," he declared. "There were no half measures—no sign of hesitation. After the job was done the stumps of the arms were tightly enclosed in oil-silk bags fastening with a thin cord threaded through. The same was done to the neck, there being enough left for the purpose. As I said just now, the head was severed just under the angle of the chin, though whether deliberately or not I can't say. The legs were not tied up, however. And that's about all, I think, except that I'm prepared to state definitely that the trunk of the body wasn't moved later than five hours after death. The development of rigor and lividity leave no doubt on that point."

Dr. Duncan smiled, returned his notes to his pocket, and sat down.

"Has anyone any questions?" queried Bagshaw.

"Several," answered Beale quietly. "First, Doctor, were you acquainted with Miss Saunderson?"

"No, I'm afraid not. I fancy I've seen her about, but I've certainly never spoken to her."

"Next, when the feet were severed, was the body wearing stockings or not?"

"Oh yes, undoubtedly."

"And have you any idea about what they may have been resting on at the time? Or the arms and neck too, for that matter?"

Duncan looked thoughtful.

"There weren't any explicit indications," he said, "but it couldn't have been anything very rigid, since the cuts were so clean in every case. That's particularly true of the legs—the stockings were very little frayed. On the other hand, it couldn't have been anything too yielding—scarcely earth, and certainly not sand. It may sound a trifle silly, but I'm really inclined to think something like a block of wood was used, the body being on its back."

"And the person who did the job would get quite a lot of blood on him?"

"I should think so—it would be a messy business."

"But I thought dead bodies didn't bleed," objected Tony.

"It depends," Duncan told him. "Never to anything like the same extent as living ones, of course, but when veins are severed like that within a short time of death, then there will usually be some bleeding. As it happens, with death from CO poisoning—which is really only a form of asphyxia—the blood remains fluid considerably longer than is normally the case, and that will naturally increase the post-mortem effusion. As a matter of fact, when just now I said the dismemberment was carried out within two hours of death, that was an outside estimate. I would place the time as being most probably from twenty minutes to half an hour after."

"Thank you," said Beale, partly on Tony's behalf: he was anxious to get on. "Now another point: had the girl been interfered with at all?"

"Oh no, nothing like that."

"In your opinion, was she married or single? Or didn't you get so far with your examination?"

The doctor's manner became distinctly apologetic.

"Really, I don't seem to have been so very thorough after all," he murmured.

"Rot," said Beale kindly. "Please don't think I'm criticizing—you couldn't be expected to mention everything in a short verbal résumé."

"Oh well, it's nice of you to put it that way. In answer to your question, she was more likely to have been married than single, but she had never had a child."

"Which, in view of what I've already told you, doesn't shake my idea about her identity as much as I'd like it to," put in Harrington, a little distastefully.

"And one more thing: from the general condition of the flesh, when would you say that she last had a bath?"

Matthews saluted the point with a quick nod of appreciation: it was one, he knew, which he would never have thought of raising.

"Well, I wouldn't care to be positive," said Duncan, "but at a guess, within twenty-four hours of death."

"Hell!" grunted the novelist. "For what it's worth, also in favour of my suggestion," he declared. "If you remember, Alice Carter's rent included one bath a week, and once-a-weeker's don't choose Wednesday."

"Why not?" asked Tony.

"Well, I'm not quite sure, but they don't, take it from me. When I was young and penniless I had plenty of experience of furnished rooms, and I always came in the Saturday-night class. For one thing, landladies usually change the bed-linen at the week-end—or pretend they do. Still, I think I'd better shut up for a bit: I do seem to be twisting all available evidence to my way of thinking. Only please don't imagine I'm doing it because I *want* to be right—I emphatically don't. It's rather that I'm terrified because I can't convince myself I'm wrong. If only Philippa would turn up!"

# VIII

T HE COLONEL MADE a perfunctory if sympathetic noise, and glanced at his watch.

"Just 11.15," he said. "Now, Inspector, I dare say you're keen to get moving, but first I'd very much like you to hear what somebody else has to report. And you as well, Charles—it'll interest you especially."

"Very well," agreed Beale resignedly, and settled himself more comfortably in his chair. The room they were in was the Chief-constable's study, blue with tobacco smoke and extremely untidy, and during the owner's temporary absence to fetch his new witness he turned to Duncan.

"I forgot something," he said. "Were there any vaccination marks?"

"Yes, on the left arm in the usual place, but not at all outstanding."

A moment later Bagshaw returned accompanied by John Best, no longer wearing uniform but clad in grey flannels and a sports coat. He gave Harrington a pleasant smile of recognition, was introduced to the others, and was then requested to tell what he knew about Philippa Saunderson's compromising letters to Robert Oakes. That brought the plump novelist upright with a jerk.

"Oh!" he exclaimed, staring hard at the young policeman. "So *you* were the go-between, were you?"

"Yes sir," said Best, straightening his tie unnecessarily. He seemed inclined to be self-conscious under the fixed regard of so many pairs of eyes.

"Well I'm hanged! But I suppose I might have guessed. Yes, let's hear what you're got to say. And this won't be for publication either," he added, glancing for a second at Dickie's busy pencil sharpener.

"Oh, not more than a tenth of what *I* write ever gets into print," the reporter assured him calmly.

Best began with a brief reference to his engagement, explaining that he went up to Cairngorm to see Mary Adams about twice a week.

"Well, somewhere about the middle of August Miss Saunderson met me outside in the garden one evening just as I was coming away," he said. "She stopped and chatted for a bit, and then suddenly asked when Mary and I were going to get married. I told her as soon as I'd got enough money saved—in the New Year, I hoped. She said she was sure Mary'd be pleased, and then she suddenly took hold of my arm.

" 'Look here, John,' she said, 'a hundred pounds would make a bit of difference to your plans, wouldn't it?' I said of course it would, and asked what she meant, and before very long she was telling me in confidence how she'd written some silly letters to Mr. Oakes the actor, the man whose bungalow we found that body in last night. She said something about a painting too, only apparently that wasn't so important.

"Well, the long and the short of it was that she wanted those letters back, and she asked me would I keep watch for her one night while she went through the bungalow to see if she could find them."

"Good lord!" muttered Harrington. "Then she *did* have a key!"

"Yes sir, I gathered she had one. Of course, I told her outright I couldn't possibly agree to anything like that, and at first she seemed a bit upset. Then she calmed down, and made another suggestion. First she asked me if I knew Mr. Oakes to speak to, and I said no. I'd seen him about, of course, sometimes with her, and he was in a film I went to once, so I knew who he was all right. Then she wanted to know when my holiday was, and I told her, in about ten days' time, and that I was going to London. I used to live there, you know.

"Well, her new idea was that while I was up in town I should go to see Oakes, and do what I could about getting the letters back. She said he was a bit of a coward, and might let me have them if I bluffed hard enough, and she offered me two hundred pounds if I managed it."

He paused, looking worried and eyeing first Harrington and then the colonel dubiously.

"It sounds a bit queer, put like that," he went on, "but I think I'd have had a shot even if she hadn't offered me a penny. She seemed so terribly worried and upset, and explained how Oakes wanted far too big a price—he'd been blackmailing her—and how she hadn't anyone to turn to that was capable of standing up to the man. Naturally before I promised anything I asked if you'd been told anything, sir,"—again regarding Harrington. "She said you knew but that you wouldn't let her have anywhere near as much money as Oakes wanted, and that you couldn't be expected to do any rough stuff. Then I suggested telling you, Colonel, and she said she didn't feel she could do that because you'd be sure to want to do something officially, and that would mean publicity, and—well, she didn't actually say so, but I got the idea she was keen on somebody else who wouldn't have cared much about that.

"At any rate, in the end I agreed to go and see the chap, and do what I could."

"Just a second," broke in the novelist. "Forgive me for asking, but did she put her promise to pay you £200 for the letters into writing?"

Best looked almost offended.

"No sir," he answered with quiet severity. "It wasn't as business-like as all that. I said I'd try and help her chiefly because I was sorry for her, though of course the money would be a great thing for Mary and me if I was lucky. Well, I went up to London on August 27th, and then something that happened almost as soon as I arrived spoilt any idea of keeping my identity secret."

"Ah, now I remember" said Beale with interest. "You made a stout attempt to stop a smash-and-grab in Victoria Street, didn't you?"

"Yes, I knew I'd seen your face before, or a photo of it," declared Dickie. "We gave you half the front page, 4.30 edition—*Evening Sentinel,* I mean. I wrote it myself, as a matter of fact, and did you rather well: occupation, hobbies, handsome appearance, where you were staying, all about your gallant efforts—everything except what you thought of London policemen."

"You all made a sight too much fuss," said Best bluntly, at which Bagshaw smiled.

"You'd better watch out" he advised Donovan. "John hates reporters worse than Mr. Harrington here hates sopranos."

"Well, I know quite a lot of reporters who don't care about coppers," was the rejoinder. "But don't let's spoil the story."

"So I went to see Oakes," resumed Best at once, patently glad to close the subject of his own past notoriety. "I rang up and made an appointment for the following Tuesday, the first afternoon he had free, and when I got there he spotted me immediately. That was rather muddling for a while, but I soon saw the best way to tackle him would be to act as if I was about ten times as tough as you newspaper people had tried to make out. And it worked. There was a bit of a scrap—he didn't seem such a coward after all—but in the end he suddenly went very white and shaky, and handed over the letters without much fuss."

"How many?" asked Harrington quickly.

"Twenty-five, sir,"

"And the price?"

"Nothing—unless you count threats about what he'd look like on the stage that night with his nose round somewhere under his ear. And then, just as I was going, he turned nasty.

" 'Tell Miss Saunderson there's still the portrait,' he said. 'And you might also mention that I've got half a dozen photos of her posing for it, too. I was keeping them as a little surprise, but now I don't think I will.'

"Well, I wasn't quite sure what to make of that, because Miss Philippa hadn't told me what the picture was like. It didn't sound the sort you'd hang on your drawing-room wall, though, so I decided I'd better try to find out something about these photos. She hadn't mentioned them at all, and by the way he was talking it looked as if she mightn't even know they existed. I asked him to show me a copy of one, to prove he wasn't talking through his hat, and he said he'd give me copies of the lot—which he did."

"Still got 'em?" asked Bagshaw, as Best paused for breath.

"Yes sir—I'll come to that in a minute. Oakes didn't do them up, just unlocked a drawer in his desk and passed them over, and of course I couldn't help seeing, and—well, they were pretty awful. It looked to be Miss Philippa all right by the face, and without hardly a stitch on, and he was in one of them too, giving her a nasty sort of smile. I don't know what I ought to have done, but what I did do was lose my temper and go for him bald-headed. He finished up a mess on the floor, and then I started hunting through his desk for the negatives. I suppose I oughtn't to have done, what with being a policeman and all, but I reckoned he wouldn't make a row. Anyway, I didn't find them, and when he came round he began sneering at me, and said I was wasting my time because they were all safe at his bank. So I came away after that, seeing I couldn't do any more.

"The arrangement with Miss Philippa was that if I had any luck I should keep the letters till I got back here, but send her a line to let her know. I did that the next day, and got a short note saying she was very pleased, but worried about the photos, which she didn't understand. She also said she was just off to Scotland on holiday with Mr. Harrington here and Mary, and she asked me not to forward anything in case somebody saw by accident, but to look after everything I'd managed to get from Oakes till she came back. And not tell anyone, of course.

"She said she'd write again when she knew the date she'd be home, and I had another letter from her on Saturday of last week. She wanted me to say where I could meet her on Thursday, the day before yesterday, preferably not in Belling. I ought to have said before that she agreed nobody should know I was seeing Oakes for her, in case it got me into trouble. I wrote back suggesting Craybourne in the afternoon—I knew I'd be off duty. I said I couldn't bring the letters or photos because I'd taken a leaf out of Oakes's book and given them to *her* bank to take care of.

"Well, I caught the half past four bus from here on Thursday and met her outside the Craybourne post-office at 5.00, and she told me at once that she'd already been to fetch the packet of letters and photos. She thanked me for what I'd done, and said she'd never dreamt the photos had ever been taken, and now she seemed to be in a worse hole than ever. She asked if I could think of anything for her to do, and I said I couldn't, unless she were to find some way of getting the negatives from Oakes's bank without him knowing. We talked about it for a long time, and then she wrote me out a cheque for £200, and went off in her car, and that's all I know.

"Oh, I forgot: she asked me would I look after the photos, as it was too late to go back to the bank, and she'd hate Mr. Harrington or Mary to see them. All except the one which had Oakes in it too, that is. She said she might be able to do something with that, but I can't say what she meant. I didn't like the idea, but I couldn't very well refuse after her giving me all that money, so I agreed. I never saw her again after about quarter to six in Craybourne Thursday, and I'm sorry I told you a lie last night, sir,"—to Colonel Bagshaw. "About not having seen her at all, I mean."

"Oh, don't bother about that—you couldn't have done much else, in the circumstances. What's this?"

Best was taking an envelope from his pocket.

"The last letter I had from Miss Philippa, sir. I destroyed the first one—she asked me to because it had all about her private affairs in it. And then there's the photographs: but I don't know if I ought to give those up."

He looked round the room with a questioning frown.

"After all, we can't be *sure* she's dead," he added. "I don't see how she possibly can be."

"Dead?" echoed Harrington, staring. "Where the devil did you get hold of that idea from?"

"You," answered Bagshaw shortly. "*Via* me. I told John that was why he'd have to explain everything—because you believed the body was Philippa's."

"And why are you certain she's alive, Best?" asked Beale.

"Well, I'm not," answered the constable, turning to him and frowning even more. "I didn't mean quite that, sir. I meant I don't see how the body we found last night can be hers, when it'd got that other girl's garters and things on. At least, that's what the Chief told me."

Meanwhile the novelist was glaring fixedly at the table.

"It's awkward," he said. "If you hand over the photographs, and then Philippa comes back, she'll never forgive any of us; but if she's dead, they may just possibly help."

It was at this juncture that Beale decided to become more active. He was beginning to be the least bit weary of Harrington's continued harping on the one aspect of the situation.

"It doesn't seem to me worth wasting time about," he remarked, in the silence that followed. Then he addressed the novelist with a bland smile.

"Presumably you didn't see your niece naked very often?" he asked.

"What? Certainly not!"

"Then it won't be much good for you to examine these photographs, will it? I don't suppose there's much room for doubt, but what we want is someone who can tell us whether they're authentic or not."

"Good lord, I know that," said Harrington irritably. "The trouble is there isn't anyone. She hasn't been to a doctor since she was eleven, to my certain knowledge—"

"Then she jolly well ought to have" interrupted Duncan unexpectedly. "The way people put off—Oh, sorry."

"And who else is there bar Oakes?" continued the novelist, ignoring him.

Beale shrugged, and turned to Best.

"Did Miss Saunderson give you to understand on Thursday, after she'd seen them, that the photographs *were* of her?" he queried.

"Well—I don't know, Inspector. She certainly never said they weren't, or even hinted it, and if not, she wouldn't hardly have been so upset and frightened."

"Frightened?"

"Of Oakes, sir—of what he was meaning to do with the negatives. I can't remember exactly what she said, but it was something like this: 'Unless I get them back, it'll just about put the lid on everything.' "

"I see: that does look as if she accepted them, which means that we'll be fairly safe in doing the same. I suggest then that only Dr. Duncan sees them, Mr. Harrington, for the present. If he says the body was never that shape or size, well and good: it'll ease your mind, and allow us to assume that for once we can rely on appearances. I can't help feeling there are several very big points against your theory, you know, and I'm wondering if you haven't perhaps overlooked some of them.

"For instance, how do you explain away the underclothing, especially the almost unmistakable garters? Either they're actually those that Mrs. Topley saw Alice Carter wearing, or they're improbably identical. In both cases there would appear to be some clear connection between these two disappearances, and therefore between Oakes and 14 Weatherall Road, in spite of what you said earlier. The man Ellis, of course, and the absence of any gas-supply at the bungalow, just come in to make it harder. Incidentally, have you attempted to identify the underclothes yet? Surely this young man's fiancée should know, being your niece's maid."

"Not yet," said Harrington. "Don't forget I haven't had much time to go round asking questions, will you? I agree it ought to be done, though, and I appreciate what you say about the need for some link between Philippa and Alice Carter, if I should be right. Apparently that puts you right off, but it doesn't worry me so much: as far as I'm concerned, it would come under the heading of trickery.

"As I hinted earlier, after writing about a couple of dozen detective stories I tend to think of murder not as a straightforward bash on the head with the inevitable blunt instrument, but as a complicated and carefully planned procedure designed to attain two almost equally important objects: the elimination of the victim, and the befuddlement of the police. The latter is usually attained by such devices as apparently unbreakable alibis, apparently sealed rooms, the employment of highly unsuspicious weapons like poisoned postage-stamps or crossbows that discharge or-

namental stilettos, and mutilation of the remains in order to prevent identification, hocus about the time and manner of death, and
so on. You make your corpse seem to have been executed with a
rusty battle-axe in Piccadilly Circus on All Souls' Day by an arm-
less man in Nova Scotia at the time, whereas in fact it was suffo-
cated in a tub of self-raising flour on board a Channel steamer the
previous Christmas."

He paused, and when he resumed put off something of his lec-
turer's air.

"I dare say the truth is that I've become incapable of treating
sudden death in terms of real life," he observed, "and if that's what
you're thinking, then you won't take any notice of me. All the
same, there'll be several tricky points for you to work on, too.
What I'm chiefly concerned with at the moment is Philippa's
whereabouts. If that body is Alice Carter's—whoever Alice Carter
may be—then where's my niece? I shall be most grateful for a
satisfactory answer. As for the photographs, your plan seems
about the best possible as things stand. Let Dr. Duncan examine
them, and give us his opinion. I suppose you'll agree to that,
Best?"

"Yes sir—if you say it's all right, Colonel? And I forgot something just now—the cheque Miss Philippa gave me Thursday. Perhaps you'd take charge of it, Mr. Harrington? If she's dead, which
I hope to goodness she isn't, then I won't be able to cash it, will I?
And if she's alive, I'd rather she wrote me another one—if she still
wants to. Only she mayn't feel I've earned it, telling everybody
about things like this, and giving up the stuff she asked me to look
after."

"Well, I hope she'd be fair enough to appreciate the facts," said
the novelist a little doubtfully, and smiled almost for the first time.
"I'm sure you've nothing to reproach yourself about, and personally I'm very much obliged to you—especially for sloshing
Oakes."

# IX

THE DOCTOR WENT OFF WITH THE PHOTOGRAPHS, and Harrington said he was going home to look through his niece's papers, in the hope of finding some clue to her disappearance. Dickie Donovan, regretfully, decided that he would need at least a couple of hours to string together into a passable sequence those facts which he was allowed to disclose, and asked the Chief-constable to recommend him a suitable hotel. Bagshaw first stared, and then laughed.

"We'll start building you one," he said: "be ready about 1942. No, seriously, all Selling's got is a couple of pubs, and I don't think they do visitors. People who stay here either stay with friends or move on. We've no tourist population, thank heaven, and no commercial travellers, and there's never been a murder here before in my time, so we've no accommodation for the Press. You'll have to go to Craybourne, or else sit on the beach. Unless you care to use this room?"

"Ha ha!" grunted Dickie mirthlessly, not for a moment believing in the offer.

"No, really. I'm a bachelor, and I like a bit of company now and again, and if I decide I don't care for yours I can always turn you out. All of you, of course. It'd be different if my sister were here—she's a holy terror: she behaves like I look. Luckily she's away, and the housekeeper's quite human. If the four of you can make do with two bedrooms, please stay."

"That's jolly generous of you, sir," said Beale warmly, amid the chorus of surprised acceptance. It was seldom that he met with anything approaching such kindness from provincial police officials.

"Nonsense—I like being eccentric," was the rather disconcerting reply. "Do you feel called upon to view the body, Inspector?"

"Well, quite frankly I'd rather not, unless you advise it."

"No, can't say I do. It's a most unpleasant sight, and it isn't as if it were still *in situ.* Or even *in toto,*" he added.

"Then for the time being I'll give it a miss."

"And me the same, only permanently," declared Tony. "Corpses are only bearable so long as you can pretend they're asleep. Corpses without heads are definitely revolting. What's the bill of fare?"

Beale thought for a moment.

"First the bungalow, I think," he decided. "Then Craybourne, in case there's anything to be picked up there. And by that time I wouldn't be surprised if we were wanted back here."

"Meaning what?" asked Bagshaw.

"Only a wild guess, Colonel: but I fancy you may have a visitor this afternoon. And would you be kind enough to have the underclothes made into a parcel? I'd like to hear what Mrs. Topley's got to say about them before I go up to Harrington's place and see the maid."

They spent an hour at Oakes's bungalow. It was an eight-roomed red-brick building with a small garden, well kept considering the poor quality of the soil: Matthews occupied some minutes examining it, and also the path leading from the coast road, but found nothing to report. Inside, the place had already been searched for fingerprints, the colonel said, but with surprising lack of success as far as the studio and kitchen went. All the rooms bore signs—dust, cobwebs, a scattering of soot in the grates—that no one had been in residence lately, and all were furnished in aggressively modern style. The main room had what looked like a cocktail cabinet and turned out to be a radiogram, and the one next door reversed the situation. In a cupboard off the hall were deck-chairs, a collapsible raft, a dozen expensive pneumatic cushions flat in a pile, a medicine ball, and two comprehensive picnic baskets. Another cupboard provided perhaps their most interesting find: several score of large sawn logs.

"So the Doc was right," murmured Matthews. "That's something to think about, that is."

The kitchen, whose floor still bore manifest traces of blood, was fitted with a large refrigerator and also with running water. In view of the bungalow's position, as Tony pointed out, this installation indicated a considerable outlay on someone's part: probably Oakes's, since the pipes seemed fairly new. The back door was locked, and the bolts rusted into place—proof that they had not been drawn recently. All the floors were of polished parquet, haphazardly covered with costly rugs and mats, the pastel wall-papers were of the highest quality parchment, and most of the chairs matched the bed which Bagshaw had seen the night before.

"He must have spent about £1500 on the furnishings," estimated Tony, "and the rugs are the only things I'd buy a threepenny raffle-ticket for."

Beale walked round idly for a while, fingering the double velvet curtains, sniffing at some cigarettes in a silver box, climbing on to his friend's back to scrutinize the electric-light bulbs. Using his handkerchief he carefully detached them one by one.

"The smallest is a 75-watt," he said. "Take a look at them, Matthews: especially those from the kitchen and the studio."

He then devoted five minutes to the canvases resting against the walls. The paintings were all of people, and all more than competently done. The majority depicted girls in or near the nude, but the colonel assured him that none had Philippa Saunderson for subject.

"Gives you some idea of what the fellow's like, doesn't it?" he remarked, surveying a pert bare bosom which he said probably belonged to a Craybourne bar-maid, since it was undoubtedly her face above it. "Should have thought she was fatter," he added irrelevantly.

"He has an appropriate reputation in town," Tony observed. "This Philippa wench must be a bit of an ass."

Bagshaw described her briefly and unflatteringly, and turned to where 'Horsey' Matthews was now examining the window.

"Anything to help, Sergeant?" he asked.

"No sir—I'll bet five pounds none of 'em have been touched, bar the one in the bedroom. Nor the door. Nor the light bulbs. I reckon the glove trade must be pretty good in Belling."

"That's an idea" said Tony. "I'd better float a company: finger-stalls for felons, gauntlets for garrotters, mittens for murderers. I wonder how many people have got a key."

"Apparently Miss Saunderson has, or had," answered Beale. "And by the way, Colonel, there's one point that hasn't been explained at all. What made you decide to enter this place?"

"Guess-work," was the prompt reply. "Same as the van, and spotting young Best as Philippa's agent—and that visitor I'm going to have presently. John said the car he heard about 2.15 might have been anything between a quarter and half a mile off. I fished out a map and saw this place was about right, and in view of what Harrington had told me earlier I thought it might be worth investigating."

"Thank you. I can only hope you go on guessing right—I rather think we may need some luck. And what about the sodden gentleman in the black overcoat? The one by the Martello Tower?"

The Chief-constable looked a little guilty.

"I'm afraid I haven't done anything about that yet," he admitted. "There's been so much else—sorry. What do you suggest?"

"I don't quite know. The fact that he was standing in the rain seems to indicate he had no car: then how did he get here? Did someone drop him, or could he have come by train?"

"Why, yes, he could have done: the 11.25 might fit. There's a sort of station, only it's a good mile from anywhere. I'll have enquiries made, coming and going."

"Thanks—it may help. You can't think of anybody off-hand who answers to his description, I suppose?"

Bagshaw smiled.

"I know a dozen people who've got black overcoats and could pass for gentlemen on a dark night," he said: "but I can't say I know one daft enough to get soaking wet like that. D'you think he might be Ellis?"

"I doubt it: Ellis doesn't sound the sort of person to wait for a policeman to come up and speak to him. Quite possibly this man's nothing to do with the bungalow or the body, but all the same he may easily have noticed something. The Tower's about half a mile from here, isn't it?"

"All but a hundred yards or so: his eyes wouldn't have been much good, but his ears might."

"Yes—we'll hope. At the moment I'm somewhat in the same boat—daylight is very dim. I don't even know how many murders I'm suppose to be investigating, nor whose they are, nor even if there ever were any, if it comes to that. Alice Carter *may* have committed suicide.

"All the same, things aren't by any means hopeless," he added quickly, as the colonel's face grew longer. "For instance, there's that bit of brown fibre you talked of. To me that suggests— possibly—a trunk, and if there's anything in that idea then I shall want to know who helped Ellis carry the thing out of 14 Weatherall Road. I'm pretty certain he couldn't have managed it by himself, unless he's a porter or a furniture-remover in private life. Then I want to see Miss Saunderson's maid, and Mrs. Topley too, about the clothes. Again, I'd like Sergeant Matthews' opinion on all the fingerprint side of the business—it's what he was allowed to be a policeman for. Finally, there's the question of the car Best heard: but I'm hoping to get a line on that for nothing. Throw in your enquiries about the man in the black coat, and the doctor's comparison of the photographs with the body, and we might be a lot worse off."

"Good man!" said Bagshaw admiringly. "I'm glad you've got a head on you. Oh, sorry—heads aren't a very nice subject."

"Nor are feet," muttered Tony mysteriously. He had been standing quietly by, and was now smiling.

"And before I forget, I believe I can answer at least three of your points, Ted, if you aren't too proud to listen."

It was Beale's turn to smile.

"I'm not proud," he asserted: "answer the lot, if you can. All your threats coming true at last?"

"What threats?"

"Well, you once said that the day would come when you, with your simple mind, would interpret a simple situation simply and correctly, while I pursued a maze of intricacy just for the fun of the thing."

"Did I really? Good for me—it must have been special beer. Anyway, here goes. The clothes are Alice Carter's—that covers two queries. Over the body, on the other hand, I'm inclined to agree with Mr. Harrington, though for a different reason—see my note-book. Finally, the car belongs to Oakes, who is likewise your expected visitor, Colonel."

"And the murderer's name?" asked Beale politely.

"Another time, greedy."

"And the man in the black coat?" suggested Bagshaw. "Though you were brighter than I was about the visitor—I ought to have expected Oakes down here. If Charles is all wrong, and he's inno-cent, the natural thing to do would be to find out what the papers mean about bodies lying all over his bungalow, and if he isn't in-nocent—"

"He'll be down here double quick pretending he is," ended Matthews. "If 'innocent' is the right word," he added, glancing at the painting of the bar-maid.

"Unless he skips?"—from Tony. "Oughtn't you to have thought of that, Ted?"

"I did think of it, early this morning. Wherever he goes today he'll be followed, and if he hasn't started for here by 3.00 they're going to telephone—I arranged it with the Yard. If that happens, I shall get you to rush me back to town to find what's keeping him: but I fancy he'll come."

"Good—good!" declared Bagshaw. "Creevy'll like you, I think. You've got the professional touch—I haven't."

"Yet you started off pretty well, sir: finding the van, and then the body. It might have lain here for a week. By the way, can you see if the light's on in this room from the road, with the curtains drawn?"

"Only if you come really close—they're surprisingly opaque."

"And when was high tide on Thursday night?"

The colonel consulted a small diary.

"10.32," he answered—"what makes you ask?"

"Oh, just sheer curiosity. Now Tony, what about black-coat? With appropriate reasons for choice, if any."

His friend smiled.

"Instinct needs no justification—does it, Colonel? However, broadly speaking this affair can be separated into two parts at the moment. The Craybourne end consists of Alice Carter and the man Ellis, and this end of Philippa Saunderson and the man Oakes. As a link between we have the grocer's van, though I'm not certain how much I believe in that yet. Now, mysterious strangers in Belling are more likely to be connected with Philippa than with Alice. In view of her reason for being so anxious about all those compromising letters and photographs and so on, I suggest—as one blooming amateur to another, Colonel—that the gentleman dawdling by the ruins was Colin Dennison."

Bagshaw opened his eyes very wide, but did not scoff.

"Yes?" said Beale, watching his face. "You think that's possible?"

"Yes, at a guess—Best's description fits as far as it goes. Don't happen to know the man, I suppose, Mr. Purdon?"

"Now don't be unkind—I never have anything to do with diplomats on principle."

"Then apparently you may have made a lucky shot," commented Beale.

"And if I say it wasn't luck but judgement?"

"I shall require convincing. Judgement about what—Philippa's psychological processes?"

"Yes—if you can get that far you can do it all."

"I certainly think I see what you mean. The girl tried to persuade herself while she was up in Scotland that the photographs were just a scare, but wasn't confident enough about that to let Dennison propose. The minute she gets back here and sees Best, or collects them from her bank, rather, she discovers that as far as she can tell they're absolutely authentic. What does she do? Your answer is that she decides to tell Dennison the truth, and sends him a wire to meet her by the Martello Tower at midnight. Or she may even have telephoned. Before she can keep the appointment, however, she gets herself murdered, and eventually turns up in Oakes's bungalow in somebody else's underclothes and minus her head. It'd be an interesting fragment of theory if it didn't have two obvious and enormous snags."

"The first being Alice Carter's body?" suggested Bagshaw, who had persuaded himself to take the discussion seriously. "There was one, you know—Mrs. Topley saw it."

"The body and the theft of the van and the means of death," agreed Beale. "In other words, if what you found wasn't Alice, then this case is going to be about as complicated as they come."

"And Mr. Purdon can't do complicated things," put in Matthews with a grin: "therefore it *was* Alice—A.R.P."

"How much?" asked Bagshaw.

"Well then, Q.E.D., sir. Somebody told me it meant 'Which was to have been done'."

"And the second snag?" asked Tony.

"Why, the lack of a suitable murderer," said Beale.

"But there is a very suitable one—Oakes."

"That's what I mean: the apparent impossibility of fitting him to the part. As far as motive goes there isn't much difficulty, I agree. He killed her to stop her from killing him, perhaps, or because she really had found some way of upsetting him with the photograph which showed them both: though heaven knows where he got the gas from. But that's no good when you turn from motive to opportunity, because he hadn't any that I can see."

"Because you say so?"

"No, for better reasons than that. What is Oakes?"

"That depends on the sort of answer you want. A blackmailer? A body-fancier? Oh! An actor. Yes, I get you—don't rub it in. He's at the New Gaiety, which is t'other side of Cambridge Circus, so including getting out of London he'd need at least two hours to cover the seventy odd miles here, and his play doesn't finish till 11.15 or so, and he doesn't drop dead till the final curtain's half down, and he'd never risk coming in make-up like that—a cross between Bernard Shaw and John of Gaunt. He couldn't possibly get here till 1.30 at the very earliest.

"Still, on second thoughts that doesn't rule him right out, you know: it only ruins my suggested reason why Philippa didn't meet Dennison as agreed."

"If it *was* Dennison," Matthews reminded him sceptically. "And anyway, it all sounds tripe to me. Oakes couldn't have had anything to do with the Craybourne business, 'cos his blessed play starts at 8.15, and it takes just as long to go north as south. That means he didn't have a hand in it at all unless he'd got an accomplice or two down here, and if he had, then they could have kept the girl quiet till he arrived, with Alice Carter's garters all ready, and a nice long rubber tube from the nearest gas-jet . . .

"No sir, sorry, but me for common sense this time. Alice Carter died about 7.00, maybe by suicide and maybe by murder, and Ellis switched the body from Craybourne to here in the van, and took the head and things away because he didn't want anyone to find out who she really was, and that's all about it. Miss Saunderson and that old gas-bag of an uncle of hers are just coincidences. Oh, sorry, sir,"—to Bagshaw. "I forgot he's a friend of yours."

"Don't apologize," said the colonel with a grin: "though I hope you didn't mean 'gas-bag' to be sinister. He was certainly verging on monotony this morning, but I think the reason is the one he gave. He can't get used to treating murder in terms of real life instead of fiction. Read any of his later stuff? Pity—you'd know what I mean better. For instance, in his last book he started off with the body of a window-cleaner found tied to a lamp-post with long twists of white human hair. The fellow was dressed in his ordinary clothes except that he wore a pair of wooden clogs, his eyes were stuck down with sealing-wax stamped with the thumbprint of a woman who'd been dead six months, and his pockets were full of empty winkle shells. And, whether you believe it or not, there was a fairly credible explanation for the whole business, though I forget exactly what it was for the moment.

"Anyway, Sergeant, I'm inclined to agree with you: give common sense a run first."

Beale nodded.

"And I'd say the same but for one thing," he told them: "namely, the number of tennis-racket covers used."

As he spoke he glanced sideways at Tony, who spun round instantly.

"So you did get there, confound you! I was hoping I'd given myself a start."

"You may still have done, if you know why any at all were used."

But his friend expressed regretful ignorance.

"I only wish I did. There must have been a reason—or is that too much to hope for? In real life, I mean."

# X

OLONEL BAGSHAW DECIDED after all to remain in Belling, while the others went into Craybourne. He promised that if Oakes turned up he would immediately telephone through to the police-station there.

"I rather like him," said Tony, as the Bentley traversed the bumpy coast road.

"Yes," agreed Beale. "He isn't at all the usual type."

"Very decent of him to invite us all there," put in Matthews from the back, where he was curled up on the seat like a school-boy. "I fancy him a sight more than his pal Harrington. What's he keep on keeping on about his niece for? I mean, does he *really* think that's her?"—with a glance at Tony.

"Hush!" said his superior. "Miss Saunderson was a female; the body was a female: therefore they were the same female. Similarly with Alice Carter, who was therefore Philippa, only her uncle never knew. Logic for lunatics, no charge made."

"Well, you'd have a job to charge me for it. But some time, sir, it might be an idea to ask who benefits, mightn't it?"

"By Philippa's death, if any? Yes, no harm in asking. You'd like Harrington to be the author of a really complicated murder, and drawing attention to its possible complication just to bluff us?"

The detective-sergeant chuckled softly.

"Something like that, sir—it'd make it more interesting for Mr. Purdon."

"Oh, don't bother about me," said Tony: "I take what comes. But I don't relish Harrington as unknown slayer. If you were the kind of people one could offer help to, I would. As it is, I shall merely look on and watch you blunder."

"Until you can't stand it any longer," suggested Beale: "when you'll turn the lamp on and blind us. Meanwhile I suppose we'll have to suffer your suppressed knowledge: though I admit you may have been on form just now. Speculo, the Guess-Work

King—a penny to see, twopence to touch. Prophecies organized thrice daily after meals, bring your own salt."

"All right, all right," said Tony. "Bleat away—I can bear it. I will now recite poetry.

"He is the wisest who talks most—
Silence but covers emptiness:
To have a thought and hide it, mute,
Till time confirm it, or refute,
Is undiscerning foolishness."

"And yet on the other hand," objected Beale, "what about this?

"A little silence is a dangerous thing,
For contemplation may disturb the veil
Of truth, and bare such blinding nakedness
That all our careful lines and curves and points—
So nicely calculated, eyes half closed—
Appear irregular, awry, misplaced,
Inaccurate; and grave morality
As less than worms obey untaught; and law
As sniggering injustice holding scales
That slip and slide; and all our palaces
As crooked cardboard huts that smell of damp."

"All right," said Tony: "let's get back to prose and fresh air. Justify your presence in my nice car by explaining why Philippa didn't tell her uncle she was employing Best to get the letters back."

"He told us why—because if anybody knew he might get into trouble. Anyway, she seems to have chosen a competent young man—not many country coppers would knock a famous actor down and start looking through his desk."

"Maybe he was spreading it on a bit," suggested Matthews.

"Well, we'll see if Oakes has a different story. I think Best was telling the truth, though—he gave me that impression."

"Tut!" said Tony, drawing up outside the police-station. "What has Scotland Yard to do with impressions, other than those of fingers and feet?"

Inspector Creevy shook Beale's hand for something like half a minute, and it was plain that he expected great things from the newcomer.

"They couldn't have sent anyone I'd rather work with," he declared.

While Matthews went off to look at the material evidence from Mrs. Topley's the Inspector recounted the one important development which had taken place so far that day.

"Colonel Bagshaw mentioned the scrap of brown fibre we found in the van, perhaps?" he asked.

"Yes" said Beale. "I hope you aren't going to disappoint me about it."

"He thinks it came off a trunk," interposed Tony, with a grin at his friend. "If you're right, it'll save you the trouble of saying 'I told you so', and if you're wrong, then it may teach you the danger of making wild guesses," he added gravely.

"Well, you *were* right, Inspector" declared Creevy impressively, "quite right. The same idea occurred to me, and today I had a couple of men enquiring at all the likely shops in the town. It was a bow at venture, admittedly, but it came off, though not quite as I'd expected.

"Craybourne's like most seaside towns—one end is definitely lower-class than the other. We call it the old town, and as a matter of fact we're in it now. The only two pawnbrokers here are also this way, and in one of them, kept by a man named Haines, we struck lucky. About 4.00 one afternoon early this week—but he can't be certain whether it was Monday or Tuesday—a fellow called about a big brown cabin trunk displayed in the window. It was an unredeemed pledge, of course, the price was twenty-five shillings, and this chap offered him a pound for it, which Haines accepted like a shot: he'd been trying to get rid of the thing for the last six months. As far as we can tell, the purchaser was Ellis."

"Ah, the mysterious Mr. Ellis again" said Beale. "Identified by the same tell-tale characteristics?"

"Yes—coloured glasses, check cap, and long blue trench coat. He was carrying a suit-case as well, incidentally. That's as far as Haines could get with a description, except that the man wore gloves, and having seen the shop myself I'm not surprised. It's a dark poky place where you might easily fail to recognize your best friend."

"Even if you wanted to," remarked Tony.

"Quite, sir; and anyway, Haines is getting on for half blind. Now, Inspector, Ellis's subsequent moves were a little peculiar. Having bought the trunk, which had a key, for five shillings below the advertised price, he proceeded to offer the full money on condition that instead of taking his purchase away then and there he should be allowed to collect it some time on Thursday afternoon or early evening. Haines at once pointed out that the shop would be closed, but Ellis waved that objection aside. Next door is a narrow alley, and the trunk was to be put there near some dust-bins, to be removed when convenient. This arrangement was duly agreed to, the extra five shillings paid over, Ellis went off, and that's all we've found out at present. What happened on Thursday is very vague. After he shut up at 1.00 Haines put the trunk in the alley as promised, and later went out for the afternoon. There was actually no one on the premises between 2.30 and 7.00, by which time the thing was gone."

"Splendid work!" said Beale warmly, to Creevy's satisfaction. "I think that news is going to help considerably."

"I hope so. It's a pity we don't know what time the collection took place, though. I've enquired in all the houses nearby, but no one noticed anything."

"People don't when it might have been useful. The assumption to make is that Ellis went round as soon as he'd stolen the van, I suppose: some time after five o'clock, when it was dark."

"Yes," agreed Creevy: "which means we need hardly consider suicide any more. There's far too much forethought displayed in buying the trunk for it to be anything but cold-blooded murder. All the same, I wish I understood the presence of the wireless set."

"To befuddle you, of course," declared Tony, remembering Harrington's word. "By the way, what mileage did the van cover while it was absent?"

"It's hard to say—the speedometer packed up a long time ago. By the amount of petrol missing, about eight miles: probably less, if the thing was stopped and restarted often. I don't think there's much to worry about in that direction."

Beale made a note of the pawnbroker's address, and then with less than his usual directness broached a subject he had had in mind for some time: ever since the idea of a trunk had first occurred to him, in fact.

"Have you many unemployed in Craybourne?" he asked.

The local inspector showed his surprise at this abrupt change of topic, but answered readily and to the point.

"Far too many—seven hundred and thirty-four last month. Why do you ask?"

"Because I'm trying a long shot of my own," was the smiling reply. "Whereabouts is the station here?"

"Railway? About three hundred yards off."

"Really? Quite near Mrs. Topley's, then. And when is the next London train due in?"

Creevy, almost without looking, selected a time-table from his well-ordered desk.

"At 2.25," he said: "in half an hour's time."

"I see. Have you a couple of men you can spare? Preferably in plain clothes. I'd like them sent along to the station about five or ten past, with instructions to watch out for and question anyone who looks as if he's waiting to carry passengers' bags. You know the kind of person I mean?"

"Yes, rather. In the summer there's a dozen or more, but I don't think there'll be so many now. Yes, the idea has possibilities: that trunk would have been pretty heavy, I don't doubt. You'll want to know if any of them were anywhere near 14 Weatherall Road about seven o'clock on Thursday?"

"Yes please: and there won't be much harm in offering a reward of ten shillings for information about the theft of a trunk from that address. Don't make it more, though, or you may get a lot of optimistic cock-and-bull stories. By the way, do any of your constables normally pass Mrs. Topley's house between 7.00 and 7.30 on Thursday evenings?"

"No. Except in the case of a street accident or anything like that, the nearest would be here at the station."

"I see—thank you. Hullo, here's my sergeant, and looking as if he's found out something. Any luck, Matthews?"

"Not the sort you mean, sir," was the reply. "All the prints seem okay—and the ones on the tooth-glass *were* left-hands. But I've been reading that list of the girl's personal belongings you made out, sir "—glancing for a moment at Creevy. "The colonel missed some of it out this morning."

"Ah, my list: it turned out useful after all, you know."

"And it may do again," said Matthews, ignoring any latent meaning the remark might hold. He turned to Beale, and his eyes were bright with animation.

"It's my turn to have a blinder, sir, isn't it? Right: then I say that Alice Carter's real name was Alice West, and that last February she was living with a man named Drake round the back of Kennington Oval."

"Nonsense," interrupted Tony: "you mean Highbury."

"Don't burble," said his friend. "This sounds good."

"Very good," agreed Creevy, smiling. "Details do count—I don't care what anybody says. Alice Carter specifically mentioned the Oval to Mrs. Topley, but perhaps Colonel Bagshaw left that out too. Go on, Sergeant."

"Well, as it happens I had the job of arresting an Alice West for shoplifting, and she fits Mrs. Topley's description all right. I also had the job of searching their rooms—hers and Drake's. You never saw such a collection of stuff: umbrellas, clocks, clothes by the hundredweight, bits and pieces of cheap jewellery, hot-water bottles, cutlery, enough crocks for a canteen, and a twenty-guinea vacuum cleaner—though how in the world she got away with that I can't imagine. Anyway, while I was hunting round I came across a china ornament just like the one in the Inspector's report: a girl with nothing on balancing on a sundial. Naturally I took it for something else she'd lifted, but she swore it was her own, and no-body ever managed to prove it wasn't. And that still isn't all. While she was arguing about it she said it was a wedding-present from her husband, and it was worth four pound ten. I asked why she didn't make it a fiver and have done with it, but she answered quite serious: it was hers, and the price was four pound ten."

He paused, regarding them expectantly, and Inspector Creevy's smile was broad.

"How long did she get?" he asked.

"Six months, sir. She was a first offender, so *she* said, and she spun the beak a hard-luck tale."

"And the man Drake?" enquired Beale. "Was he mixed up in it?"

"No sir—at least, he didn't get as far as the dock. But he's a shady customer all right—been pinched three times, only there was never enough evidence. What's more, I saw him, and as far as size and things go there's nothing to stop him being Ellis."

Beale was pleased.

"Would you mind having another look at your timetable, Inspector?" he requested.

"Oh lor, I don't want to go back!" protested Matthews, perceiving what was in the air.

"But you'll have to," said Tony. "It's no good kicking—off with you, tooth-mug clutched tightly in one chubby hand and bed-post in the other."

"Ah, not a bad idea," remarked Beale: "taking the mug, I mean."

"Tain't a mug," said Matthews: "it's a glass. I'm the only mug here—if I'd dreamt you were going to pack me off home I wouldn't have said a word."

There was a train at 3.00, which the detective-sergeant was instructed to catch. It would be his job while in London to find out, by comparing the fingerprints on the tooth-glass with those in the records at Scotland Yard, if Alice Carter and Alice West were the same person. If so, said Beale, then before returning to Craybourne he must try to trace the girl's movements recently, since her release from prison.

"And get hold of something about Drake too," he was told. "You're sure he wasn't her husband?"

"Well, they both said he wasn't," Matthews answered.

Beale and Tony then received from Creevy directions for reaching Mrs. Topley's. They departed with a promise to return not later than 3.15, in case of telephone messages about Oakes. Their first stop, well out of their way, was at a cafe in the town, where they had a quick meal.

"Things are looking brighter" observed Tony presently. "As Creevy says, this trunk business definitely points to murder, though I suppose there was never much doubt."

"But it'll be apt to spoil one or two of your favourite theories, won't it? Especially if she turns out to be Alice West."

"Well, I can always start again: but I'm hanged if I can get over those tennis-racket covers. Want to know what I wrote in my note-book?"

"I dare say I can guess, thanks: something to the effect that there shouldn't have been three."

"Ah, then I wasn't as clever as I thought. But if one for the neck and two for the arms, why on earth not two for the legs? Similarly, if none for the legs, why bother about arms and neck? And I think the second question's by far the harder. I can't imagine one single reason for hiding the amputations."

"But—provided there was one—from the fact that the feet were left uncovered you deduce that X hadn't bargained for removing them?"

"Exactly: which is why I'm still a bit inclined to believe Harrington may be right. The presence of Alice Carter's vest and things shows that X wishes us to think the body was hers, but the absence of the feet shows it isn't: that's my present fancy. And incidentally, curse the fellow for using that trunk—it does me out of the obvious word to describe what they found. 'Remains' sounds like an undertaker, and 'remnants' like a white sale. If it hadn't got legs and arms you could call it a torso: I think I shall change to 'hulk'."

"Why not carcase?" suggested Beale.

"Yes, that's it—the beautiful carcase: she was supposed to be fairly pretty, wasn't she? Anyway, to go back: feet are tell-tale things. Get hold of, say, a debutante and a kitchen-maid, and it's a fair bet that if you covered up everything but their heads, a stranger might easily guess wrong these days, what with one thing and another. And he might do the same if you stood 'em both naked in a bath-tub, as long as you hid the hands. X may have removed them because of fingerprints, but I've a feeling he forgot the feet till he was actually on the job. If the—the carcase were really Alice Carter's, he wouldn't have needed to bother, but he took one look at Philippa's and saw they were far too clean and well cared-for."

Beale frowned.

"You're definitely improving," he said. "I like it, except for one thing. To 'take one look', as you suggest, would mean first removing the stockings; and then, before remedying his oversight, putting them back on again. Agree?"

"Yes, I suppose so. Perhaps we can find out about that, though. What are the odds that if he did that he'd replace the garters in exactly the same position? Pretty negligible. Right: then if Dr. Duncan can swear the garters weren't touched after death it'll wash my theory out."

"Or else leave us with another mystery to solve: how could X possibly know, *without* taking one look, that the feet had to go too, and why, if he did know, didn't he provide bags for the ankles the same as he'd done for the wrists and neck? But the trouble's going to be that Duncan won't be able to tell us—you see if I'm not right."

# XI

**T**HEY FOUND 14 WEATHERALL ROAD without trouble, but before ringing the bell Beale decided to look round the builders' yard next door. There was no one about, since it was Saturday afternoon, and he and Tony had the place to themselves for ten minutes. They easily located the shed rented by Deacon, and when they opened the rickety door, there was the van inside. Tony expressed surprise at this, but Beale pointed out that the grocer employed it in his business, and asked what use it could be to the police once it had been thoroughly examined for traces of its adventures.

"Oh, I don't know, only it seems odd to see the thing back where it started from" was the answer. "I'd have expected it to have been kept for the trial, and brought into court labelled Exhibit 44. Anyway, it looks to be the simplest job in the world to steal it, if one had a mind to. Personally I haven't, but a chap with a carcase to get rid of could hardly have a better conveyance. Who'd notice a shabby old wreck like that trundling along in a shabby town like this? Yet there's plenty of room inside."

After inspecting the nail which had jagged the trunk, Beale walked outside again and stared over the wall opposite at the back of the house next door.

"Yes, you'd be able to see all right from the first-floor windows he remarked. "In fact, we *are* being seen—presumably by Mrs. Topley herself. If she sticks her nose against the glass much harder she'll bust it, and find herself flying headlong into the next world."

They went out of the yard past piles of bricks and rubble, rows of brown drain-pipes and unwieldy stacks of rough timber, and a minute later were entering the cold hall of No. 14. On the inner mat Beale paused for a quick survey: to the right a hat-stand and a low table, then the stairs, then a dark passage probably leading to the kitchen, and farther round to the left two doors. Through the more distant of these they were shown into the cheerless drawing-room, Mrs. Topley herself leading the way: a small grey-haired woman with a lagging step, a weak mouth, and a thoroughly frightened expression.

"Oh sir, it's been terrible!" she repeated. "I don't know what I shall do, I'm sure. The house'll never seem the same again—I keep fancying I can smell gas all day long, and last night I woke up screaming. Was there something you wanted, sir?"

"Yes, I can understand how unpleasant it must have been for you," said Beale, not without genuine pity: she looked so unfitted to cope with serious trouble. "I hear you've been extremely helpful, and I'm only sorry I've got to bother you again."

"Oh, don't mention it, please—I know it isn't your fault."

"Thank you. Now, I suppose you've heard about the discovery at Belling last night?"

But Mrs. Topley had not: it appeared that she had been without the heart to take even a glance at her morning newspaper. Briefly Beale told her, causing her expression to change from timidness to wide-eyed horror.

"Oh the poor thing!" was all she could say when he had done. "You're sure it *is* her?"

"Not absolutely sure—that's really why we're here. It's about the clothes: would you mind looking at them, and telling me if you recognize them?"

"Oh dear! Yes, if you want me to. Oh dear! Is there—are they—will there be much *blood?*"

"Not a lot. You need only see the petticoat—the other things obviously match. But please remember this, Mrs. Topley: on no account say you can identify the garment as your lodger's unless you're quite positive. If you've the least doubt, then you must tell me."

He undid the parcel, selected the petticoat, and handed it to her. She took it reluctantly, as if it might be capable of suddenly becoming animate; then, after a moment's hesitation, she shook the shoulder-straps free and leant over her lap to compare them.

"Yes, it's hers—it's Miss Carter's," she said in a whisper. "See? The ribbons don't quite match—the darker one's a bit I gave her. I dare say I've got some left—just let me fetch my work-basket and look."

In a moment she was back with a second longer piece of ribbon, and as far as Beale and Tony could tell, this exactly matched the left shoulder-strap of the petticoat. He thanked her, learnt that as far as she knew the dead girl had last taken a bath on the previous Sunday morning, and obtained permission to see the room up-stairs.

It was bleak and desolate, and both shivered a little when they stood inside. The bed leant drunkenly against the left-hand wall, its head having been removed; nearby on the dusty wooden floor lay the striped mattress, rolled and secured with string, and upon this was a pile of folded blankets. The blind was down, the curtains drawn, the dressing-table and mantel-piece bare, and the gas-fire disconnected. For some moments Beale walked idly round: he looked in the cupboards, he got down on his hands and knees to peer under the furniture, he opened the window and put his head out. Then he turned his attention to the glass partition running along the top of the wall above the bed. It was about eighteen inches deep, and from inside seemed quite opaque, though there were obvious gaps in the dirty frosted paper pasted over it; but when he stood on a chair in the passage he found that he could see the far side of the room without difficulty, even without the electric light on.

After inspecting the bathroom, and determining that Ribleys' yard was clearly visible from the window, they returned down-stairs. Mrs. Topley was waiting for them in the hall, and at once began to speak.

"Oh sir, there's something I think I ought to tell you, while I remember. Would you step inside and sit down again for a minute?"

"Of course," said Beale, wondering what was coming. From the woman's manner he judged that it was in her opinion important.

"Well sir, it's like this," she whispered, sitting very upright in her chair twisting her hands nervously in her lap. "When the other gentlemen were here I said my guest had never had but the one visitor, Mr. Ellis, her cousin—at least, that's what she said he was. And I honestly believed she hadn't, or I'd never have said so, but yesterday evening I was on my way to buy some sugar, having run out, and a woman I know to speak to stopped me in the street. Well, she's a lady really, Mrs. Amos her name is, and her husband was Mayor five years ago. She told me how sorry she was about all this, and we got talking, and she happened to ask me did Alice Carter ever have any callers. I said only one, her cousin, the Inspector having told me not to be too free to people, and then she said 'Oh no, surely, aren't you mistaken, Mrs. Topley?'. I asked her why, and she said she'd been passing the house one afternoon several weeks back and seen a young lady on the doorstep, and as she knew I was out, it being a Thursday, she just stepped inside the gate to tell her in case she didn't know, and the young lady said she didn't want to see me, she wanted to see Miss Carter. Well, of course Mrs. Amos didn't know who Miss Carter was, so she just said 'Oh I see' and walked away, and thought no more about it till this morning, when seeing me brought it back to her. But more than that I don't know. I dare say perhaps Mrs. Amos might, though, and I thought I ought to tell you. She lives at 25 Sea-View Gardens, quite a big house: near Nelson Square it is."

"Thank you very much," said Beale, having grasped the essentials of her story. "I'll send somebody round to see her, just in case it proves important."

When they got back to the police-station just after half past three Inspector Creevy greeted them with even more enthusiasm than he had previously displayed. Beale—rightly—assumed that something must have developed from his suggestion about unofficial porters.

"It was a brilliant idea, sir," declared Creevy, unconsciously giving the impression that ideas were to be judged solely on the results they produced. "But first, there's been a telephone call from Colonel Bagshaw. He says that Mr. Oakes arrived just after 3.00, and please will you go over there as soon as possible? He also asked me to tell you that Mr. Burden guessed right—he said you'd understand."

"The new name suits you, Tony," remarked Beale. "But I wonder which guess he was referring to."

"Why, about Dennison, of course—need you ask?"

"Well, there were so many. You'd better write a book, and call it *Oneiromancy by Onus*. And now for business: I'll go first, Inspector, shall I?"

He summarized in a few words what he had learnt from Mrs. Topley, and repeated Mrs. Amos's address.

"Do you know the woman?" he asked.

"Yes, slightly. She talks a lot—there shouldn't be any trouble."

"Good: and one more point, before I let you start. And is Sergeant Turner here? If so, I'd like him to come in for a moment."

The sergeant was sent for, and Beale found his heavy matter-of-fact manner reassuring.

"I take it you know Mrs. Topley fairly well?" he asked.

"Yes sir—her husband was a good friend of mine."

"Then I think you'll be just the man to carry out an experiment I want tried."

He turned to Creevy again.

"At the moment Mrs. Topley's a very nervous woman," he said, "and the thing she's most nervous about is naturally gas. What I'm anxious to find out, as near as possible, is how strong the smell was on the landing when she entered the house about 7.00. To get that information out of her will need care and tact, and as she knows Sergeant Turner I suggest you give him the job."

"Certainly: but what exactly is it you're after?"

"Principally, the time taken for gas from the bedroom to reach the landing through the key-hole or any other outlets. Get the men who actually broke in to see that the conditions are approximately the same as far as the windows and door go. Then connect a rubber tube to the supply, turn the tap on full, and rest the other end on, say, a pillow with a blanket over it. After that close the door and wait on the landing till the smell becomes perceptible, and then get Mrs. Topley to indicate as accurately as she can when it's as strong as it was when it first attracted her attention on Thursday. She'll probably give the word when she notices anything at all, but even so we shall get some idea how keen her sense of smell is: it varies enormously with different people.

"To provide some comparison, have two or three other witnesses on the landing. Take the time when the tap's turned on, and then let each make a note of exactly when his nose starts working. For preference they'll be near the door, and behind Mrs. Topley so that she can't crib. Synchronize their watches first, of course—it may just conceivably be a matter of seconds."

"And if they haven't got watches, sir?" enquired Sergeant Turner solidly: but Creevy's impatient snort was answer enough.

"And don't rely on the chap who turns the gas on," advised Tony: "otherwise he'll win by a mile."

"No sir, that's sense," agreed the Inspector. "Very well, I'll see that that's arranged. What sort of a result do you think you'll get? Or oughtn't one to ask?"

"By all means," said Beale. "I know very little from experience about the penetrating properties of household gas. In view of the conditions as noticed by Mrs. Topley, though, and the good fit of the door, which I saw for myself just now, I shall be surprised if anyone smells anything within seven or eight minutes."

"Seven or eight minutes!" echoed Creevy, astounded. "But that'll spoil everything."

"If it does, I'm sorry: but I do like facts I can be sure about. And now it's your turn," he added, when the sergeant had marched resonantly out. "I gather you picked up something?"

"Yes, rather—he's waiting for you next door. William Prince by name, a queer old man who's been about the place ever since I was a boy. He's not quite as bright as he might be, but on the other hand he isn't too soft to be extremely useful. Will you see him?"

"Well, suppose you tell me yourself," suggested Beale. "I've got to get back to Belling as soon as I can."

"Oh yes, of course. Well, it seems that last Tuesday about half past four, just as it was getting dusk, Prince was hanging about the station waiting for the 4.38 from Brighton in the hope of earning a few coppers. While he was there a man came up and asked if he's like to make five bob. Of course Prince did like: he'd pretty fond of his beer, and next time he's pulled in for d. and d. will be his forty-ninth.

"This man, who was a stranger to him and answers to Ellis's description, then said that to earn the money Prince must be on the opposite side of the road from Mrs. Topley's place at seven o'clock on Thursday night. He was to wait there until Ellis opened the door and signalled to him, and then go across to help carry out a trunk. Of course, the old man wanted to know what the dickens it was all about—why he couldn't come and knock at the door in the normal way. Ellis immediately became very mysterious, told Prince he wouldn't get a penny unless he followed his instructions exactly, and added something about shooting the moon—clearing out without paying his rent, in other words.

"Well, on Thursday Prince duly turned up, only unfortunately for us he was five minutes late—he must have got there just after Mrs. Topley. He saw her come running out after he'd been there a few minutes, and very soon afterwards Ellis opened the door and beckoned to him as arranged. They both went upstairs, and outside the first-floor front was a large brown trunk—obviously the one Haines told me about. This they carried down, out of the house, and round to the yard next door, just inside the gate of which was the van. The moment the trunk was safely inside Prince was given his five bob, and an extra one for luck, and told to clear off and keep his mouth shut, and that's all he knows."

Beale had been paying careful attention, and now asked the inevitable questions.

"Prince didn't do anything when he saw Mrs. Topley run out?"

"No—he'd been expressly told to stay where he was until he saw Ellis."

"How heavy was the trunk?"

"A fair weight, he says."

"There was nothing else on the landing?"

"Nothing, and the bedroom door was shut."

"Did he notice any smell of gas?"

"No, he says not, but he's had a shocking cold for a week, apparently."

"Did Ellis shut the front door behind them?"

"Yes."

"And what about the wireless?"

Creevy shook his head with a smile.

"It's a pity, but the chap's almost stone deaf," he replied. "He says he fancied he heard some sort of noise somewhere, but he wouldn't be sure what kind."

"Gosh!" exclaimed Tony. "That must have been a bit awkward for Ellis—at the station, I mean. He'd have to bawl his instructions like a toastmaster."

But again the Inspector shook his head.

"I found out the answer to that one for myself," he said. "He doesn't really hear people talking, he sees it: lip-reading."

"Ah, then he can see all right?" asked Beale.

"His sight's very good, I believe."

"Splendid: then how tall did he say Ellis was?"

The Inspector frowned suddenly, and muttered under his breath; for a second he turned from a cool urbane police-officer into a youngish man very much annoyed with himself.

"I forgot to ask," he said ruefully, and Tony half expected him to reduce himself then and there to the rank of sergeant.

"Well, it's the only omission I've noticed so far," Beale told him, and watched the frown give way to something approaching a smile again.

"I'll go and find out," said Creevy: "only it occurs to me that you mayn't get a very satisfactory answer. William Prince has the misfortune to be almost a dwarf: he's as strong as a gorilla, but I doubt if he stands five foot."

"Fairly good psychology," remarked Tony to Beale. "To the short, all men are tall, and it's a darned sight harder to say how much taller than it would be t'other way round for a giant. But that's only natural human egotism, of course. Theoretically it's as easy to say that you come up to someone's front-collar stud as to say that someone else comes up to yours, only people never do."

And Creevy's report bore out his opinion.

"Prince stands four foot ten," he told them, "and all he can say about Ellis is that he was 'a good bit taller than me'. All the same, we've learnt a great deal from him, thanks to your inspiration."

"Inspiration!" scoffed Tony, in the car again. "Next it'll be genius, and after that some Sunday-paper astrologer will come along to prove you were the seventh son of a seventh son, and foster-brother to all the warlocks in West Sussex."

# XII

OBERT OAKES was a tall and somewhat florid man of forty with a good figure; the smartness of his double-breasted suit made Colonel Bagshaw's baggy tweeds seem positively disreputable by comparison. He had the mobile face of the character-actor, and at times while he talked his dark eyes flickered restlessly: as if, thought Beale, he were continually looking for the appreciation of some shadowy audience which only he could see. He rose at their entry, and his manner seemed to show that he had not enjoyed his wait.

"So you do exist!" he announced, in a full expressive baritone, and glanced at his watch with studied naturalness. "I understand that you're in charge of the proceedings, and humble nobodies like myself must attend your pleasure. However, I won't waste time in recrimination now you are here. Rightly, or wrongly, I feel entitled to some explanation with regard to this,"—and with a gesture which startled everyone but Beale he produced from his inner pocket a folded newspaper.

"Which is why you've come?" he was asked quietly—almost vapidly as far as tone went; yet Beale's grey eyes remained perfectly steady on Oakes's face.

"Of course, of course. The Chief-constable here referred me to you—hence my presence."

"Colonel Bagshaw referred you to me—hence your presence. I'm sorry, but I don't quite follow that, Mr. Oakes—put it down to my official dullness if you will. It doesn't seem to me to make sense unless you telephoned here before you left town, and I'm pretty sure you didn't, or I should have heard. But don't let's quarrel about trifles, when there's so much else to discuss. You ask me for an explanation: very well. My answer is, in as few words as possible, sudden death. What's yours?"

Tony and the colonel smiled at one another, and settled themselves more comfortably, independently sensing that before them was the pleasure of witnessing a duel between two fairly-matched antagonists. Their part would be that of spectators, and each was content with it. Bagshaw was thinking 'Dammit, the chap's got a lot more in him than you'd ever suspect: he knows what he's doing all right.' Tony was thinking 'I wonder where Dickie's got to—he'll be sick he missed this.'

"What's my what?" demanded the actor, a little testily; but his eyes were wary, and his face as rigid as a plaster mask.

"Why, your explanation—I'm sorry if I wasn't clear. Or perhaps the plural would be better, because there's more than one point about which I want your help. Let's begin with the simplest, shall we? You read in a London daily newspaper that a body has been discovered in your seaside bungalow, and Scotland-Yard detectives are investigating the discovery. Correct?"

A little to Tony's surprise, Oakes merely nodded.

"Thank you. Then why, please, do you set about satisfying your curiosity in so roundabout a way? Surely the direct and natural thing to have done would be to ring up the Yard, instead of coming all the way down here."

"Why? And why not, pray? Is it any legitimate concern of yours, Inspector? I chose to come here myself—I came."

"I see: in other words, no explanation offered."

"And none likely to be," said Oakes, flushing. "Look here, my man, my time's valuable, and I don't intend to be played about with. As the owner of the bungalow in question, am I or am I not entitled to know what's alleged to have been found there, and how long the police propose to commandeer the premises for?"

"Oh, is *that* what's bothering you?" murmured Beale, as if the major part of the whole mystery had just been solved. "We shan't keep you off your own property a second longer than is absolutely necessary, Mr. Oakes. The moment the exact connection between body and bungalow is clear, we'll depart; but until then, as I dare say you know already, we have a perfect right to take possession. Murder happens to be a serious affair in real life. As for the discovery, I can give you the main details rather more fully than your newspaper."

He went on to do so, Oakes listening attentively with his left elbow resting on the arm of his chair and his chin cupped in his hand. His face was almost expressionless, and Beale, watching, wondered how he could best stir the man into some positive display of emotion again. By annoying him, probably, he decided: he judged that Oakes would be satisfactory as a witness only when he could be induced to relax his self-control. In view of his attitude so far, there was little chance that he would be willingly helpful: unless he could somehow be frightened.

"Thank you," said the actor presently. "If you'd only been as open to begin with," he added, smiling for the first time, "I should have understood the position."

Beale too smiled.

"Then you'd understand a great deal more than I do," he remarked. "Still, I've only just begun to try, so I mustn't be pessimistic. Now, Mr. Oakes, perhaps you won't mind answering a few questions? In the first place, how long has the bungalow been your property?"

"Since 1929—why?"

"Because I wanted to know. How many keys to it exist?"

"Three, as far as I'm aware."

"All in your possession?"

Oakes hesitated for the fraction of a second.

"No," he answered: "only one. My manservant has another, and I lent the third to a friend some time ago."

"Where is your servant?"

"At my flat in town, of course—44 Brook Court."

"I see. And this friend—was it a man or a woman?"

"A woman—a Miss Saunderson. I believe you know her, Colonel"—turning to Bagshaw. "She lives down here."

"Ah, that's interesting," said Beale. "Do you mind telling me when you gave her the key?"

"Not at all—about this time last year, as far as I remember. As a matter of fact, she and I aren't especially friendly any longer, and I've been meaning to ask for the thing back."

"And can you tell me where Miss Saunderson is now, by any chance?"

"No, I'm afraid not. I haven't seen her for some months, but I imagine she's at home."

"Why did you cease to be friends with her?"

At this the actor frowned, and tapped his chair impatiently with his long shapely fingers.

"I don't object to being asked questions about the keys," he said, "because I'm not quite a fool, and it's pretty obvious that bodies don't just fly through walls. On the other hand, Inspector, I should hate to think you were prying into my personal affairs. I dislike people who do that sort of thing intensely."

Beale gave a credible imitation of a man attempting to conceal a feeling of amusement.

"I bet you would," he observed, with almost vulgar jocularity.

"I beg your pardon! Exactly what do you mean by that?"

"Nothing much: only I fancy your personal affairs wouldn't stand much daylight, Mr. Oakes—especially with regard to Miss Saunderson. However, we'll go back to the keys: have you yours here?"

Without speaking the other pulled from his pocket a bunch of a dozen, and indicated one of Yale pattern. He had outwardly retained his composure in the face of Beale's pointed remarks, but the three men watching felt sure that they had given him cause to think.

"May I borrow this for the time being?"

"So long as you return it eventually."

"Of course: you shall have it the day I arrest the man I'm after."

"Thanks," said Oakes: "I dare say I can wait."

For a moment there was silence, spent by Tony in attempting to forecast the turn the conversation would take. That his friend would deliberately bring it to a close for the time being was the last thing in the world he expected: but it happened.

"Well, we're both busy men, Mr. Oakes," observed Beale. "At present I don't think I need trouble you any more, except for one thing. Before you go I must ask you please to make me out a brief written summary of your movements between six o'clock on Thursday night and six o'clock on Friday morning."

"Why?" demanded the actor, so quickly that it seemed the request had been anticipated.

"Surely you shouldn't need to ask, since you understand my interest in the keys. From that it follows, I think, that I shall be interested in everybody who possesses one: namely yourself, your manservant, and Miss Saunderson. If only as a matter of common-sense routine, I must be able to eliminate you from any suspicion of having used your key on Thursday night. While you're inscribing your alibi, I shall be telephoning for someone to go round to your flat and interrogate your servant."

Oakes glowered at this, but apparently decided not to comment on Beale's phrasing. Instead he shrugged and got up.

"I suppose it's the way they taught you to do things," he sneered. "And what about Miss Saunderson? Or don't ladies get asked what they do in the dark hours?"

Beale steadied himself: it was the opportunity for which he had been looking, but had almost abandoned hope of getting. Now it would be his turn to act, and with a silent invocation to the others not to spoil things he began to answer the actor's question within two seconds of its being put.

"Oh, I know all about *her* movements Thursday, thanks," he said, in matter-of-fact disinterested tones.

There was a moment more of silence, during which Oakes stood very still: his expression might have been incredulity, or perhaps no more than disbelief. Then he turned pale, put his hand to his mouth, coughed, and looked away.

"Where would you like me to perform?" he asked casually.

Three minutes later Beale and Tony were walking down Bagshaw's gravel drive.

"It shook him!" exclaimed the former, in a fierce whisper. "We mustn't let him go back yet, only how the devil are we going to stop him?"

"Why mustn't he go back?" asked his friend.

"Because he knows something, and we've got to get it out of him. He rather gave himself away just now—maybe you weren't noticing, and that was why you kept quiet. He gaped at me when I said I knew all about Philippa Saunderson's movements on Thursday: which may mean nothing, or may be infernally important. Anyway, his behaviour's not quite normal, coming here instead of tackling the Yard."

"Actors prefer drama," suggested Tony.

"Possibly. How can we keep him here?"

"Can't say, unless you arrest him, or run off with his magneto, or something."

"Yes, that's another reason," agreed Beale obliquely. "That's his car outside, I suppose? We must get young Best to listen to it starting up, in case he can recognize the noise. I wonder where the fellow is—I ought to have asked."

They moved across the road to Oakes's car, a two-seater Daimler of impressive appearance.

"Rather nice," said Tony, "and confoundedly expensive, whether he got it for cash or on the h.p. All the same, I'd rather have my own bus."

For a moment Beale merely stared at its sleek lines and brilliant coach-work; then, after hesitating, he opened the near-side door and put his head inside. A few seconds later he was on the pavement again, and his manner had become tense.

"Look!" he commanded, pointing to the seat beside the driver's. Tony did so, and immediately observed that on the dark-blue leather was a slightly darker stain about the size of a saucer. Without quite knowing why he glanced at the floor-covering, and saw a similar mark, smaller and rather lighter. Then, not waiting to be asked, he knelt down on the running-board and sniffed.

"Interesting" he said, when he had straightened himself.

"Petrol?" enquired Beale.

"No—carbolic."

"Good man! And probably fairly recent, or you wouldn't notice anything."

"What was it originally—blood, d'you think?"

"I hope so: I mean, we'll find out. If it is, we've got our excuse to detain him. Now how's it to be managed? I expect the fellow can be kept quiet for another half an hour: till 5.00, say. We shall have to be thundering quick. Get the Bentley started while I have a word with Bagshaw."

He hurried indoors, secured the colonel from the study, and spoke urgently.

"Is there a decent analyst in Craybourne?" he asked.

"Yes," came the prompt answer: "Atkins, lives opposite the town hall. Why?"

"I must see him, and there's no time to lose. Look here, sir, can you keep Oakes busy till I get back, and not only that, but away from his car? It's really important. Any excuse will do: tell him his statement's got to be amended, or written upside down—anything. He simply mustn't go near the Daimler till I've had five minutes with it, and first I've got to see Atkins. There's a stain or two that may be blood, at a guess. Oh lord, I was forgetting it's Saturday afternoon—"

"He'll be there," said the colonel confidently. "He's working on some patent idea that's going to revolutionize the treatment of diabetes—he'll be there."

"Good: then will you ring him at once, please? Tell him to have ready materials for the leuco-malachite blood-test."

"Leuco-malachite? Right: and tell your pal to step on it. Oakes said he wanted to be away by 5.00, but I'll keep him somehow even if I have to turn nasty."

"Yes, tackle him about Miss Saunderson if necessary. Say she's disappeared, and he's got to look at the body."

"Fairly fast?" asked Tony, ten seconds later.

"Only more so: we want Craybourne town hall, and that ought to be easy, because it's bound to be the ugliest building in the place."

On the perilous way he explained in some detail the object of their journey.

"There are several preliminary tests for determining if blood is present on any particular substance or not," he said, "and the leuco-malachite is one of the best. This chap Atkins will give us some of the reagent, which as far as I remember consists of 1 grain of leuco-malachite green, 100 c.c. of glacial acetic acid, and 150 c.c. of distilled water. Anyway, those are about the proportions. To four parts of that mixture you add one part of a 1% solution of peroxide of hydrogen, and there you are. Whenever the result comes in contact with blood, either animal or human, it first of all turns green, and then dark greeny-blue."

"Why?" asked Tony primly. "Not to mention how, if it was green to begin with."

"Only faintly. And don't expect me to explain, because I can't. It's what happens."

"In other words, it's science, and therefore a mystery. Well, I hope Oakes's Daimler turns a very bright green, because I don't like the fellow. If you told me the right shade I'd go and buy a pot of paint in case the stains are something ordinary like an egg that somebody overlooked, or a pound of butter.

"All the same," he went on, more seriously, "there'll be a lot of fresh complications if your magic comes off. How can it be the corpse's blood, when we decided that Oakes couldn't have killed her?"

"Oh no we didn't," contradicted Beale: "only that he couldn't have done it before half past one. And it needn't have been the same person, you know."

"You mean that X administers the gas and Oakes removes the head? But that's turning the business into an absolute nightmare."

"Well, it isn't exactly a bed-time story, whichever way you look at it."

"True: and the position of the stains certainly makes it look as if something fairly small was put first on the seat and then on the floor. A bag, say—one of those collapsible shopping-baskets with the head and so on inside."

"Now don't fill in all the gory details," advised Beale. "It may not be blood, and if it is it may not be human blood; and if it is human, there may be some perfectly harmless explanation. I shall certainly make Oakes produce it, though, before I let him do any public acting tonight."

The analyst had the required materials ready, and they were back outside the colonel's house at 4.55. The test, from start to finish, took three minutes. For each stain Beale took two pieces of clean white blotting-paper, soaking one in distilled water provided by Atkins, and the other in the leuco-malachite reagent. The first he pressed for a few seconds against the suspected mark, and then placed it in close contact with the second: in each case the characteristic green stain denoting the presence of blood was almost immediately noticeable.

"That settles it," he said. "Come on—we may as well have the bust-up right away."

Indoors they met Bagshaw in the hall, and learnt that although the actor was beginning to get restive, he had been put off with a story about Beale's urgent desire to see him again before he left. There had thus been no need for further mention of Philippa Saunderson.

"What's going to happen?" he asked. "Was it blood?"

"Yes, and I expect he'll be a bit peeved, sir. It may mean an arrest."

The colonel scratched his chin dubiously.

"Without a warrant?" he queried. "For what?"

"I can't say yet—I'll have to see how he shapes."

The actor rose as they entered the study.

"Well, I've done what you asked," he said conversationally, "and Colonel Bagshaw tells me it ought to do, so if it's all the same to you I'll be getting back to town. Perhaps you aren't aware that my play begins at 8.15, and I'm on ten minutes after the curtain goes up."

Beale pondered for a moment: he had not expected Oakes to ignore so completely the fact that he had again been kept waiting. Did the man imagine that Bagshaw had been bluffing, unwilling to release him until he knew if Beale approved? Or was his attitude the outwardly bold front of someone inwardly desperate to escape?

"I'm sorry," he said briskly. "I'm afraid it's quite out of the question for you to leave just yet, Mr. Oakes. I have a great deal more to discuss with you. I dare say the colonel will let you use his telephone, if you care to make the necessary arrangements with your theatre."

The actor drew himself up to his full height; his eyes narrowed, and a spot of colour was visible on either cheek.

"What the hell!" he snapped, all trace of urbanity gone. "If you've got two pennorth of sense in your fat head you'll know the play can't go on without me."

"Then it'll have to come off," Beale told him firmly.

"My God, you must think you're somebody! I don't give one single little damn what you want to discuss—you aren't going to do it now. I shall be available all day tomorrow, Sunday, and if you care to call after midday I may spare you an hour. Meanwhile you'll kindly remember that you've no authority whatever to detain me."

"And yet, you know, I propose to do just that" he was informed. "I don't think you can quite appreciate your somewhat delicate position, Mr. Oakes, or you'd hardly take up such an unhelpful attitude."

"I appreciate it perfectly. Having committed no crime, except apparently to fall foul of you, I'm free to come and go as I please. Unless they changed the law during the lunch-hour, of course."

"Ah, perhaps that means you refreshed your memory of it before you came?" suggested Beale. "But that wasn't quite what I was driving at. I was referring to your possible connection with the events of Thursday night."

He stared at Oakes keenly as he said this, and thought he saw a momentary flicker of fear in the actor's dark eyes.

"I was in London the whole of Thursday night," came the swift answer, in a rising voice. "What grounds have you for daring to suggest otherwise? Especially as you haven't even had the decency to read my statement."

"Very well, I'll give you the grounds," Beale told him severely. "In the first place, we have reliable evidence that a powerful car drove away from your bungalow in a suspicious manner about 2.15 A.M. on Friday; and you possess a powerful car. So do thousands of other people, you may say: but they emphatically don't also possess keys to the bungalow. Secondly, it has been suggested that the body about which I told you earlier is Miss Saunderson's, and you may care to know that I'm fully informed about your recent dealings with her."

"What d'you mean by that?"

"Exactly what I say, Mr. Oakes. I know all about the twenty-five letters, price £100 each, about the compromising portrait, and about the even more compromising photographs. It wouldn't be the hardest job in the world to land you with a blackmail charge, and I'm sure that wouldn't make the best publicity for your distinguished career."

The only answer to that was a cold malevolent stare, and a request to go on.

"Thirdly, then, your powerful car bears stains on the near-side front seat and the floor-covering just in front which are of obviously recent origin. In spite of some optimist's attempt to remove them with carbolic, I've been able to satisfy myself that those stains were caused by blood."

"Ha! He's a witch-doctor!" sneered Oakes. "You just smelt them, I suppose?"

"No, as a matter of fact it was my friend who did that" Beale contradicted. "I shall want a thorough explanation."

The hint was ignored.

"And who the devil says they were blood?" demanded the actor. "Does nothing else make a stain?"

"Well, suppose you tell me something else that could have made those particular ones."

"All right, that's easy: if you must know, a friend of mine leant against some red paint the other day, and then got in my car."

"Dear me! And presumably trod against it too: he must be a very acrobatic sort of person. Needless to say, I don't believe you. It so happens that just before five o'clock I tested those stains myself in what my friend would tell you was a highly scientific manner, and the reagent I used responds only to blood, not to red paint."

"You damned interfering swine!" cried Oakes violently. "You—"

"Steady!" cut in Beale. "That won't do you any good. Just sit still for a minute and reconsider your decision. Will you stay here tonight and give me what help you can, or do you prefer me to take steps to make you? Don't forget that the case I'm on is one of murder, not petty larceny or exceeding the speed limit."

"Hear hear!" barked the colonel suddenly. "You have my fullest support, Inspector."

"Thank you: but I think that possibly Mr. Oakes will behave sensibly after all."

The actor now was obviously deep in thought; he glared steadily at the floor, and for a moment Tony wondered how anyone could sit so still with three pairs of eyes watching him. Then he recollected that Oakes was used to being stared at. 'He'd have a good head if it weren't for that sensual mouth,' he thought. 'I can see why he's got such a following of adoring young females, though.'

Presently Oakes looked up, and his face seemed suddenly strained and weary.

"All right, I'll stay if you insist," he said. "But why tomorrow won't do I can't imagine."

"Tomorrow we may all be dead" Beale observed cheerfully. "I'd rather talk to you tonight, and I think you've chosen wisely. You have an understudy?"

"What passes for one: but don't blame me if my manager brings an action against you for damages."

# XIII

FTER THE ACTOR HAD TELEPHONED the New Gaiety, under unobtrusive supervision from Bagshaw, they went into the drawing-room for tea. Tony took the first opportunity to enquire about Dickie Donovan's whereabouts.

"Oh, him!" said the colonel with a smile. "He spent a couple of hours trying to smash my typewriter, and then he sloped off. Said he'd had an idea, and didn't know how far it would take him or when he'd be back, and as it was Saturday he wouldn't need to have any more news ready till after midnight tomorrow."

Soon afterwards Beale rang up Scotland Yard, to ensure that due attention should be given to the dumb manservant at 44 Brook Court, and his bungalow key. He refrained from dictating Oakes's account of his movements on Thursday night because he expected to receive a different and more interesting version shortly. 'Horsey' Matthews, he was told, had just arrived, and seemed to have recovered his usual good spirits.

"Tell him to ring me here at 6.00 tomorrow" said Beale: "unless he's lost in the wilds of Kennington."

Ten seconds after he had hung up the receiver, and while he was still touching the study door-handle, the telephone bell rang. It was Inspector Creevy, jubilantly informative.

"I interviewed Mrs. Amos myself, sir," he began, and Beale smiled: since they were equal in rank, he must be going up in Creevy's estimation, which possibly argued another successful shot in the dark.

"She described the young woman she saw on the steps of 14 Weatherall Road, and says the date was Thursday September 1st—the day after Alice Carter moved in. And if you ask my opinion, her visitor was none other than Miss Saunderson."

"Is that a guess?" he was asked eagerly: the promise of some definite connection between the two missing girls was unexpected and stimulating.

"Only in part," answered Creevy. "You'll remember I have Miss Saunderson's description, which Colonel Bagshaw gave me on Friday. But what seems to me more significant is that Mrs. Amos says she was using a small red sports car. I took the chance of telephoning her uncle—Mr. Charles Harrington, the celebrated crime-novelist, you know—and he tells me that his niece runs just such a car."

"You didn't explain why you wanted to find out?" queried Beale quickly.

"Oh no, I was quite vague."

"I see. It's certainly interesting news, and good work on your part."

"And that isn't all," came Creevy's purr. "Sergeant Turner carried out the gas-test you suggested, without much trouble as far as Mrs. Topley was concerned. The result bears out your forecast amazingly well: no one on the landing smelt anything until eight and a half minutes after the tap inside the room was turned on. The space of time covered, for five witnesses, was thirty-three seconds, Mrs. Topley being the third to notice the odour."

"Again, good work."

"Excellent—on *your* part. I should very much like to know what it means, though."

His distant voice held a hint of enquiry, but the bait was refused.

"I'm not a bit sure," Beale told him. "Now I can give you some news, for a change."

He related the developments with regard to Oakes and the stains in the car, and rang off thoughtfully. What in the world would Philippa Saunderson have had to do with Alice Carter? He wondered if Matthews would be able to provide an answer from London. Tomorrow might show: meanwhile he must return to the task of extracting information from Oakes.

The moment he was inside the drawing-room again his hopes sank, however: the actor seemed to have regained full control of himself. He even smiled confidently as he himself began the discussion.

"I've decided to come clean, as they say," he asserted, "and I apologize for any trouble I may have caused you by not doing that in the first place. If you can see things from my point of view, though, perhaps you'll understand. After all, I *am* something of a public figure, and publicity to an actor is almost the same thing as livelihood, provided it's the right sort. Getting oneself mixed up in a sordid crime definitely isn't, in my opinion, which was why I tried to keep clear."

He said this with such unctuous blandness that Tony almost laughed; but a second later his face clouded a little.

"Hasn't rehearsed his part enough,' thought Beale, and was glad.

"How much you've been told about my relations with Miss Saunderson I don't know," continued Oakes. "Nor how true that much is, though I can guess it's a bit one-sided. If you're fancying she was any kind of a lily till she met me, though, you're dead wrong. She may have been as pure as the proverbial snow once, but she'd drifted a good deal before I even knew she existed. Still, I don't want to give away secrets, so the less said about that the better.

"When she terminated our association she hurt me. I don't mind admitting it—nor that I don't like being hurt. Some people would probably have let it go at a bit of plain speaking, but I'm afraid I'm not quite that type. I'm no braggart, but I am a man, and a man doesn't like being dismissed for a bit of animated red-tape in a wing-collar. And not even red at that: if you cut him open you'd probably find soda-and-milk inside, and one or two white-papers. I made up my mind to get a little of my own back on Miss Philippa, and if you don't think I chose a very pretty way, all I can say is that I wasn't feeling pretty.

"In brief, I determined to frighten her, and I rather think I suc-ceeded—anyway, I'm sure I hope so. There was never any real intention to blackmail her—that goes without saying: all that hap-pened was that I played the part thoroughly. Until lately, that is, when I began to think the joke had gone far enough. She was apt to be the sort of hysterical young fool who might throw over the traces if she were goaded too far, and so I decided to call it a day. And then, the very next evening, last Thursday, I had a telegram from her: here it is."

From his waistcoat pocket he took a slip of white paper, and held it out.

"Read it yourself," he invited. "Keep it if you like—make sure it's a genuine telegram, and not some subtle trick to take in the hounds of justice."

Without comment Beale reached for the proffered form, and examined it, but could detect no sign of falsity. The office of ori-gin was Craybourne, the time of handing in 5.49 P.M. on Thursday October 20th, and the addressee Robert Oakes, New Gaiety Thea-tre, London, W.C.I.

*Urgent see you studio tonight have decided buy pretty pictures will wait two till three only opportunity Phil.*

"Thank you," he said, passing it on to Bagshaw. "I'll be glad to take charge of it for the time being, but it certainly seems all right."

" 'Nay, it is; I know not seems,' " retorted Oakes in his deep mellow voice. "Dear me, how the late lamented bard does clog the tongue at times. Or do you prefer the Earl-of-Oxford theory?"

"I don't give a bare bodkin," Beale told him truthfully. "He's too dead to interest me as a case of doubtful identity."

"Well, there I disagree: it would clear up a great many doubtful points in the plays themselves, and stimulate public interest. However, don't let me side track you. As I was saying, I received that telegram when I reached the theatre at 7.30, and I understand it was delivered about twenty minutes earlier. I'd half a mind not to go, but on thinking it over I decided it would be a good opportunity to put things straight. And as well, to be quite frank, I didn't like the words 'only opportunity'. It sounded as if she might be getting too worked up.

"I duly set out at ten minutes to midnight, alone: I arranged for sandwiches and a flask of coffee to be put on board, and as I wasn't hungry I didn't bother with a meal before starting. It would have made me rather late, anyway, as it takes a good two hours at night. The road was quite clear except for a bit of fog near Purley, and I drew up outside the bungalow at five past two. There was no sign of Philippa, and no lights showing, but I knew she'd still got my key if she hadn't lost it, so I assumed she was inside all right, but had drawn the curtains carefully so that nobody should spot her.

"Well, I walked round and opened the door, and the moment I was in I realized that there really weren't any lights on—you can always tell there when the hall's in darkness. That puzzled me, because I was a bit late, and she was always an aggressively punctual person. Automatically I went into the studio, since it was the room she'd mentioned, touched the switch, and saw—it."

He paused, though whether with deliberately dramatic intent or not Beale could not be sure. The actor's words had been coming more slowly, and his eyes now held more than a suggestion of horror: it seemed possible that for once he was being sincere.

"It was a ghastly sight," he went on expressively, "and I'd rather not attempt to describe it in detail. The body was lying on the rug with its feet cut off, and yellow bags on the hands and round the head; it had cheap green undies on, and an appalling pair of garters."

He halted again, and then laughed a trifle unsteadily.

"That alone was enough to tell me it wasn't Philippa," he said. "She'd never have been seen even dead in such things, and anyway she never wore green. Well, I just stood and stared, I don't know for how long, and then I found myself shivering from head to foot. After that I'm not absolutely sure what happened: if the light was out, then I suppose I must have switched it off, but I don't remember. All I knew was that I wanted to get away, and I had my foot down hard once I got my nerve back. I was home by 4.30—my man will confirm that—and I didn't sleep a wink."

He stopped, sighed, and took out his cigarette-case.

"Have one?" he asked, but Beale refused, taking out his pipe instead and slowly beginning to fill it. During the operation he thought deeply, speculating about Oakes's story, and wondering how much of it might need subsequent revision. He felt vaguely uncomfortable in his mind, and disliked the feeling, for which he knew the cause. He was at the moment quite unable to assess the value of the actor's evidence, and the admission riled him. Agreed that acting was the man's job, at which he had proved himself highly successful; yet he could not honestly accept that as sufficient excuse for his uncertainty. For some years he had spent about a quarter of his working time in learning to recognize sincerity when he encountered it, and now he was stumped by the first professional he came across.

After all, he told himself, Oakes had been clearly ill at ease at one time; but somehow he—Beale—had allowed him to regain his confidence. He was sitting there now puffing at his cigarette with an air almost approaching conscious virtue: a distasteful task had been accomplished, it seemed to say, and his mind was at rest.

"Curse the fellow,' thought Beale. 'Was he genuine or not? But surely the fact that I've any doubts means he probably wasn't. And yet his story makes sense, except for the stains which he hasn't attempted to explain. Of course, he's used to being looked at, and that's why I miss the normal witness's embarrassment at being the centre of attention. Duncan and Best showed it this morning, and Harrington too, a little.'

"Did you wear gloves?" he asked abruptly, glancing up; and the actor received the question as if he had had five minutes' notice of it.

"In the bungalow, d'you mean? Yes. You see, when I'm driving I always have a thin pair of chammy-leather ones under my gauntlets, and naturally I can manage keys and things all right in them. I have to look after my hands, you know—I play the piano quite a bit."

"Of course," agreed Beale, recalling that Oakes was reputed to be high in the second grade of amateurs. And then he understood suddenly just what it was which troubled him: wherein the man differed from Best and Harrington and Dr. Duncan. His hands had been almost perfectly controlled during the whole time he was speaking, and the realization was some comfort.

"I shall have to check your story where I can," he said.

"Naturally. Perhaps I'd better jot down the times and so on, in place of this afternoon's effort?"

"Yes, please. And there'll be something else, too—something unpleasant, I'm afraid."

"Yes? What would that be?"

"To view the—the carcase. You see, Mr. Oakes, you happen to have one clear advantage over the rest of us: you know what Miss Saunderson looks like, or looked like, unclothed, and we don't."

"Ah!" murmured the actor, with a faint smile. "If you call it an advantage, though I admit I've seen uglier women."

"I didn't mean my remark that way. I want to know if the body can possibly be hers."

"Of course not—I've told you Philippa was superstitious about never wearing green. And incidentally, I don't think it would be too soon if I were allowed a question or two of my own. I gather that she's disappeared: but what exactly do you mean by that?"

"She hasn't been seen or heard of specifically since Thursday evening, somewhere about eleven o'clock."

"Really? But I thought you knew all about her movements?"

He smiled pointedly as he said this, but Beale merely shrugged.

"I meant up till that time," he declared untruthfully.

"Ah. And while you're being generous, who suggests that the body is hers?"

"Mr. Harrington, her uncle."

"Good lord, that old goat! It's just the sort of thing he *would* think of—why people read his muck beats me."

"For the same reason that they watch you act, perhaps: it's a cheap way of leading an unfamiliar life for a few hours. While I remember, have I your permission to get the stains on your upholstery analysed?"

"Oh, by all means," said Oakes readily. "Only I shall expect a new seat if you cut mine to bits, you know."

"We'll try not to go as far as that" Beale promised. "Incidentally, how *did* the stains get there?"

He put the question half jokingly and half in earnest. It was a point about which he particularly wanted information, and he felt fairly sure that the actor could supply some if he should be willing; yet equally sure that he would do so only under a degree of pressure which they were not at present in a position to apply.

"Lord, *I* don't know!" said Oakes, with an admirable gesture of ignorance. "If I did I'd tell you, honest I would."

# XIV

I T WAS NOW ALMOST SEVEN O'CLOCK. At Beale's request the Chief-constable offered Oakes the room which was to have been occupied by Matthews and the absent reporter, and the offer was accepted.

"I won't give you any trouble," the actor promised smilingly. "My mind's quite clear now, so why should I?"

"And what next?" asked Bagshaw, when they could speak freely: a question which Beale countered with another.

"Where's young Best likely to be?" he enquired.

"Don't know—up at Harrington's with his girl, perhaps. You want him about the car, I suppose? He'll be parading for duty to-night about 9.45."

"Good: and meanwhile I must arrange for those stains to be analysed. Now, Colonel, what about some of the news you've been bottling up?"

"News? What news?"

"Oh, come! Dr. Duncan's report on the photographs, to begin with."

Bagshaw nodded, his face gloomy.

"Creevy's right—I shall never make a policeman," he declared. "The doctor said he didn't know. There aren't any marked differences between the photographic body and the real one, but on the other hand, in the nature of things, there aren't any very striking resemblances."

"In other words," put in Tony, "what he really said was 'Find the body and I'll tell you'?"

"Yes, roughly. Now, what comes next?"

"The moist man in the overcoat, or *Mr. Burden was Right,*" suggested Beale.

"Ah yes. I rang up Dennison at the F.O., and found Harrington had done the same half an hour earlier. He was just about as stuffed as usual: profoundly shocked at the news of Miss Saunderson's disappearance, and all the rest of it. Still, he did propose coming down here tomorrow—said he thought he had some information which might help, but he'd rather keep it till he saw me, thank you very much. Diplomacy *par excellence* in a really high-class accent."

"I see—pity he didn't suggest coming tonight."

"I did myself, but apparently he was full up with work and couldn't get away."

"Did he go as far as admitting he was down here on Thursday?" enquired Tony.

"No, and I didn't like to ask direct for fear of frightening him. I rang the railway station, however, and a man in a black coat and hat and carrying a small bag was seen getting off the 11.25, which was three minutes late. Incidentally, I think one of us ought to stand you a really good cigar, Mr. Purdon—I've no doubt he was here."

"One of you? Why not both? But maybe you'd better wait till tomorrow, just in case I'm wrong—only I shan't be."

"And finally, did you hear if Mr. Harrington had any luck?" asked Beale.

"Yes: he telephoned to say he found a letter from Best, much as expected, and the one from Oakes about showing the portrait in town."

"Good—that sounds interesting. No trace of the ones he was blackmailing her about?"

"No—I expect she destroyed them. He didn't come across the photo with Oakes in, either. Why didn't you run up and see him?"

"Yes, I will, and I can get the maid's opinion of the clothes at the same time."

"Right. There'll be food here from 8.00 onwards. I suppose I'd better take our friend next door down to view the corpse. And what in the world do I do if Donovan turns up?"

"I don't know—it's queer he hasn't telephoned."

When Beale and Tony reached *Cairngorm,* a pleasant unsymmetrical house about a quarter of a mile from the sea-front, they were told that John Best had only just gone. This information came from Mary Adams, and their first sight of her provided an agreeable surprise. She was a tall graceful girl of about twenty-four with a small straight nose and dark lustrous hair. Her eyes too were bright, and both men fancied that her smile would be worth seeing. At the moment her face was quite sober, though; it seemed that she was suitably concerned over the disappearance of Philippa Saunderson.

'Handsome,' thought Tony—'Best's got good taste. I only hope she doesn't spoil it all when she opens her mouth.'

But he need not have feared: her low pleasant voice was in harmony with her looks.

"Good-evening, sir. Mr. Harrington says you want me to see some clothes."

"Yes, please. I've got a parcel here with a petticoat and the remains of some stockings inside. I should like you to examine them carefully, and then tell me if Miss Saunderson ever possessed anything similar, to your knowledge."

As he spoke he took out the clothes he had mentioned, and put them on the table. They were in the novelist's dining-room, and the green artificial silk at once seemed shoddy by comparison with the cloth on which it lay. Mary Adams merely glanced at the stockings distastefully, and shook her head.

"Miss Philippa would never have worn cheap ones like that," she declared. Then she picked up the petticoat, and Tony noticed that her hands were well cared for; as also the fact that on her engagement finger was a neat diamond ring, relatively inexpensive but tastefully designed. She scrutinized the material, fingered the shoulder-straps, and finally examined the hems.

"No sir," she said with a quiet smile, "this isn't hers either."

"You're quite sure?"

"Quite: and not only because I don't recognize it. Miss Philippa's inclined to be rather particular about her underclothes, and this isn't very good quality stuff. It's ready-made, too—you can see by the way it's finished off, but she mostly has hers to measure. And not in green—she's a bit superstitious, and won't wear the colour."

"Well, that sounds pretty conclusive," remarked Beale—"thank you. I've one or two other things to ask about while I'm here, and then I'll stop bothering you. Did Miss Saunderson ever wear garters?"

"Well, she's got a pair, but she only uses them in the summer when it's really hot and she's down on the sands. And they're not like the ones on the—the body: John told me about them. He found it, you know."

"Yes, and I don't envy him. And now a rather curious question, and if it strikes you as being indelicate you must forgive me. Have you ever seen Miss Saunderson naked?"

The girl pleased Tony by treating the query sensibly.

"No, never," she said: "Mr. Harrington asked me this afternoon. I've often seen her with very little on, and once or twice in her bath when she's forgotten her dressing-gown or something, but I honestly couldn't say I'd recognize her if she wasn't wearing anything and her face was covered."

"So you can't tell me if she had any distinguishing marks anywhere—scars or moles?"

Mary Adams thought for a few seconds.

"She hadn't any scars," she answered. "I remember her saying so one day when she was talking about a friend who'd been thrown while riding. I'm fairly certain she had no moles either, but she did have some vaccination marks on her left arm."

"Ah, thanks. In the usual place?"

"Yes sir."

"Are they very noticeable?"

"Not very. When she goes out in the evening she puts a dab of liquid powder on, and then they don't show at all."

Beale nodded at the information, and stared unseeingly at the carpet before turning to the girl again.

"I won't ask you to look at the body," he said, "but if I can arrange for a photograph of the left arm which shows the vaccination marks I'll get your opinion on it. It's just possible that you might be able to say definitely by the shape that it couldn't be Miss Saunderson, or alternatively that it could easily be, don't you think?"

"Yes sir. Only—"

"Yes?"

"I was going to say, how *can* it be? In somebody else's undies?"

"I'm afraid I can't tell you, but all the same we've got to consider the possibility. Dead bodies *do* sometimes turn up in the wrong clothes, unfortunately. Well, that's all for now, Miss Adams, and many thanks. Oh lord, are *you* going to start?"—as Tony cleared his throat ominously.

"It'll soon be over," promised his friend. "All I want to know is the approximate price of that garment; or, better still, of the three together—the complete set. You needn't go into details," he added hastily, to save the girl any possible embarrassment. "For instance, would ten bob cover the lot?"

She smiled, and nodded.

"Two and eleven, and twice one and eleven," she said. "What's that—less than ten shillings, anyway. I think that would be about the price."

From the dining-room they went to Harrington's study, where the stout novelist was obviously awaiting them. For some minutes he listened while Beale briefly related the afternoon's events, and at the end he was frowning.

"You'll check the telegram, of course?"

"Yes, but first I'm curious to know if Mr. Dennison also received one."

"Ah. Bagshaw told you he's coming tomorrow?"

"Yes—was it your suggestion, then?"

"Partly—mind?"

"Not a bit—I'm very glad. I shall probably telephone him myself later tonight, though, and ask him to make it early. Can you give me his home number? Thanks.

"And now may I see the letters you found this afternoon?" he asked presently.

Best's was little more than a note, written on cheap lined paper in a round hand.

> *October 15th*
>
> *Dear Miss Saunderson, Thank you for your letter. I shall be off duty next Thursday afternoon, and can meet you in Craybourne. Will five o'clock outside the general Post Office be convenient? The things I told you about are at your Bank in Belling, I left them there in the Manager's charge. I hope you have a nice journey, and that Mary is well. Yours Truly, J. Best.*

The second was longer, and the writing more mature. Beale was not surprised to see that it displayed a certain amount of flourish, the effect being a combination of vanity and dashing boldness. The ink used was a brilliant violet, and the paper verged towards lemon rather than cream.

> *44 Brook Court, W.i*
>
> *7: x: 38*
>
> *Dear Phil, Really, I wish you would send a gentler envoy next time. I dislike these uncouth amateur bruisers, and am more than a little peeved about it. Still, don't let's talk about him, though I fancy he may have a surprise for you when you*

*see him next—unless he's told you already? I know I've been
dilatory in writing. And now I have a piece of news which I
hasten to pass on. The day before yesterday I was talking to
Garstein, the art dealer. As you may remember, he's always
bestowed a kindly interest on my poor daubs, and must certainly have had news of a legacy or something, for he actually
offered to give me a part show with Gordon Cocklewhite. Or
perhaps he was binged, because as you probably know they
call Gordon the pastel prince, and would a sober man contem-
plate pastels in the same room with my lurid oils? I shan't be at
all amazed if poor G's delicacies curl up in their dainty frames,
and that'll be a bit expensive for him at ten guineas a time. I
understand him to be a most earnest and god-fearing young
man with a brilliant future as far as the anaemic depiction of
oranges and flat fish goes: unlike myself, whose future lies in
the past, so to speak, and whose choice would be figures instead of fish any day—or night.*

*But I wander. I am allowed a round dozen paintings, but am
cruelly restricted to a meagre four nudes. Garstein says he
can't bear to think of his chaste gallery becoming the haunt of
pimply young men agape and agog, waiting for the too too
solid flesh to materialize miraculously, if only in their imagina-
tions. I have decided to exhibit the female publican about whom
we quarrelled so violently, and two more of which you know
nothing—which is perhaps just as well, or would have been.
And the fourth—can you guess, my sweet? Not strictly a nude,
of course, but what's in a veil? No impossible guess, given average eyesight. Nevertheless, it will look very jolly, and people
may begin to think I really can paint a little, perchance. It is
undoubtedly one of the best things I ever did, as I tell myself
every time I happen to glance that way. My brushes for once
behaved; though what brush would not, desired to illustrate
your nordic loveliness?*

*I trust you are well, and those near and dear to you. When
the date of the show is fixed I shall certainly send you and your
current cavalier tickets for the private view.*

*Yours in memory, Robert.*
*P.S. Unless—dare I mention it?—you would prefer a very pri-
vate view only. The price remains the same, but if a 5% dis-
count should help, merely say and it is yours. What is 5% between those déjà 100%? Please indicate your pleasure by the
end of the month.*

"A thoroughly nasty letter," said Beale, when he had finished reading it.

"Extremely," agreed Harrington. "It was written by a nasty specimen, that's why. His personality comes out quite clearly."

"Yes, I feel now that I'm beginning to understand him. May I keep it for the time being?"

"By all means," said the novelist, and relapsed into a troubled silence. His dumpy form was huddled in an arm-chair as if he were cold, and he had his legs curled under him out of sight.

"Something on your mind?" suggested Beale at last. "I mean, something fresh?"

For a moment Harrington stared at him, eyebrows meeting in a frown. Then he bounced up in the chair abruptly and leant forward.

"You're right," he said, and his voice seemed less gentle than before. "I think I'll tell you. After all, if she is alive still then it's her own damned fault for not showing up and proving it. *Must be.*"

"Unless she's lost her memory," put in Tony. "People do."

"Not people like Philippa," declared the novelist, shaking his head emphatically. "No, my opinion grows firmer: I believe she's dead. I believe it's her body that's being messed about by Dr. Duncan—that we're up against a really cunning murder, Beale: something good enough for fiction. Murder in real life's apt to be pretty poor stuff on the whole, don't you think? Inartistic and clumsy more often than not—a wallop and a bash and the job's done.

"It takes us writer fellows to be really subtle: and do you know why? Because if we make a howler we stand to lose nothing but a few readers next time. The worst that can happen to us is a snarky remark in a Sunday paper: we don't have to lie in bed shivering at night because there may be a car-load of coppers coming up the drive to make us pay for our mistake. If you could persuade one of us—Bailey or Sayers or Christie, MacDonald or Ellery Queen or Carter Dickson, to go out and do a real murder with real knives and bullets and blood and prussic acid, I bet it would be a flop. Or make 'em do one apiece, and you wouldn't get more than a hint of artistry in the lot."

"You mean one that appealed to them, I suppose?" said Tony. "Not just a mere exhibition murder?"

"Of course not: one done for a real motive in order to remove a particular victim. Dammit, there'd be nothing to it if you didn't mind who you killed and provided you were capable of being callous enough. Just think of the scores of times you yourself could have polished off some poor unsuspecting wretch whose name you didn't even know, and not a soul the wiser. If you don't believe me, try it. Wait till there's a good thick fog, and then wander round with a hatchet under your coat: you'll be a bit of a duffer if you can't cut half a dozen notches in it by evening. Or get hold of some poison—weed-killer or what-not: doctor some chocolates, and then dump 'em three at a time in every sweet-shop you can find when the owner isn't looking. You'll get enough bodies to start a crematorium.

"But I'm just talking—sorry. I dare say it's because I don't really want to tell you what's on my mind: but I will. When my niece first mentioned this affair of hers with Oakes, and asked me to lend her the £5000 to buy him off with, I said I couldn't possibly raise that much, but that I'd let her have £1000 if it would help—I told you this morning. But what I haven't told anyone yet is that I actually got hold of that much in cash, in case it were wanted. All in small notes, of course: blackmailers never touch big stuff in the story-books, so why should they be expected to in real life? I put the money in an old biscuit tin, and the tin I hid in that cupboard under the window.

"All this was back in the summer, mind, before we went to Scotland, and at the time I said nothing to Philippa about it. She was apt to be, well, extravagant over money, and I saw no sense in putting temptation in her way."

He halted for a moment, frowning again and glaring at Beale with obvious unhappiness.

"I don't know your views about trusting people," he went on at last: "and if it comes to that, I'm not even sure I know my own. On the whole I think I agree with the chap who said, 'Trust yourself when sober, sometimes, but others only when they're sufficiently drunk to be unnatural'. Anyway, let that go. The point is that I preferred not to let Philippa know there was a thousand pounds in the house, though I wanted it handy in case of emergency. It was as safe in that cupboard as anywhere, because the maids never do more than dust the outside now and again, and who'd think of looking for hard cash in an old biscuit tin? It'd be only slightly more reasonable than looking for biscuits.

"Well, I'll cut it short. When I returned from Scotland by myself I remembered the money, and opened the tin, and it was still there. On Thursday afternoon when Philippa told me about the letter you've just read, and the photographs, she kept saying 'I've got to do something—I've got to do something.' Then, just as she was going, she turned to me suddenly and asked how quick I could let her have what I'd promised, provided I hadn't changed my mind. Without thinking I told her that as it happened she could have it in cash then and there if she liked, only I'd rather she tried to spend less if possible. She looked at me a bit queerly, said thank you, and walked out.

"That was about half past four, I suppose. I stayed here working till a good bit past seven, and then put on my hat and coat and went for a stroll—the rain had stopped for a while, and I hadn't been out all day. As far as I can work it out I left the house about 7.35, walked down to the shops to get some pipe-cleaners, and met young Best on the way—quarter to eight that was. I had a bit of a chat with him, and got back here about twenty past, which means I was absent from this room for some forty-five minutes. After that I didn't stir till I went to bed—had my meal on a tray, and was still here when Philippa looked in about 11.00 to say good-night and tell me she was off 'on business'. As far as I know, she hasn't set foot in this place since. The next morning, when she was missing, something made me open the biscuit tin. It was empty except for a scrap of paper torn from my writing-pad, which said, 'I.O.U. £1000—Philippa. Don't be cross.' This is it."

"Her writing all right?" enquired Beale, examining it.

"Not a doubt—I'm sorry I didn't tell you earlier."

"Why didn't you?" he was asked, gently but pointedly, and the question made him shuffle a little.

"Because it hurt me almost more than anything," he said. "Maybe I'm a moral eccentric—I don't know: but it seems to me very near plain stealing to go snooping round looking for money that someone's said he'll lend you, and taking it without his knowledge or permission when there's nothing to stop you being open. Maybe you won't agree, but to me that's got a twist in it."

"Yes, I think I understand. Anyway, I'm glad you've told me now. Combined with Oakes's apparently genuine telegram, it certainly gives us some idea of what your niece may have had in mind when she set out."

"And mightn't it also put an entirely new construction on things?" asked Tony. "I don't want to hurt your feelings any more, Mr. Harrington, but you can go quite a long way on a thousand pounds."

The novelist regarded him with greater attention than hitherto.

"That hadn't occurred to me," he admitted. "But why the telegram? Just to throw dust in our eyes?"

"Or in Oakes's. Here, wait a second! Suppose the telegram was intended solely to get Oakes down here while she dashed up to town and tried to get the negatives back? With a wad of money to bribe the servant, perhaps. I say, this sounds good!"

"And how did she go?" queried Beale mildly.

"Pooh! That's easy. She got Dennison down here too, a bit earlier, and borrowed his car."

"Which he hasn't got" said Harrington. "He can't even drive. And anyway he came by train, if it was him: off the 11.25, so Bagshaw told me."

"Then he hired a car," continued Tony obstinately. "He got here earlier still, just after 11.00, when Philippa left you she went straight out to meet him, they drove back to the next station the train stops at before Belling, and he got in while she cleared off to town."

But the novelist was already shaking his head.

"It's ingenious," he conceded, "but I'm afraid it won't work. You see, the next station back is Craybourne, eight miles by rail, and—believe it or not—the train leaves there at 11.08. I'm certain Philippa wasn't out of here before the hour, which rather puts the lid on."

Tony had still a card to play, however.

"The train was three minutes late arriving here," he said: "the colonel told us. Yes, I know the idea's as full of snags as a newspaper is of misprints—what was Dennison to do with himself, and how would she get back, and banks don't open at night and give other people's rude photos away. All the same, tomorrow I shall go round asking questions."

"I may hold you to that," Beale warned him. "It would keep you quiet. Well Mr. Harrington, we don't seem to have got very far yet, but I don't think the outlook's any blacker, do you?"

"I don't know. I keep worrying about it all till my head buzzes. Oh, there's something else too, if you haven't already heard: something about Philippa knowing the girl in Craybourne—Alice Carter."

"Yes, Inspector Creevy told me—I was going to ask you about that. Is it possible, do you think?"

Harrington made a gesture of helplessness.

"Almost anything's possible with her," he said. "It sounds like her car, anyway, and she was here all right on September and, because we set off by road for Scotland that evening."

"Was that a long-standing arrangement?"

"Yes, a matter of weeks. I don't know if it would be any good asking Mary whether she remembers what Philippa did earlier in the day—perhaps. She's generally better informed about her comings and goings than I am."

"Did she know about the Oakes affair?" asked Beale sharply.

"No, I don't think so. You see, Mary isn't that way inclined at all, so you could probably tell for yourself. She certainly wouldn't approve of anything the least bit unsavoury, and might easily have given notice or something, which would have landed Philippa in a pretty sort of a mess."

"Why? I'm afraid I don't quite understand Mary Adams's position. Does she do nothing but look after your niece's welfare?"

"Good heavens no!" exclaimed Harrington, almost with a laugh. "Technically, I believe, she's a parlourmaid, or was when she came here two and a half years ago. Only, Philippa being Philippa, with one of those fancy educations behind her which include a year on the Continent hob-nobbing with millionaires' daughters and minor royalty and so on, it wasn't many weeks before Mary was being roped in to deal with her clothes and her general welfare, as you put it."

And then his tone changed abruptly.

"The trouble is, she's been thoroughly spoilt," he declared: "and it's my fault. The only woman I've ever cared tuppence about in my life was her mother—and unsuccessfully at that. However rich or famous I may live to be, I shall still count myself a failure because Julia turned me down. But she's dead now, a long time, and it's no good being sorry for myself. For her sake I tried to give Philippa a decent time, and it begins to be evident what a howling mess I've made of it."

He sighed, scowled, and then sighed again.

"Have a drink, won't you?" he asked. "Only about an hour late—forgive me."

They stayed for another ten minutes, during which Beale obtained undoubted samples of the missing girl's handwriting, both in pencil and ink, and learnt that she had never kept a diary. He also ascertained four things from Mary Adams: that she had never heard of Alice Carter until the day before, that she did not remember what Philippa Saunderson had done on the afternoon of September 2nd, that she had not been in her confidence with regard to Robert Oakes, and that the red sports-car's maximum speed, seldom reached, was rather under 60 m.p.h. on a good road.

"I knew she was friendly with Mr. Oakes this time last year," she said, "and I knew they weren't so friendly afterwards, but I'm afraid she never told me why."

"Have you ever seen him to speak to?"

"Once or twice when I've been out with Miss Philippa in the car. She used to run me over to my grandmother at Tilgate sometimes."

"Did you like him?"

Mary Adams hesitated.

"No," she replied. "It was little enough I saw of him, of course, but I'm sure I wouldn't want to know him better."

# XV

**B**EFORE RETURNING TO BAGSHAW'S for supper they ran into Craybourne, where they arranged for the picking-up of Oakes's car, and the analysis of the stains by Atkins. A call at the police-station obtained from Station-sergeant Turner the news that nothing further had happened. Creevy, he said, was now off duty.

"And that's where I feel I ought to be," murmured Beale outside. "You know, I can hardly believe it's still today: we seem to have done such a lot."

"If you say so," agreed Tony, with obtrusive politeness.

"Why, do you think I should have done more?"

"Lord, no! I mean that I'm not especially encouraged by results so far. You still don't know whose the body is, you know."

"Yes, I know I don't: but you think you do, so what does it matter? Unless you really believed your suggestion about Philippa's starting life afresh on the contents of her uncle's biscuit tin?"

"No, not really. Only he seemed so miserable, and I still think it was worth making."

"Not if you didn't believe it yourself."

"Rot."

"Except if you had some definite object in view, such as to find out how Harrington received the idea."

"But not because it *might* be true—oh dear no! I repeat, rot."

"Then you can't be as certain you're right about the carcase as you implied."

"Can't say—how right was that?"

"About eighty-nine degrees."

"Then the odd one fairly represents my belief in the theory of absconsion."

"All right, you win. Any theory which produces a word like that automatically justifies itself."

When they reached the Chief-constable's house they were told that he and Oakes were still out. During the subsequent discussion about whether hunger or courtesy should come first, John Best arrived, this time in uniform.

"You wanted to see me about a car, sir?" he said.

"Yes," agreed Beale: "I'm glad you've come. Did you notice a two-seater Daimler outside?"

"Yes sir—Mr. Oakes's, isn't it?"

"Oh, you've seen it before?"

"Yes sir, in the summer. It's rather noticeable."

"Well, don't let the owner's identity prejudice you. I'll get my friend to try the self-starter, and I want you to listen carefully. We'll go into a back room, and then we shall get the effect of distance, more or less."

The moment the whirr of the machinery became audible the young policeman's manner grew tense.

"It sounds very like," he said. "It was just that high-pitched sort of noise, only I can't be absolutely sure. I dare say there'd be a lot of cars'd do the same."

"Well, it's good enough for me, as it happens. Now look here, Best, how do you feel about meeting Oakes again? He'll be back here soon, and if you'd rather hop it before he turns up, I'll make it all right with the colonel."

Best smiled.

"I wouldn't mind meeting him," he asserted, "only I've got to be on duty pretty soon."

"Yes, of course. And one more thing, while we're alone. What did you do after Miss Saunderson drove away from the post-office? Or did she give you a lift back here?"

"No sir. You see, I do a bit of running, and I was supposed to be training that afternoon, so after she went I walked down to the beach and ran home."

"Ran home?" echoed Beale, puzzled: but Tony nodded.

"So you know that tip, do you?" he remarked. "I tried it once—nearly killed me."

"Ay, it takes it out of you all right," agreed Best.

"Now wait a bit," said Beale: "you two are leaving me behind. What nearly killed Mr. Purdon? I'd love to hear."

"Do your knees knock together as you walk?" enquired his friend. "Are you splay-footed or bow-legged? Do your ankles creak going upstairs? Have your arches no underneath? Yet in no more than ten years I can build you fine rippling muscles from toe-cap to tibia that will make you the envy of all your friends. Send twenty pounds for my free book, *How to Kick a Cannon Ball and Like it.*"

Beale shook his head dismally, and turned to the policeman for an explanation.

"He means running on shingle, sir," said Best, when he had stopped laughing. "The chap who told me about it swore that if I did a couple of miles a day regular for a month I'd feel I was walking on feathers. And there's something in it, too. When I come off duty nowadays I reckon I could do a ten-mile walk and not mind—much."

"Well, rather you than me. So you ran back to Belling?"

"Well, not *all* the way, but a good four miles of it."

"See anything?"

"No sir, nothing funny. It was dark by then, of course, but I had a torch. I can't say I was looking out for murders, though," he added.

Beale smiled.

"Well, next time you'd better: it would come in thundering useful. And where did you meet Mr. Harrington? He tells me he saw you that evening."

"In Belling, sir, near Mrs. Goodwin's. That's a tobacconist—I forgot you don't know the place."

"What time?"

Best stared a little, as if he thought he could guess at the reason for the question, but preferred not to.

"About quarter to eight," he replied. "Maybe a minute or two before."

"Thanks: and one more thing, very strictly between ourselves. Did Mr. Harrington give you the impression that he was purposely delaying you? Or do you get that impression now, looking back?"

"Why, no, I don't think so. No—he just went on talking much the same as he generally does."

"What did you ask him that for?" demanded Tony afterwards; but Beale refused to be illuminating.

"I thought it would make a nice question," was all he would say.

A few minutes after Best had gone Oakes returned, and assured them vehemently that the headless body was not Philippa's.

"She was slimmer about the hips when I knew her," he said, as if it were the most natural comment in the world. "And I'm pretty sure she was longer in the thigh, too. No, I'll bet anything that's not Phil, and I must say I'm damned glad."

Beale merely nodded.

"If only we knew where the head was, we could be quite sure about the identity," he observed quietly.

"Yes," agreed the actor, with one of his coldest stares. "I suppose you *are* looking for it?"

A little later Sergeant Tukes came round with the photographs which had been taken in the bungalow early that morning. One look at the first was enough for Tony, but Beale compelled himself to study all ten for some minutes before handing them to Bagshaw.

"And I'd like another of the left arm, showing the vaccination marks," he said. "Can you arrange for one? Thanks. I also want to ask the doctor a question—was he still down there?"

"No, but I'll give you his phone number."

As expected, Duncan was disappointing.

"I'm sorry, but I can't possibly tell you that," he said. "The garters weren't moved later than two or three hours after death, in my opinion, but I don't care to be more precise. Are you having Sir Douglas down? Good—I'll be handy if I'm wanted."

Subsequently Beale spent the best part of an hour in Colonel Bagshaw's study telephoning. From Scotland Yard he received the news that apparently Oakes's servant had done nothing suspicious. He had readily produced his bungalow key, and denied having been out of London for the last month. In particular, he had an unimpeachable alibi for the whole of Thursday evening.

"Right," said Beale: "but I haven't quite finished with the fellow. Tomorrow I want him questioned about a set of half a dozen photographs which I believe he may have taken some time last year."

He gave details, and then dictated Oakes's second story of his movements Thursday night: it was to be checked where possible. Next he rang up Sir Douglas Henderson, the Home-Office pathologist, and arranged for him to conduct a post-mortem on the headless body the next morning. Third on his list of calls was one to Colin Dennison, at his flat in St James's.

"I understand you're coming down here tomorrow," he observed. "Please make it as early as possible, by 11.00 if you can manage it, and please bring with you any correspondence you may have received from Miss Saunderson this week. Post-cards, letters, telegrams, cables—everything."

"Why not ask him for details outright?" queried Tony. "Presumably there'll only be the wire, as he was staying with the girl in Scotland till Tuesday."

"Oh, there's no need to rush things," said Beale: "especially as I've had just about all I can digest in the way of information for one day."

His final call was to the postmaster in Craybourne, from whom —in bed and grumpy—he obtained the names of two girls who might have been dealing with telegrams on Thursday afternoon. It was also arranged that before lunch next day he should receive confidential copies of all messages handed in there between 5.00 and 7.00 P.M. which bore the signature 'Philippa', or anything that could reasonably be termed a synonym.

"Bah!" exclaimed Tony. "How d'you know Dennison doesn't call her Twinkletocs or Bluebell?"

"If you don't stop being awkward" he was told, "you'll get a called lot worse than that. I wish I knew where Dickie was."

"Gone fishing, I dare say."

"Then he'll get wet, because it's blowing up for a storm. Oh—fishing!" as his friend continued to regard him significantly. "Yes, I wonder: does a severed head float or sink?"

# XVI

ALL THROUGH THE NIGHT the wind blew strongly, but dropped with the dawn. From their bedroom window the next morning Beale and Tony could see the sea stretching away towards the rim of the horizon, a shifting white-ridged restlessness beneath a sullen sky.

At nine o'clock Dickie Donovan telephoned.

"Hullo, is that you, Ted? How's the mystery going?"

"About the average: where are you?"

"Tilgate—other side of Craybourne. The air's better here."

"And that's all you've got to say?"

"At the moment, but I may be ringing you again later. Sure nothing's happened?"

"Very little that's publishable. And you'd better stop in Tilgate, because there's no room for you here. Your room's booked by a man called Oakes."

"Gosh! Oakes and Matthews bedfellows? It can't be true."

"It isn't. Matthews has gone back to London."

"Why?"

"Why not? If you must know, he felt home-sick."

An hour later there arrived a messenger-boy from the Craybourne post-master. He brought with him a sealed envelope containing three telegram forms, and a covering note which said that they were the originals handed in on Thursday at 5.49. All were in pencil, and as far as Beale could tell by comparing them with the specimens of her writing he had got from Harrington, all were written by Philippa. The first contained the message which he had already been shown by Oakes. The second and third were both addressed to Colin Dennison, one at his flat and the other at the Foreign Office.

*Urgent see you tonight by old Marietta catch 8.50 and will give you my answer do come Colin love Philippa.*

Dennison himself turned up in a chauffeur-driven car at quarter to eleven.

"Where's Oakes?" asked Beale quickly, as he caught sight of a slim figure in a smart black overcoat approaching the front door.

"Still in bed," was the answer: "said he'd take it easy for a bit, if it was all the same to everyone."

"Good: but I'll have Dennison in the study, I think, out of the way. And you'd better push off and ask your questions, Tony, if you don't mind."

The newcomer was young and of medium height, well but quietly dressed and intensely serious in manner. He looked as if he rarely smiled and never laughed, and he spoke in a clipped impersonal voice. After studying him unobtrusively for some moments, Beale decided that Philippa must have, or have had, a queer taste in men if she could turn so rapidly from Oakes to Dennison. Something in the latter's bearing gave him the impression that there was nervousness under its apparently businesslike coolness, and accordingly he opened fire abruptly.

"I'm glad you came," he said. "I think you owe us an explanation, Mr. Dennison, and so perhaps you'll start with that."

"I don't follow," retorted the other, continuing to sit upright. "First you must tell me what has happened to Miss Saunderson. Is she in Belling?"

"We can't say. She hasn't been seen since about 11.00 on Thursday night."

"You mean she's disappeared completely? It's absurd."

"But surely Mr. Harrington told you as much?"

"Of course, but I naturally thought she would have returned by now."

"Really? Does that mean you have some theory to account for her absence?"

Dennison's manner became even more distant.

"I hardly think we need discuss that," he said. "The point is, what steps are being taken to locate Miss Saunderson?"

"Quite adequate ones," Beale told him. "Now, when did you last see her, and where?"

"On Tuesday morning in Edinburgh: she saw me off on the 9.30 express."

This information was jotted down at once in a notebook, an action which caused the young man to frown.

"And when did she communicate with you next?" he was asked.

"Two days afterwards. I received a telegram from her on Thursday evening. I have it with me, if you care to see, and a similar one which was delivered at the Foreign Office: though she should have known better than to embarrass me like that, of course."

Beale glanced at the two forms, and saw as he expected that the wording of the message on each was identical with that delivered to him earlier from Craybourne.

"Thank you: and now I should like to know what steps you took as a result of the telegram: in detail, please."

Dennison pursed his thin bloodless lips.

"I assumed the message to be genuine" he said. "Accordingly I caught the 8.50 from town as requested, and reached the station here at about 11.30. From there I walked towards the old Martello Tower on the sea-front, a distance of roughly a mile and a quarter. It was raining hard, and I had omitted to bring my umbrella with me, so I hurried, in the hope that Miss Saunderson would be early. I was at the Tower by quarter to twelve, and I waited there for almost an hour and three-quarters. Just before half past one a policeman came up from the direction of Craybourne, and asked me what I was doing. I told him I had had an appointment with a friend who had failed to keep it."

"And then?" prompted Beale, as Dennison relapsed into silence.

"And then it occurred to me what a fool I must be looking," the clipped voice went on, more bitterly. "I realized that for some reason Philippa—Miss Saunderson—had played a stupid trick on me, and I determined then and there to have nothing further to do with her. I said good-night to the constable and walked away, as cross and uncomfortable as I think I have been for years. I had half a mind to call at her home and demand some explanation, but decided against it: I felt that nothing could excuse such conduct. Instead I walked across the footpath to the railway line, from there to the by-pass, and thence in the direction of London until I managed to stop a car and obtain a lift. I was put down in Sutton at five o'clock, and took a taxi home, arriving a few minutes before 6.00."

"I see—thank you. Should Miss Saunderson turn up again, what will your attitude be?"

"I can't imagine why you want to know, but if she offers me some satisfactory explanation of her failure to meet me on Thursday as arranged, I shall of course accept it. Otherwise I shall keep to my resolution to discontinue our friendship."

Beale nodded.

"Then obviously I've been misinformed about your feelings towards her, Mr. Dennison."

"I beg your pardon—what does that mean?"

"Well, I was told you were fond of her: yet at a time like this, when she may perhaps have met a violent death, all you can think of is your own self-esteem."

The young man reddened.

"What on earth are you talking about?" he demanded. "Met a violent death? Are you referring to the body found in a bungalow here? The one the newspapers are full of? How can that be Philippa's, pray? For heaven's sake say what you mean, man."

Beale complied, explaining that since the body in question was headless, it had not yet been possible to identify it.

"The coincidence of Miss Saunderson's disappearance during the period when death occurred," he went on, "has caused Mr. Harrington to put forward the theory that the body is hers."

"Oh, ridiculous! It's the sort of thing he would suggest. You don't believe such nonsense yourself, I can see."

"Because I used the word 'coincidence'? Don't be too sure. Quite frankly, Mr. Dennison, I'm in an awkward position. I simply don't know whose the body is: therefore I have to take into account the chance that it may be Miss Saunderson's. The description fits, as far as it goes."

"But the clothes!" objected the other. "If they're as reported, then they're certainly not hers."

"Why not?"

Dennison picked up the Sunday paper he had brought with him.

" 'The remains were clad in cheap green underwear,' " he read. "There you have your answer. Philippa never wore cheap clothes, and she never never wore green. Ask her uncle, ask her maid, ask anyone who knows her. Why, she was most upset once because without consulting her I purchased a jade necklace for her use."

"You're the third person who's mentioned her dislike for green," observed Beale. "Now, please be kind enough to answer one or two further questions. What information was it you expected to receive by the Martello Tower?"

Dennison again coloured.

"Does that matter?" he asked coldly.

"I should like to know."

"Oh, very well. While in Scotland with Miss Saunderson recently I approached the subject of matrimony."

"Thank you. Then presumably you expected to stay the night at *Cairngorm?*"

"Naturally: I brought my things with me in an attaché case. She would have taken me to the station in the morning to catch the 8.05 to town, which would enable me to be at the Foreign Office by 11.00. Normally I'm expected there before that, of course, but I was ready to run the risk of a reprimand."

'There's heroism under fire for you,' thought Beale tartly.

"And how did you know there was an 8.05 to town?" he asked mildly.

"Because I consulted a time-table before I set out," replied Dennison seriously. "Had there been no train, I should have wired back postponing her suggested meeting until the week-end. As it was, I felt I could fall in with Philippa's whim."

"Even to the extent of walking a mile and a bit in the rain. That's the part I don't quite understand, you know. Why didn't she meet you at Belling Station in her car? It would seem to be a more normal procedure."

"Good heavens, how should I know? Why didn't she keep the appointment at the Tower, if it comes to that?"

"I'm sorry—I must have expressed myself badly. What I mean is, why should she ever have chosen that particular rendezvous? Can you suggest a reason?"

"No, frankly I can't. I was wondering about it all the way down, and came to the conclusion that perhaps she had some personal incentive which would emerge later."

Beale examined the sentence mentally, and found it as vacuous as he had suspected.

"You took it to be a whim on her part?"

"Yes—it was not out of keeping with her character."

"You knew where the Tower was all right?"

"Of course. I've stayed at *Cairngorm* for week-ends, and I have relatives not far away. As a matter of fact, it was almost opposite the Tower that Philippa and I first met, as the result of a minor accident between her car and one belonging to my uncle, Sir Peter Dennison."

Beale nodded.

"And finally, what *is* your explanation of her disappearance? I'm sure you have one."

The young man hesitated before leaning forward, pallidly profound.

"I have," he agreed. "It is her misfortune to be a person of moods, never quite certain of her own mind. I think myself that when she sent me the telegram she fully intended to permit me to propose to her, and then for some reason reconsidered her decision later, between eleven o'clock and midnight—the times respectively of her leaving her home and the appointment at the Tower. By then, of course, it was too late for her to warn me against coming, and I have no doubt that rather than meet me as arranged, and explain frankly that she found she needed more time to prepare her answer, she chose to disappear."

Beale's face remained creditably grave.

"And has so far felt shy of returning?" he suggested.

"Exactly: though I think 'ashamed' would be the better word."

Dennison departed soon afterwards without encountering Oakes. He was going up to see Harrington, he said, and would probably not return to London before the evening. Just on lunch-time Tony came back in the Bentley, and admitted when asked that he had been unable to obtain the slightest confirmation of his former theory.

"But I've got a better one than that now" he asserted. "Wait till it hatches out a bit, and I'll tell you."

Oakes appeared for the meal, and during it chatted to everyone so cheerfully that Beale wondered what had caused his change of manner. The previous night they had parted on very distant terms.

"How're they getting on with the car?" he asked, almost gaily. "Got down to the chassis yet?"

"I don't know, but I'll run over and find out this afternoon."

"Good—I'd like to get back this week."

"Well, I dare say we can manage that, but how soon rather depends on you. To be quite plain, Mr. Oakes, I don't understand your attitude over the stains. There's no possible doubt that they were originally caused by blood, and I'm still waiting for some explanation of how they got there."

But even such direct speaking failed to curb the actor's high spirits.

"Explanation?" he echoed. "My dear good fellow, I'd like one just as much as you would. I give you my word I've only got yours for it that there ever were any stains. I certainly never noticed any, and please don't throw yesterday's red paint in my face, because that was only a gag. You annoyed me, and I thought I'd try to annoy you."

"I see," said Beale, untruthfully. He was not in the least convinced by Oakes's denial, and could think of no sensible reason why the actor should expect him to be.

'What's the fellow playing at?' he asked himself. 'He looks as if it was his birthday or something, but I'm sure he oughtn't to.'

He began the afternoon by asking the colonel if he felt like undertaking some detective-work.

"Who, me?" said Bagshaw, apparently aghast. "Real magnifying-glass stuff?"

"No, nothing so interesting, I'm afraid. What I want is as complete an account as possible of Miss Saunderson's movements from the time she arrived in Belling on Thursday afternoon to the time she left the house after saying good-night to Harrington. The people most likely to help are Harrington himself, Mary Adams, Best, whoever handed over the packet at her bank, and anyone with bright eyes who happened to see her outside the post-office, especially after Best had gone. I'll look after that end if you'll tackle this—will you?"

"I'll try," declared the Chief-constable. "At least I may begin to grasp what Creevy means when he talks blandly about instituting enquiries. I take it you want a detailed report all neatly typed out and signed by as many different people as possible?"

"Something like that," agreed Beale with a smile. "Place seen, time seen, by whom, clothes worn, gist of remarks made, actions performed, manner of doing same, and so on—you know the sort of thing. You needn't bother with what we've already been told about, of course, such as her talks with Best and Harrington. Concentrate on the others, especially the bank, and get the times as accurate as you can."

"Any helpmates allowed?"

"Of course—only pick somebody reliable."

"All my men are reliable," said the colonel with mock severity. "I'll take John, then. Or no, perhaps not—he'd probably rather run round with his girl than me."

"And while I remember, where can I get hold of him? There's a couple of things I want to ask before I get going myself."

"He lodges with Sergeant Tukes. I could take him, couldn't I? Then you can follow me round when I pick him up. In a hurry? Right—provided the beggars aren't still snoring. I always forget they have to make up for night-duty some time."

Tukes was not only awake but dressed, but Beale found Best preparing to shave by the sink in the cottage kitchen, the ginger kitten dancing excitedly about his feet.

"Sorry to interrupt," he said, "but do you remember what Miss Saunderson was wearing in Craybourne on Thursday?"

"Oh lor!" exclaimed the young policeman, frowning. "I'm not much of a one for noticing," he added in explanation. "Mary's always laughing at me because I don't know if her frock's new or a year old."

He pondered for some moments, brush in hand, and then nodded.

"I remember," he said. "She had a raincoat on, buttoned right up, and a brown hat she took off—we sat in her car and talked, out of the rain."

"Outside the post-office?"

"Yes sir—they don't mind things like that over there."

"Nor over here, surely?"

"Oh, you mean the van. But they weren't in anybody's way, stuck out there in that lane."

"No, I suppose not. Who arrived first on Thursday, you or Miss Saunderson?"

"I did, sir, five minutes early, and she was a couple of minutes or so late—nothing much."

"And when you'd finished your conversation, what happened? I mean, did you watch her drive off, or did you walk away and leave her still outside the post-office? What I really want to find out is whether she went inside or not."

Again Best thought.

"Not before quarter to six, sir, she couldn't have. And I left her in the car outside. She asked if I wanted a lift, but I said no I'd rather not. I never actually saw her move away, but she had her engine running again."

"Thanks. And now to go on a few hours, can you say at all accurately at what times during the night you were within sight or earshot of the bungalow?"

"Yes sir—I've been trying to work it out. I reckon I walked by it towards Craybourne about 11.15, and back past it just over half an hour later: say 11.50. For the best part of an hour after that I wasn't more than three or four hundred yards away, while I was messing about by the beach huts because I thought I'd heard someone there. Then I went to meet Sergeant Tukes, which was when I spotted that chap standing by the old Martello, and I wasn't anywhere near the bungalow again till twenty to three."

"That was after you'd heard the car?"

"Yes sir—it was that made me go so far down."

"So far?"

"Past the chalets. You see sir, they were burgled last month, and since then we've had to keep our eyes open. There wasn't much taken—a couple of watches, and a box of cigars, and drink and stuff—but the people made a fuss. They said they were paying rates, and why didn't we look after 'em?"

"Did Mr. Oakes lose anything?"

"No sir—at least, he never reported anything missing. There's a nice bit of takings there, too, and the sergeant reckons it was left alone because they couldn't get in."

He said this with the hint of a smile, and Beale appreciated the point.

"And what's your own opinion about the mystery?" he asked. "Is the body Miss Saunderson?"

"Well sir, I'm beginning to wonder since I heard that car last night. It's a bit awkward me saying anything after being mixed up with Mr. Oakes, but suppose it wasn't him—just someone with a bus that makes the same kind of noise."

He paused, furrowing his forehead.

"Go on," Beale urged him. "If you can clear up even a bit of the muddle, I shall be jolly grateful."

"Well sir, my idea is that there *was* someone on the beach when I thought I heard a noise. When I went down to look he slipped by me somehow, going back the Craybourne way, then up on to the road, and along past me very quietly to the Tower, where he'd arranged to be picked up by the bloke in the car. Only *he* was late, and I frightened the other chap away, and when the car turned up there wasn't anyone left to pick up."

"I see—I hadn't thought of that. Then the man you met by the Tower would presumably be the one we're after?"

"Yes sir, that's how it works out."

"Which is a pity, because at the moment it doesn't look as if he can be."

"Why, have you found out who he was?"

"Yes—thanks to a brilliant guess by Mr. Purdon. The name is Mr. Colin Dennison."

"Colin Dennison," repeated the constable. "Isn't that the chap—the gentleman—Miss Saunderson was in Scotland with?"

"Yes."

"Well I never! What on earth—Still, it doesn't matter, because it couldn't have been him."

"Why not?" asked Beale quietly.

"Oh well sir, I mean to say. Mary told me they were practically engaged."

# XVII

T HEY TOOK THE COAST ROAD to Craybourne past Oakes's bungalow, and as they went by Tony turned to his friend. "Odd how it still looks all right from outside," he remarked. "You'd never associate the place with headless corpses if you didn't know. And while I remember, what do you make of dear Robert?"

"I wish I knew."

"Well then, about things in general, if you prefer it. You're not being very communicative, you know."

"Because I haven't very much to communicate," said Beale. "At present I can see nothing but a lot of loose ends that won't tie up. You start at Mrs. Topley's, and that gives rise to the Ellis mystery. The scene then shifts to the bungalow, and that leads to Oakes and Dennison. Then you're told that Philippa Saunderson's disappeared, which also leads to Oakes. For the time being, naturally, we're getting on better with the Belling end than the Craybourne one. There are people we can ask about Philippa, but nobody we can ask about Alice Carter—yet.

"The thing I'm trying not to do is to let fancy browbeat common sense. After all, if it hadn't been for Harrington, who's a professional plot-concocter, there'd never have been any doubt about the identity of the carcase. Mrs. Topley saw it—rather more of it than anyone else, even though it was wrapped up—in front of the gas fire, the man Prince helped to carry it out of the house in the trunk and dump it in Deacon's van, Best and the colonel found it on Friday night in the bungalow. Or they found *a* carcase. You and Harrington say airily that it isn't Alice Carter any more, but Philippa Saunderson, but I think you might at least try to explain what happened to poor Alice. She couldn't have been Philippa all the time, because Philippa was alive at eleven o'clock that night and Alice wasn't. So what? Maybe there never was such a person? Maybe Mrs. Topley invented the whole story just to get her name in the papers?"

"Oh, rot!" said Tony. "You've only got to spend five minutes with the woman to see she isn't remotely capable of doing that. Of course there was an Alice Carter, and a corresponding body which was done up in the trunk and put on board the van: no one disputes that much. But to my mind there's so close a connection between Oakes and Philippa Saunderson that any body turning up in his bungalow, whatever its condition or raiment, ought surely to be hers: especially when she can't otherwise be accounted for. And there's all that business with the yellow bags and the feet, pointing the same way.

"At least, that's how I did feel about things, but as I said this morning, I've been hatching out a new idea. Would it bore you terribly to pull up for a few minutes and let me expound?"

Beale looked at his watch and frowned a little doubtfully.

"I'm not sure we ought to spare the time," he said. "Won't it keep till tonight? I was thinking we might rope the colonel in, and Dickie too—he'll probably be back because he'll have to find out what's happened here before he telephones his rag."

"Well, no, I'm afraid not. You see, Bagshaw mightn't approve of my idea."

"Really? That sounds more interesting. All right, only we mustn't be too long."

So Tony drew the Bentley to a standstill, on one side of them grassland, and on the other the grey-green sea beyond the dunes, lapping dismally at the shore.

"Well, who do you think I think it is?" he began tortuously.

"Now none of that! I'm not stopping here to be asked questions: I want to be given a rational solution—order out of chaos, and plenty of supporting evidence."

"Oh! Well, I'm not sure there'll be much of that to spare, but you shall have as big a ration as I can manage, Briefly, the name is Best—P.c. John Best."

"Good God!" said Beale, really shocked. "But I was talking to the man not ten minutes ago. My dear imbecile, why in the name of insanity pick on him? You must have used a very bent pin."

"Pin nothing: let me explain before you start snorting. This morning while you were badgering Dennison I roamed round asking very tactful questions. I couldn't get anywhere with the train idea, so I thought I'd try something else I thought of in bed last night. What I'm now going to tell you is the result, beginning with a short history of Best.

"He was born in Belling in 1912, and orphaned the year the War broke out. That is, he lost his mother: they never finally decided who his father was. He was adopted by a childless couple named Best, who kept a small greengrocer's shop, and he naturally got called after them. He grew up in the normal way till he was sixteen, except that he never got on particularly well with his adopted father, apparently a bit of a ruffian. In 1928 Mrs. Best died, and it was found that what little money she had of her own, about £200, was left to John and not to the husband. That didn't make things any better between them, and after another six months young Best cleared out. He said he was fed up with the old man's snarling, and was off to London to make his fortune. Quite how he got hold of the £200 in cash, at that age, I don't know, but he did, whereupon comes the usual gap of five years. During this Best senior also died, leaving nothing to anyone but a few bad debts and a hundredweight of seed potatoes the rats wouldn't eat. In 1932, that was.

"Switch to 1935; scene, Belling: re-enter John, now a good-looking young man with next to nothing of his £200 remaining and rather reticent about his immediate past. He owns to having tried his hand at a number of jobs, but without much luck, in view of which, will they please take him for a policeman? Well, they did, and everyone agrees he's settled down very well, especially since Mary Adams arrived from Tilgate to work at Harrington's. They were engaged within four months, which means that to date the engagement has lasted just over two years, and I don't want you to lose sight of that point. You are still awake, I hope?" he added politely, regarding Beale's closed eyes.

"Quite awake—carry on with this astounding melodrama. *The Copper and his Chopper*—one performance only."

"Well, as I say, the theory depends upon that as one of its main supports: the incredible length of the engagement, in view of Mary Adams's, undoubted charms as witnessed by ourselves. The other is the fact that whoever dumped the body in the bungalow seems to have had the use of a key. That would come from Philippa, of course: Best could easily spin her some yarn about looking round the place for her while she was in Scotland."

"That sounds reasonably possible," agreed Beale: "not that I believe it for one moment. But go back to prop number one—I don't get the hang of that at all."

"I was going to explain," Tony told him. "You saw Mary Adams yesterday evening. If you were in Best's position, would you talk twaddle about saving up till you had enough money? I wouldn't: I'd marry the girl quick, before some other blighter sidled in and cut me out. She struck me as being extraordinarily attractive, even though I only saw her for a few minutes."

"Certainly—I won't quarrel with that."

"Good, then I can get on. An engagement of that length seemed to me unnatural. I therefore tried to find a reason for it, and the only one I could think of was that Best couldn't marry the girl because he was married already. The name of his hypothetic hidden wife, of course, is Alice, she being Matthews's wedded shoplifter."

Beale opened one eye.

"Alternative title, *From Altar to Halter,*" he remarked. "It sounds exactly like one of Harrington's efforts to me. Is Best Ellis, by any chance?"

"I wouldn't think so—the height's all wrong. But he was Ellis for the purpose of the murder at 14 Weatherall Road. I needn't go into details about that, because you can guess for yourself what happened, but I'd better dwell lightly on the reason for Alice's being in Craybourne at all.

"Best spent his holiday in London for the purpose of getting in touch with his wife somehow. They'd obviously married while he was living there, and separated before he came back to Belling in 1935. Because of that smash-and-grab affair he got his name in the papers, and through that succeeded. I imagine this Alice as a nasty bit of stuff who guessed he wouldn't want her hanging round his neck for the rest of his life, and was out to see how much she could make him pay for his freedom. Best suggests a divorce, they squabble, he blurts put something about Mary Adams, and the final result is Alice in Craybourne, keeping her mouth shut just as long as he provides two or three pounds a week on which she can entertain her pal Ellis. He's really nothing to do with the story at all, of course."

"Really? Don't simplify it too much—you may find you've nothing left but vapour. But go on."

"Well, I won't drag it out. Best, disguised as Ellis, does all that business with the trunk—after he's seen Philippa in his own likeness, of course. We can then pass to about half past seven, when he's parking the van in Smuggler's Lane: the trunk and body he's already deposited in the bungalow, but so far there's been no bloodshed. He next goes home on foot, returns later that night on duty, and completes the operation with regard to Alice Carter by removing her head and hands. And then, to his discomfiture, in walks Philippa Saunderson."

"Hurray!" said Beale. "Using the same key he's just opened the door with himself. Or did she merely put her hand down the chimney and let herself in that way?"

"As a matter of fact, no: and it's useless your trying to trip me up like that, because it won't work. Best gave her the key back by the post-office that afternoon, but an evening or two beforehand took the precaution to put the catch up on the lock, so that he could come and go as he pleased. Well, any other objections? The rest is fairly plain, I think. Philippa has to die too, and that gives him the idea of switching the bodies."

"And Alice? What happened to her?"

"In the sea."

"With or without feet?"

"I don't know—probably he left them on."

"Kind of him. And the yellow oilskin bags?"

"Again I don't know, but obviously something to do with the original plan, before Philippa butted in and spoilt it. He then had to transfer them to her, and there weren't enough to go round."

"And the stains in Oakes's car? I suppose they were caused by the bagful of bits. Best just happened to be walking round looking for somewhere to put it when Oakes conveniently turned up."

"Oh—well: I haven't sorted that part out yet."

"I bet you haven't. And one final point: presumably Best was far-sighted enough—or second-sighted—to provide himself with a pocketful of gas from Mrs. Topley's, with which he later assisted Philippa hence? There's none at the bungalow, you know."

Tony laughed in spite of his desire not to.

"Trust you to leap on the feeble bits," he said. "No: I now confess. My whole theory depends on the fact that the CO didn't come from household gas in Philippa's case, but from a car-exhaust: i.e., the van. However, there's nothing like being prepared, so if the medical gent from London says it *was* household gas, I shall then become common-sensical, and agree that the bungalow body is Alice's. I don't really see that it matters much: everything else will still fit."

"Oh no it won't!" declared Beale firmly, sitting up and stretching. "Your whole fabrication relies on car-exhaust."

"But why? I don't see it."

"Then allow me to explain. You agree that Alice Carter died by inhaling coal-gas?"

"Yes—who said she didn't?"

"Nobody—yet: but I shall soon be ready to be button-holed by practically anyone and told that she really got in the way of a steam-roller. The position seems to me to be this. Alice Carter died at or about 7.00. If it isn't her body in the bungalow, then the doctor was wrong, which I doubt. If it is her body, then your theory's ruled right out, because Duncan said specifically yesterday that the beheading and so forth took place within two hours of death at the very most, and that would make Best a magician. No one else could be at Mrs. Topley's at 7.12, the time she went for the police, then get the trunk out and into the van, drive to the bungalow, get rid of his load, do the butchery, take the van back to Smuggler's Lane, and thence reach Belling on foot in time to meet Harrington at quarter to eight."

"Curse!" said Tony. "I'd forgotten all about Harrington. Yes, that dishes it—but I tried hard."

"Oh, undoubtedly: nobody questions your energy, only your results. I'm afraid you've gone for motive at the expense of everything else, which hardly seems wise till we can at least be sure whose body is which."

"All right, then suppose you give your views. Who do you back—Ellis?"

"He certainly seems the likeliest choice—for Alice Carter's murder, that is. Where exactly Philippa comes into it I can't say, but I expect I'll find out eventually. At the moment I'm chiefly interested in the car stains. I'm convinced they'll turn out to be human blood, and the question will then be, whose blood was it? If Atkins can show it didn't originate from the body we *have* found, then we'll know almost for sure that there's another body about that we haven't found."

"Why not make Oakes tell you? He must be able to."

Beale frowned.

"I'm not even satisfied about that," he said. "Both girls were fair, and the light couldn't have been very good. Imagine yourself in a similar position. You enter the bungalow, switch on the light, and see the carcase. As soon as you can move again you rush out to the Daimler, and on the seat you find a bag or basket which certainly wasn't there a few minutes earlier. You look inside, and this time see a human head—the head of a girl with fair hair. Do you examine it closely, to make sure it *is* Philippa's? Or do you gurgle and drop it back quick, and stop on the way back to bury it, taking the identity as proved?"

By now Tony was staring.

"But that means you believe the man!" he expostulated. "That there *was* a body in the studio when he put the light on."

Beale nodded thoughtfully.

"It seems he certainly couldn't have murdered Alice Carter, and I've yet to be convinced that Philippa's dead."

"I bet you she is."

"Maybe—but bets aren't evidence. As I keep saying, the whole affair's bedlam at the moment. All the same, if I were picking an outsider to put my money on I think I could do better than young Best. No, I certainly shan't mention any names: after all, guess-work comes in your department,"

# XVIII

THE NEXT HOUR WAS A BUSY ONE. First Beale called at the police-station, and asked Creevy to find out if any of the constables on duty in the town Thursday afternoon remembered seeing Philippa's car, either outside the post-office or elsewhere. Then, after learning that Atkins would not be ready to report before evening, he went round to interview the two girls whose names and addresses he had been given by the postmaster. The first was out, but it proved unimportant, since the second remembered dealing with the three telegrams. She seemed intelligent and observant, and he felt that he could probably rely on her evidence. The sender of the telegrams, she said, had been a fair-haired young woman dressed in a fawn mackintosh or raincoat. She had worn no hat, and was very wet.

"But that's no wonder," added his informant. "It simply pelted between 5.00 and 6.00, and all the people came in looking like drowned rats."

"Did she write the messages out in the office?"

"Oh no—I happened to see her walk in. She came straight up to the counter and waited her turn behind an old man of about ninety-something with no roof to his mouth. He kept her two or three minutes."

The time she estimated to have been just before ten minutes to six, and she assured him that there had been no occasion for the fair-haired girl to speak. She had paid for the telegrams with a ten-shilling note, and at once walked away after receiving the change.

"Was she what's called a lady?" asked Beale, and the post-office assistant laughed.

"I haven't the least idea," she told him—"awfully sorry."

"And had she gloves on?"

"No, I don't think so, but I wouldn't be sure. She may have had."

He thanked her, and returned to the police-station, where Creevy had news for him.

"You're lucky" he said. "P.c. Grey remembers seeing a small red sports-car outside the General at twenty to six. There were two people inside, a man and a girl, and he recognized the man as being stationed at Belling, though he didn't know his name."

Back at the colonel's house, they found Sir Douglas Henderson ready with his post-mortem report. The Home-Office pathologist was a keen-eyed man with an authoritative manner; he greeted Beale with a casual nod of recognition and a cloud of pungent cigar-smoke.

"Nice little job you've got here," he observed: "needn't have messed up my week-end, though—this Duncan chap seems to know his stuff. She's been dead now something under seventy-two hours. The cause was asphyxiation by carbon-monoxide, and the source household gas."

"Blast!" murmured Tony, but made no effort to answer Henderson's arched eyebrows.

"The severing of the head and the extremities of the limbs was done shortly after death," he went on: "I should say within an hour myself, and I happen to have some small experience of such things. The weapon used was a chopper of some kind, one with a straight edge."

"Dr. Duncan suggested a butcher's cleaver," said Beale.

"Yes, that would do very well" agreed Sir Douglas graciously. "Therefore the person who did it was a butcher. Really, you know, your job's much simpler than mine,"—and he laughed genially. "And a butcher who was fond of tennis," he added as an afterthought.

"But where *would* one get hold of a cleaver from?" asked Tony.

"If I were an ingenious man," said the pathologist, after an appreciative puff at his cigar, "I think I could contrive to steal one. Naturally I'd choose my shop with care, and have a fiver and a plausible yarn about a bet with a friend ready in case I were nabbed. Or I might make friends with a butcher purely in order to borrow a cleaver. Or I might apprentice myself to a blacksmith and learn to make one. Or hang round the Caledonian market till I saw what I wanted—you can get anything there. However,"—with a wave of the cigar, "as I'm not an ingenious man I should probably do the sane and obvious thing: go into a large ironmonger's and buy one."

"You certainly seem to know all about it," he was told.

"On the contrary: we prefer knives to choppers in my kind of butchery."

"And you're positive about the source of the CO?" queried Beale. "It couldn't in any circumstances have come from car-exhaust?"

Henderson shrugged, and became sarcastic.

"Possibly someone's invented a new kind of automobile that I haven't heard about" he said. "It uses hot air, perhaps, and discharges household gas in the face of pursuit. Not otherwise."

"I see—I beg your pardon."

"Oh, please don't—you always were a sceptical sort of fellow, what I remember of you. As a matter of fact, there isn't room for even a grain of doubt. In the normal way all the gas present in the lungs at the time of death would escape in about twenty-four hours, but in this particular instance that didn't happen because the head was tied up in a racket-cover. The effect was to collect the blood and so seal the trachea with a clot: a case of putting the cork in the bottle *before* the horse had flown. Consequently Duncan was able to obtain samples of the lung-contents: hydrogen formed a definite constituent, and that ruled car-exhaust right out."

Soon afterwards there was a telephone call from Scotland Yard. Where checking was possible, the second account of Oakes's movements had been borne out by independent witnesses. The Daimler had finally returned to the actor's lock-up garage, within a hundred yards of Brook Court, at 4.35 A.M. Friday, the caretaker having heard it arrive. The man responsible for the upkeep of the car stated that he had first noticed the stains on seat and floor late in the following afternoon. His description made it obvious that they must then have been in approximately the same condition as when viewed by Beale and Tony twenty-four hours later; but as he had used his eyes only, and not his nose, he could not answer for the presence of carbolic.

With regard to the six photographs of Philippa Saunderson as *Salome,* Oakes's servant reluctantly admitted having taken them, after repeated questioning. He said he had done so on the actor's orders, at the bungalow about a year previously, and he was sure that the girl had neither known of nor suspected their existence at the time. He denied possessing any idea of the present whereabouts of the negatives, and asserted that his employer had done the developing and enlarging and printing himself. In only one had

Oakes figured: three of the rest had portrayed the girl with a veil in her hands, and in the other two she was completely nude.

Finally, said the voice the other end, Detective-sergeant Matthews had unexpectedly been called away to Woking, but would telephone later that night.

"What on earth's he gone to Woking for?" demanded Beale.

"After the man Ellis, sir, I believe," was the startling reply.

To judge by results, Colonel Bagshaw was much more of a policeman than he pretended. With Tukes's help he obtained a considerable amount of information, which he rapidly typed out after tea. In the finished document he incorporated what Beale had learnt earlier in Craybourne.

*Known movements of Philippa Frances Saunderson between approx. 3.00 P.M. and 11.00 P.M. on Thursday, October 20th.*

| Times | Movements etc. | Clothes | Witnesses |
|---|---|---|---|
| 3.00 ——— 3.20 | Arrives in Belling by car. Calls on bank manager in South St, gets from him sealed packet addressed to her and deposited by P.c. Best on September 25th. Ace. by Mary Adams, who sat outside in car. P.S. seemed normal, perhaps somewhat worried. | Fawn raincoat, grey tweed coat and skirt, brown shoes, driving-gloves, hat-less. | Manager. (W.J. Kerr Esq.) Mary Adams. |
| 3.25 | Arrives at *Cairngorm.* | Ditto | Mary Adams and Charles Harrington. |
| 3.25 ——— 4.40 | At *Cairngorm.* | ——— | Ditto |
| 4.45 | Leaves alone in car, not mentioning destination. | Raincoat, different costume, dark brown, fawn jumper, same shoes and gloves, brown felt hat. | Mary Adams. |

| 5.02 | Arrives outside G.P.O. Craybourne in car. | Ditto | P.c. Best. |
|---|---|---|---|
| 5.02 | In car talking to Best. | Ditto | P.c. Best for both. P.c. Grey saw car with man & girl in at 5.40: recognized man as Belling P.c. |
| 5.45 approx. | Starts engine outside G.P.O. Best leaves her. | Ditto | P.c. Best. |
| 6.00 | Calls at Dibdin's garage, Belling for petrol, oil. Manner absent-minded. | Ditto | Samuel Walker, garage hand. Is sure of time as he was about to go off duty, and so was watching clock. |
| 6.08 approx. | Arrived at *Cairngorm,* put car away in garage. | Ditto | Mary Adams. |
| 6.08 —— 11.00 | Stayed indoors, dined alone at 7.30. Movements unchecked between 7.30 and 11.00, but spent much of this period in her sitting-room leading off bedroom. Could not have had visitors without Mary Adams's knowledge. Manner preoccupied. | Changed into dark frock, etc., and different shoes. | Mary Adams. |
| 11.00 approx. | Puts her head round study door to say good-night to Harrington and that she was going out 'on business'. | Brown hat and raincoat. | Harrington. |

*Remarks:* Subsequent to Philippa Saunderson's departure Mary Adams went into the bedroom and found there the dark frock and indoor shoes. The dark-brown costume, fawn jumper, and heavy brown shoes were missing from wardrobe where Mary had put them away earlier (but this was not discovered till Friday after breakfast, in answer to Harrington's query). Pigskin handbag, umbrella, and brown felt hat also missing. Contents of bag (probably) make-up materials, bunch of keys, driving-licence, fountain-pen, small change, £2-£3 in notes. The other garments she was wearing do not include anything remotely resembling those found on the headless body in the bungalow. She is not believed to have used the telephone between 6.08 and 11.00. There are two at *Cairngorm,* one in the study and one in the hall. The exchange has no record of any outgoing calls since 3.00 P.M., and the servants are all positive there were none after midday. Both bells are audible in their quarters.

"Thank you," said Beale, when he had finished reading. He made no comment aloud on Harrington's apparent omission to mention the £1000 which had disappeared from the biscuit tin. It was understandable that while there was still hope of the girl's being alive, the novelist might hesitate to bring what he considered a shady action on her part to the notice of someone who knew her personally.

# XIX

**B**Y THE WAY, COLONEL, where's Oakes?" asked Beale presently. "He doesn't seem to be giving much trouble."

"Don't understand the chap," was the puzzled answer. "You saw how he was at lunch, all bright and perky as if he'd just laid an egg. Well, he must have taken a dose of tonic or something, and the effect didn't last, because when I got back from my wanderings he was sitting hunched up in a chair in the lounge as if he had about two minutes to live. I asked if he felt all right, and he snapped my head off, so I left him to it."

"Did he say anything more about wanting to go?"

"Oddly enough, no. What's his game, d'you think?"

"I'm not sure yet, but I fancy that for some reason he's watching his step."

"Oh well, I don't suppose he'll have to wait much longer. Atkins'll let us know the minute he's got any news, and then we may have a handle to pull. Ah, maybe that's him now,"—as they heard the ringing of the frontdoor bell. "I expect he'll come himself."

They heard a maid cross the hall, the mumble of voices, then the maid's returning footsteps, and a moment later the heavier ones of a man. Then followed a pause, surprisingly succeeded by a shout and a scuffle. When they opened the study door they beheld Robert Oakes held firmly in the grip of John Best.

"What the devil's all this about?" demanded the Chief-constable.

"I don't quite know, sir," answered the younger man, still in plain clothes. "I was coming through the hall when this—this gentleman saw me from in there,"—nodding towards the lounge. "He suddenly yelled, and came charging out."

"Take your hands off me, curse you!" shouted Oakes, his face pale and perspiring. "Stand up and fight, you—!"

"Not on a Sunday," said Bagshaw with severity, and turned a questioning gaze on Beale.

"All right, let him go," said the latter at once to Best. "And hit the end of his nose good and hard if he starts scrapping."

The actor moved back a pace or two when he was free, straightening his clothes and feeling one arm as if it pained him. He carefully avoided looking at any of them, and from his expression it seemed possible that he regretted his recent violence without quite being able to regain his lost temper. Tony, regarding his drawn features and unhealthy pallor, could scarcely believe it was still the same man, so great was the change in the last few hours.

There was a silence of perhaps ten seconds, and then the actor spoke.

"I'd like a drink, please," he said shortly. "A good strong one— whisky. And couldn't we go somewhere less draughty?"

As they moved towards the open door of the study Beale was frowning. Oakes looked now exactly as if he had just been through a spell of acute anxiety: yet how was that possible, unless its cause were to be found within the man himself? And how likely was it that he would ever suffer from his conscience, whatever he had done?

"Either he's remembered something he doesn't like and worried his nerves to bits brooding about it' he thought, 'or he's been acting superbly up till now, and this is Oakes with his make-up off.'

He began by asking for an explanation of the attack in the hall, but the only answer he received was a scowl and an invitation to mind his own business. At this he smiled with his lips, but his grey eyes were unwavering in their stare.

"At the moment I consider you my business," he said. "If you won't tell me, I dare say Best will."

He turned to the constable with another smile, more friendly.

"You told us an interesting story yesterday morning: would you mind repeating it? Miss Saunderson asked you to approach Mr. Oakes about some compromising letters she'd written, and an indiscreet portrait she'd allowed him to paint of her. He was willing to sell them back, but the price was too high, and she hoped you might be able to do something. Go on from there."

But before his request could be obeyed the actor made a visible effort to pull himself together.

"What's the sense in that?" he muttered. "And what's any of it got to do with you? Your job's to find out who cut off some Craybourne wench's head."

"I know" said Beale quietly. "But I happen to think there may be some connection, you see. Go on, Best."

The constable did so, but no one looked at him. All eyes were upon the actor, lounging back in an arm-chair glaring at his empty glass. Presently, without asking permission, he refilled it from the decanter on the table nearby, but made no comment on Best's story until the description of the struggle in his flat.

"You're a liar," he remarked then, venomously. "You didn't knock me down—I caught my foot in a rug."

"And that's the only contradiction you have to make?" queried Beale a few moments later. "You weren't pushed, you simply fell. You don't deny anything else?"

"Why should I? Say what you like, all of you. There isn't a thing you can bring against me, and you know it. Blackmail? Bah! Story-book stuff."

He drained his glass, put it down, leant forward, and openly sneered.

" 'The great detective looked baffled!' " he said. "My God, you make me laugh. Why can't you be frank, man? First you pinch my car, and now you bleat about blackmail. I repeat, what damned business is it of yours what sort of photographs I take? Just you let me catch you giving your tongue a day off outside this room, that's all—any of you. Slander's another good word."

He paused to light the cigarette he had taken out of his thin gold case, and when he spoke again his voice was a shade higher. It seemed to all of them that he was every minute losing a little of his self-control, and their natural suspicions were put into words by Bagshaw.

"I believe my whisky must be better than I thought," he murmured.

"Ha! Now I'm drunk, am I? On three spoonfuls of that muck! Murder, blackmail, drink—you get feebler. Next you'll be telling me off because I missed Sunday-school this afternoon. But I meant what I said just now, mark you. One squeak and you'll all be selling your best pants to pay my damages. If you think I killed somebody, arrest me. If you aren't quite such howling idiots as that, then try your second string. Only let me give you a word of advice,"—and his face became suddenly tense, the eyes screwed up and the lips curled back. "Mind you've got a witness, you precious bunch of smarties."

It was then that the telephone rang. Beale took the call, made one involuntary exclamation, and listened for some five minutes.

"We'll be over right away," he said, replaced the receiver, and stood staring at it. Then he turned to Oakes once more, and his expression was inappropriately one of faint amusement.

"That was from Tilgate," he observed. "They've just found the second body—if you're interested."

The actor was on his feet in a second.

"What's that?" he cried. "What?"

"The second body: and unfortunately in the same state of incompletion as the first. I do wish you'd tell me what made those stains in your car, you know."

But afterwards he was to regret that he had said anything. Oakes turned very white, shut his eyes, and Tony was only just in time to catch him as he fell.

Dr. Duncan was sent for, and arrived within ten minutes. While they were waiting Beale repeated the information he had just received.

"Yes, another body," he said. "Just about the same as the last, too: a girl with no head or hands or feet, and no clothes on this time, and nothing to show how she died."

"Hell!" interrupted Bagshaw. "I shan't like telling Charles. One of 'em must be Philippa, mustn't it?"

"I'm afraid so—not much doubt about that. Perhaps you'd better wait till the doctor's had a look at it, though, just in case. Incidentally, the discovery was due to Donovan. Apparently he's been in touch with a friend in Brighton who runs an aeroplane, and they spent the afternoon skimming the waves after finding out the likeliest place to look."

"Huh! That shows us up a bit, doesn't it? Anything about the trunk?"

"No, he didn't mention it."

Best, who had been listening intently, shyly turned to Tony and asked what trunk the colonel referred to. His superior overheard, and explained.

"Oh, and what did you come round here for anyway?" he queried.

"Oh yes sir, I was forgetting. It was something I wanted your opinion about."

"In private?"

"Well, no, sir—it doesn't really matter. You remember that cheque for £200 that Miss Philippa gave me in Craybourne on Thursday?"

"The one you returned to Mr. Harrington yesterday?"

"Yes sir. Well, he came round this afternoon after you'd gone, and said he'd like to pay me the money just in case she didn't come—wasn't able to, and I thought I'd better ask you first, sir. Ought I to take it?"

"Search me," grunted Bagshaw. "I don't see why not. What do you say, Inspector?"

Beale smiled, and shrugged.

"I think I would, in your place," he told Best. "You certainly seem to have earnt it, even if Mr. Oakes did trip over a rug!"

The Chief-constable remained at Belling, in case of developments or important telephone calls, but Duncan accompanied Beale and Tony after first making arrangements for the actor to be conveyed to hospital.

"I'm not absolutely certain what's wrong with the chap," he said, "but I've a pretty good idea. He was bright and cheerful at lunch, and has since then grown progressively more sullen and nervy? Yes, it seems to fit. In my opinion, Inspector, he's been in the habit of taking drugs of some kind, possibly morphine, and he didn't bring enough down to see him through the week-end."

"But the minute he began to realize that," objected Tony, "wouldn't he start insisting that we let him go back to town?"

The doctor looked thoughtful.

"One would have expected him to," he agreed. "I can only suppose he had some reason for not wanting to give the impression of running away. Would that make sense?"

"It might," said Beale. "Perhaps I'll be able to let you know later."

They reached Tilgate by eight o'clock; Duncan took charge of the body, now at the local mortuary, and promised that he would have as much information as possible ready for them in an hour. In the charge-room, talking to an inspector and two sergeants, they found Dickie Donovan.

"Hullo! For once I got somewhere first," was his greeting. "Is my nosiness approved of?"

"Definitely," Beale assured him. "I'll stand you the best dinner the town can produce."

"Good—I'm about ready for a bite. But first there's a little something next door that might interest you."

"The trunk!" exclaimed Tony quickly.

"The trunk, no less," agreed the reporter. "Do I qualify for a bonus?"

"You shall eat till you bust," he was told. "Or drink, if you'd rather. Let's see the thing."

It was large and brown, and very wet. Part of one side was split at the bottom, but not badly, and the lid was still locked.

"We didn't open it, sir," said the Inspector in charge—"thought you might like first go. We looked for prints, though, but there weren't any outside. The locks are the only place that would take them, and they're both clear."

"Can you open it?" asked Beale.

"I dare say—we can have a try. Perkins, got that crow-bar handy?"

"Think there'll be any heads inside?" enquired one of the sergeants; and Tony, who had been well to the front, retreated instantly.

"I doubt it," answered Beale, and he was right. The contents, all sodden and in many places gritty with sand, consisted entirely of Alice Carter's clothes and personal possessions, as listed by Creevy. The two suitcases were there, and the shattered remains of the china statuette, but what took Beale's eye immediately were the shabby blue slippers and the long pink dressing-gown.

"That's interesting" he remarked, surveying the latter. "Pity the thing's so wretchedly wet—I'd very much like to know if there's any blood on it."

He transferred his attention to the handbags, but both were empty. Nowhere was there any sign of such articles as keys, coins, letters, private papers; nor any rubber tubing, as he had been half hoping there might be.

"A wash-out, lit. and met., I fear," murmured Tony. "Unless the dressing-gown and slippers mean anything?"

But no one attempted to reply.

Over dinner in Tilgate's best grill-room Dickie explained his plan of campaign. He had first consulted everyone in Craybourne at all likely to know about tides and currents, and then moved on to do the same along the coast. That had taken him the rest of the previous day; but the wind during the night had upset all his calculations, and he had had to spend that morning readjusting them. His friend with the aeroplane had been willing to take part in a rough and ready search, and at low tide, with dusk only a few minutes away, he had caught sight of the body wedged among some rocks.

"But the trunk was none of my doing, actually," he admitted, having safely started his third pint of beer. "The honour of finding it belongs to a retired sea-captain named Bruce who spends all day goggling through a telescope about three miles farther along the coast. How long will it be before you start back? I've got heaven knows how much telephoning to do, and I dare say you've been saving some news up, too."

He listened attentively to Beale's admirably concise account of what had happened in the last thirty hours, and then they drove to the mortuary. If the trunk had proved something of a disappointment, however, Dr. Duncan's firmly apologetic ignorance was a still severer blow to their hopes.

"I can tell you scarcely anything," he said. "She wasn't drowned—that's reliable. She hasn't been dead more than three days, and she was probably naked when she entered the water. And that's about all."

Beale sighed.

"You're making it very difficult," he grumbled. "You say she wasn't drowned: does that mean she might have died in the same way as the other?"

"Oh no," said Duncan quickly. "I'm awfully sorry—I ought to have made that clear. Naturally there hasn't been time for a thorough examination, but you can rule out carbon-monoxide poisoning all right: the signs are conspicuously absent."

Tony just refrained from scowling.

"And what would the signs be?" he enquired.

"The colour and condition of the blood. The effect of CO is to turn it pink, and it remains pink even when greatly diluted, whereas ordinary blood tends to turn yellow."

"Really?" said Beale. "I didn't know that, and I've been a policeman eighteen years. The blood isn't pink, and therefore the corpse didn't die of CO poisoning?"

"Exactly. I admit it sounds rather a negative proof, but that's only to be expected, really, since it seeks to establish an absence and not a presence."

"So when anyone says 'Strike me pink!' " remarked Tony, "what he really means is 'Put me in a gas-oven'. And would it be altogether too much to ask *why* CO turns blood pink?"

Duncan hesitated, smiling.

"Why does a candle go out if you blow it?" he countered. "It's cause and effect."

"Oh, I've heard of them; but what I'd dearly like to be told one day is *why*. All you're saying is that it happens, which I don't question. But you scientific coves are all the same. You stand a couple of candles on a table, and light one, and invite me to puff at it. When the flame disappears you tell me wisely it's because I puffed, and expect me to be satisfied: but I'm not. I still want to know why it didn't just crackle instead, or turn pink, to be topical, or reappear on the other candle. Your answer is that blowing doesn't do that. Patiently I ask why. You say that blowing doesn't do that. Then or later I begin to scream, and immediately get certified for being unscientific—i.e., irrational. It's a queer world: and why? Because it is—a totally valid answer, I fancy, since it explains nothing."

"For pity's sake stop talking," said Beale. He turned to Duncan, who was half smiling and half frowning.

"The head was removed before the body entered the water," he remarked: "even I can guess that. But how long before? Oh dear, not even a wild estimate?"

"Within a day, probably," declared the doctor gravely. "No, I'm sorry, but I can't help you there."

"But it doesn't matter, does it?" asked Tony. "In view of the non-pinkness of the blood, I mean. You're right and I'm wrong: it wasn't little boy blue."

"Really, I wasn't bothering about that" Beale told him acidly. "What about the instrument used to cut off the head, Doctor?"

"Exactly the same as before, by the look of things. As a matter of fact, practically everything I said about the first body holds good for this one: age, size, shape, physical condition, colouring. It's rather queer, really."

"You mean, they'd have been a good match in life?"

"What's survived for inspection would. I dare say there'd be observable differences if you were to lay them side by side, but seeing them separately like this, the resemblance is rather striking."

## XX

ND NOW WE'VE ONLY GOT TO LOOK FOR TWO HEADS, four hands, four feet, two motives, and one murderer," said Dickie cheerfully on the way back. "Or am I wrong? Have I left something out?"

"Well, what about Philippa Saunderson's clothes?" Beale reminded him.

"Oh lord, I'd forgotten them completely—how the devil do you remember all these things? Why weren't they in the trunk, I wonder?"

It was Dr. Duncan who suggested an answer.

"Perhaps the murderer didn't want the two deaths to be connected," he said.

"And yet he treated both bodies in the same way."

"Yes, that's true: then why didn't he complete the similarity of treatment by leaving them both in the bungalow?"

"Yes, why not?" echoed Dickie. "It's a point that's been worrying me."

Beale thought for a moment, and then turned to him with a question.

"What difference did last night's wind make, according to your tidal experts?" he asked.

"Ah, that's better. One of them was positive that normally the body would never have drifted so far in-shore so soon, and mightn't have turned up for another week or ten days; and he was a lifeboatman for twenty-eight years, so he ought to know what he's talking about. Obviously the murderer forgot to take possible storms into account."

"And yet you *would* have connected the two bodies," observed Dr. Duncan, siding against his original suggestion. "Wherever or whenever the second one appeared, the fact that it hadn't any hands or feet or a head would have been enough to relate it to the body in the bungalow."

"Then perhaps it was time that mattered," said Beale. "Given a week or ten days, he didn't mind: but I'm hanged if I can see why that should be. Tell me something: does a severed head float?"

The doctor shrugged doubtfully!

"I shouldn't expect it to, but I haven't really any experience to go by. Not for some considerable period, anyway—not till the features were quite unrecognizable. But that wouldn't matter in the case of the first body," he added. "CO turns the brain-substance bright pink as well as the blood, so that the question of which carcase it belonged to would merely be a case of thorough examination."

"By the way, Harrington called while you were gone," said Bagshaw after he had heard what Beale had to tell him. "I've been so busy listening I forgot to mention it. He left a letter for you—here it is."

"A letter? Thanks. Did he say anything about Dennison?"

"Only that he's going to stay over tonight in case there's any news. I didn't mention this second body, but I shall have to go up and tell them presently, confound it.

"I'll do it if you'd rather," Beale volunteered.

"Really? That's decent of you. But you'd better read the letter—sorry. He wrote it here, as a matter of fact, when he knew you weren't available."

*Dear Inspector Beale,* it began, *Forgive me for bothering you, but I've just had what strikes me as a possibly brilliant idea, and I feel I must tell you of it. Assume what was found in the bungalow to be Philippa in fact but Alice Carter in intention: that is, you are meant to think it A.C. by the clothing and manner of death. Remember the evidence of the woman in Craybourne, and assume also some at present unknown connection between Philippa and Alice. If your patience lasts, assume further—or invent—some extremely urgent reason why A.C. should wish to be presumed dead. Yes, it sounds drivel, but I can't help that. I'm merely trying to build a tentative framework for a trick: namely, the apparent disappearance of the body from 14 Weatherall Road. I suggest that in sober truth it had never drawn breath: that what the landlady saw consisted not of flesh and blood but a draper's dummy. All the time Mrs. Topley was in the house, Ellis hid under the bed out of her sight. The moment she went for the police he whisked the props into the trunk you told me of, and was gone like the wind. The real A.C. was of course a party to the deception, and furnished the necessary dressing-gown and underclothing. How poor Phil came to figure as a second dummy (flesh and blood this time) I can't say, and by now you're probably annoyed with the whole idea. Whether or not, will you please satisfy yourself—and so me—that the object in front of the gas-fire could not have come from displaying clothes in some shop window? Yours sincerely, C. Harrington.*

Beale's main feeling was one of impatience more than annoyance. Nevertheless, while the others were reading the letter he telephoned Creevy.

"It's been suggested that what Mrs. Topley saw wasn't Alice Carter but a draper's dummy," he said. "Will the idea bear a moment's scrutiny?"

"No sir," came the prompt reply; "and the reason is that I thought of it myself, and made a point of asking the old woman. As a matter of fact, I went even further than that, though I haven't told anyone because I didn't want to be thought all kinds of a fool. I got my sister to wrap up in a blanket this morning and lie down, and made Mrs. Topley arrange her, and after that the draper's-dummy business was right out of court. At least, I never saw one that bent double at the waist, and had its legs at an angle of about thirty degrees to one another."

"Good," said Beale—"many thanks. I never saw one like that either, and anyway, there's a stronger argument still against it."

"Yes?" queried Creevy with interest.

"A psychological one. What trickster could resist the temptation to make it look even more like a human body by showing more than the legs? There'd have been part of an arm protruding, and perhaps a tress of flaxen hair: but legs were all that Mrs. Topley actually saw."

He waited a moment longer to give Duncan's preliminary report on the Tilgate body, and then rang off. When he returned to the study the others were arguing warmly.

"We're debating the precise difference between fancy and imagination," Tony told him. "The colonel says that letter's the first, I say the second: Dickie says it's unimportant, because the thing's meaningless. Who gets the bun?"

Beale shook his head.

"I could imagine circumstances where you'd all be wrong," was his only answer.

As he had promised, he went up to *Cairngorm* later to break the news. Harrington took it badly, but Dennison seemed merely to purse his thin lips and glare more coldly. Then after a short silence he spoke.

"It's damnable," he said. "Someone shall pay for this."

"I knew it!" muttered the novelist miserably. "I knew it all along. What in the world did she want to go playing about with a swine like that for?"

"Swine? What swine?" demanded Dennison quickly.

"Oh, nothing," said Harrington wearily. "Don't take any notice of me."

"But I insist on knowing," objected the other, his face now tense. "You mean she's been doing something behind my back?"

The older man looked at him, at first vaguely and then with sudden animation in his brown eyes.

"Behind your back?" he said, and repeated the words more loudly. "Who the hell d'you think cares a cuss about your back? She's dead—don't you understand? She's dead, and all you care about is your back, you sawdust dummy!"

He would obviously have said more, but Beale intervened.

"Just a moment, please. Mr. Harrington, have you any snapshots of your niece available?"

The novelist sighed, and smiled wanly.

"Thanks—I believe I almost lost my temper then. Yes, I can let you have some. Here,"—feeling in his pocket: "I was looking at these today—will they do?"

He held out a cardboard folder with a dozen prints inside, and Beale saw that they were exactly what he wanted. They gave the girl in several different poses, both with and without a hat, and he studied one for a moment. It was strange, he thought, that not until she was certain to be dead should he know what she had looked like in life: attractively pretty, though with a hint of over-sophistication in her smile and stance.

"These will do excellently," he said. "And two other things before I go, the first being your letter."

"Oh, that: not worth troubling about now. There were snags in the idea, anyway—the disposal of the dummy, for instance, and the manner of—the way she died. I'm sorry if I've been a nuisance," he added.

"Not a bit: I understand." Harrington glanced at him keenly.

"Yes, I believe you do. Rather than face Philippa's death before I had to I'd have leant on any theory, however wild. It hits me hard, very hard."

As he spoke his eyes turned for a moment to Dennison, standing motionless by the window with his back to them.

"But you mentioned two things. What's the other?"

"This," said Beale quietly, lowering his voice. "I don't like asking, but it's a stock question I have to put, I'm afraid. Does anyone gain financially by Miss Saunderson's death? If so, who, and by how much?"

"Nobody—nothing" was the answer. "At least, nothing positive, that is. I shall spend about four hundred a year less, if that counts?"

"Of course not—thank you. By the way, are these in her handwriting?"—and he took out the three telegram forms.

"Undoubtedly, I should say," was the novelist's verdict, after close examination.

At 11.25 that night Matthews telephoned as promised, and wasted no time in coming to the point.

"I've got him, sir," he said, "and a hell of a long statement."

"Ellis? Where? When? How?"

"It'd take an hour. I ran into a pal of his, who said he'd seen him Friday evening in a pub, and after that it was just hide and seek. And you aren't going to like the next bit of news, sir."

"Oh lord!" exclaimed Beale. "Is he dead too? You killed him yourself after a long silent struggle on the edge of a cliff?"

Matthews chuckled.

"No cliffs in Woking, sir," he said. "And corpses don't make statements. Not to me, anyway—maybe I ain't psychic enough. But you won't like the news, just the same: he's gone and rubbed his fingertips smooth with pumice powder, and he's no earthly use for prints."

"Drat the fellow!"

"Yes sir, that's what I said—something like."

"Why did he do it?"

"That comes in his statement, which reads about as smooth as his fingers. Everything nicely explained, times and places for an alibi and all the rest of it."

"An alibi where?"

"Tilgate, sir: at the greyhound track there. Oh, I forgot: Ellis is Drake, and Alice Carter's Alice West. I checked that definitely from the prints—hers and the ones on the glass. It wasn't her who touched the bed-post last, though, and there was nothing funny about her feet."

"When did she come out of gaol?"

"August 9th."

"What, no remission of sentence?"

"She didn't have the chance, sir. Being under twenty-five she came in the Young Prisoners' Class, and they don't get any remission unless the Committee recommends it, and hers didn't."

"I see. Is anything known about what she did after she came out?"

"Only that she turned the D.P.A.S.[1] down flat."

"And what about her alleged husband—is he in the story?"

"Well sir, I haven't been able to find out much about him, not even his name, but according to Ellis he did the murder."

"Did he now!" said Beale. "That news won't please Mr. Purdon—he thinks young Best's our man, or did. Harrington picks Oakes, and Dennison hasn't been above suspicion."

"And who's your own fancy, sir?" asked the detective-sergeant innocently.

"Oh, I haven't got a proper one yet—I'm still too busy finding out what's been done. You'd better bring Ellis down tomorrow, plus statement. As you say it's a long one I won't make you read it now, only mind it's still long in the morning. Telephone when you know what time you'll get here, and I'll be available."

To finish the day came the report on the Daimler, provided as the colonel had prophesied by Atkins himself. He was a tall long-nosed man with an energetic air of competence, and he carried a bulky envelope.

"It's all in there," he said, tapping it: "and extraordinarily interesting, too—I haven't enjoyed myself so much for ages. The stains originated from human blood all right, and it came from the body in the bungalow—there were very definite traces of CO. All the same, some bright person did his level best to twist our tails."

"Really? How?"

The analyst smiled happily.

"I can tell you that almost as certainly as if I watched him at it," he declared, "and I repeat, it was clever. He found himself faced with human bloodstains to get rid of, and he said to himself, 'Now

---

[1] Discharged Prisoners' Aid Society.

my boy, what am I going to do about this here? Mustn't let it stay human, oh dear me no! That might be awkward—that might put ideas into people's heads.'

"So he claps on his emergency thinking-cap, and by and by he goes out and buys himself a pound of the juiciest rump-steak he can get hold of, and then back he goes to the car, and rub rub rub on the stains."

He chuckled gleefully, as if he himself had organized the deception he related.

"And the result was a monstrosity," he told them. "Something out of legend: blood with the characteristics of both bull and man. In other words, he re-invented the minotaur, and gave him a coat of carbolic for luck, and anybody who can do that is bright, I say."

"But not bright enough, apparently," remarked Beale.

"Oh, well: I'm a practical man —I don't believe in monsters. It was hard work, though, but we found a spot he'd missed at the edge of the floor-stain, and that gave a reaction for human blood alone, and blood impregnated with CO at that. If only he'd been a bit more thorough he really might have muddled me; if he'd used more steak, and rubbed harder, and put in a slice of sheep or camel or frog. All the same, he's a smart fellow, and I'd like to meet him."

"So that's what Oakes was relying on," said Bagshaw afterwards. "Only, why didn't he make up some yarn about butcher's meat?"

"No, that would have spoilt things," averred Dickie. "I like the way he did tackle things best. 'What are those stains?' you ask him. 'Red paint' says he. 'Rot' says you. 'Then I've no idea' says he. 'Find out and let me know.' Somehow I feel that's cleverer than blurting out they're best rump. It's definitely a case where pretended ignorance pays—if it comes off."

"Don't see it," objected Tony. "You've left the paint out now— that was pretended knowledge."

"No, Dickie's right," said Beale. "Oakes reckoned we'd argue that if he knew they were beefy he'd say so, instead of being funny. Therefore he didn't know. Therefore even if we spotted the human blood underneath we wouldn't hold him responsible, because if he had been he'd surely have explained when he got the chance."

"And what's going to happen to him?" asked the Chief-constable. "Arrest?"

"I don't know: I don't see how I possibly can."

He surveyed the others glumly, looking them up and down as if he were a schoolmaster with some of his more backward pupils.

"There's been too much crooked thinking about this case," he told them. "Or not enough clear thinking, which is almost as bad. I suggest we return to essentials. Now we've got both bodies we know that only one died from CO poisoning, and therefore that what you found in the bungalow, Colonel, and what Mrs. Topley saw at Craybourne, and what caused the stains in the car, were one and the same. Oakes couldn't apparently have murdered Alice Carter, because he wouldn't have been able to get to London in time for his show, so I don't see how the stains would justify an arrest. And anyway, he's safe enough in hospital—he won't run away if we do want him: for the murder of Philippa Saunderson, say."

# XXI

T HE INTERVIEW WITH ELLIS took place at the police-station. Beale had a short talk beforehand with Matthews, and learnt that on his own initiative the detective-sergeant had rung up Tilgate the evening before with regard to the wanted man's alibi.

"They'll be working on it now, sir," he said, "and I'm scared it's water-tight. Then where shall we be? Or have you got on a bit by yourself?"

"That doesn't sound very complimentary. Talk to Tony while I tackle your new friend, only don't let him lead you up the garden with any extra specially brilliant ideas."

"Not me, sir: and you'd better be careful, too. Ellis is a slick little fellow—he's got all the answers on the end of his tongue, and a few over. He could sell a pair of bellows to a one-handed man with central heating."

"Is that his line nowadays?"

"No: he says he's got some new system for playing the dogs, but I reckon myself he's up to his old games."

Beale studied the man's statement thoroughly before sending for its author about noon. Since it is always advisable for a police-officer conducting an interview to have a reliable witness present, he asked Bagshaw to fulfill the role.

"And wear your worst face, sir, if you will," he suggested. "Make him think you're wondering what he'll look like in quick-lime."

A few minutes sufficed to convince them that George Ellis, *alias* Drake, was both cool and crooked. In height he stood about five foot six, his clean-shaven face was sallow, with deep-set blue eyes and high cheek-bones, and his hands were bandaged. He was dressed in a waisted brown suit, and his shoes were very pointed. He regarded his questioner with an expression compounded partly of calculation and partly of somewhat flippant candour, and when told he might smoke if he liked he glanced for a second significantly at his covered fingers.

"Thanks, Chief," he said. "Excuse my glove."

"Which is your real name, Ellis or Drake?" began Beale.

"Ellis to you," was the reply. "I gave up bowls in fifteen-something."

"And now you play soccer on Saturday afternoons instead. Don't be too funny or I might choke myself laughing, and that'd be murder without any *possible* doubt."

He stared at the man for some moments and then turned again to the typewritten statement, skimming through it in a low monotone.

"Age thirty-seven, official occupation professional punter, resident in Tilgate since beginning of September, own a motor-cycle, unmarried. H'm. What was Alice Carter's real name, by the way—West?"

"Lor, I don't know. She was always West to me."

"And that's where she's gone—I see."

As he had half-expected, his vulgar comment obtained a reaction. Ellis's look became hostile.

"You wouldn't talk like that if we were alone and I had the use of my hands," he observed sharply.

"All right, sorry. But you don't question the fact of her death?"

"What d'you mean? I only know what the papers say—and that horse-faced little tyke who brought me down here."

"Yes, he does look a bit that way, doesn't he? Let's see, I had a parcel here somewhere—maybe it's next door."

He rang the bell on the desk, and then took out his pipe.

"Tell me something about your greyhound-racing system while we're waiting," he said. "Does it work?'

"Of course it works, else I wouldn't use it."

"No, I suppose not. Could you explain it?"

"I could—but why should I?"

"Well, why shouldn't you? Unless the chap who said you haven't got one was right."

"Well, he wasn't. All right, I don't mind—but it won't do you any good, 'cos you don't know enough about dogs. It's all to do with the forecast pool at the races: what comes in one two and three in any particular race. If they're the dogs everybody expects, then there's a lot of winning tickets, and you don't get hardly anything, and if they're outsiders you can pick up seven or eight quid, and maybe more.

"Well, first you've got to know all about form, both sides of the lights: what a dog's done in public, trials as well, and what it's done in private when nobody wasn't supposed to be watching. That bit's not so easy, but you can find out things if you ask the right bloke."

He paused while Best brought in the parcel for which Beale had asked him in a whisper a moment earlier, and was then asked to continue.

"Well, the way I work things is this. I pick a track where I know some of the dogs—and that includes their trainers and the rest of the bunch—and I only handle six-dog races. No hurdles, either—it's safer on the flat. And again, I won't touch a race that's got an absolute cert in it—that lessens the chances of a good pool. All that means I only do about three races out of the seven or eight on the card, of course. I take my pick early, long before I start out, so when I get to the track I know just what I'm going to do, pretty near. All the same, if I meet a chap who's got a bit of news to pass on when I get there, I don't shut my ears up. The main thing is to look at the six dogs in my three races, and wash out the worst two in each, which isn't always as hard as it sounds."

"Do you mean cross them out of the card, or take steps to see they don't get a chance of winning?"

"Oh, come off it! Cross 'em out, of course—you don't think I go round wringing their necks or something, do you? And they don't need to be the worst dogs, either: just two that aren't going to be in the first three. You get to hear about these things, or you work it out for yourself, if you're clever. Well, by then I've got four left in each of my races, and generally I don't rightly know which is going to be odd man out, nor yet just which order the others'll finish in: so I do the lot."

"You mean you permute all the possibilities?"

"Permute? What's that? I do 'em in threes, up and down and inside out, if that's what you're driving at, and with four dogs that costs me forty-eight bob at two bob a time. I wait near the tote till the list of runners goes up on the board, and then I start laying my bets as fast as I know how. After I've collected the winnings on the last race, that is—if any."

He halted, apparently considering that he had given away enough about his means of livelihood. By now his manner was noticeably less inimical, and Bagshaw silently applauded Beale's tactics. He knew that he himself, once on the wrong side of the man, would have stayed there, and so perhaps have lost some advantage.

"Yes, that's all very well," said Beale, with consummately feigned interest. "By limiting yourself to races where the result is likely to be fairly open, you obviously miss the poorer pools. All the same, I shouldn't think it's a very certain source of income. How many nights a week do you put in?"

"Four or five, up in London, but only three down here."

"I see. That means nine races, and an outlay of something over twenty pounds. To make it worth my while, I should want the pools I won to average about a fiver: that's assuming I drew blank once in three."

Ellis smiled for the first time.

"As a matter of fact I've been doing ten races a week," he asserted, "and only missing just over one and a half on balance. The average pool, including blanks, is three pound thirteen and ten so far, which makes about nine quid a week."

"Yes, that's not bad. I do very little better myself, and spend considerably more time at it. But why come down this way and restrict yourself to three nights a week? Oh, sorry—it's in your statement."

He returned to the typewritten sheets, and resumed his quick scrutiny.

"Lived with Alice West in Kennington for two years—she got six months for larceny last February—came out August 9th—you had a disagreement. What was that about—another woman?"

"Yes," was the rather surly answer. "How'd you know?"

"How do you think? Because of which she refused to live with you again. You begged her to change her mind, and she said she might. That was because you were really fond of her, I presume?"

"Of course—I really was."

"You didn't see her between the 22nd and the 30th, when she knocked you flat by telling you she was going to live at the seaside with her husband. She'd recently met him again after an unspecified number of years, and he'd given her the money for her fare, and she was travelling to Craybourne on the following day, the 31st."

He looked up, frowning slightly.

"Why Craybourne?" he asked. "Did she say?"

Ellis hesitated, and then shook his head.

"I thought it was because her husband had landed a job there," he said, "but it couldn't have been."

"Why not?"

"Well, he was to follow her down a few days after—that was her story. Only he never did, so he couldn't have had a job ready to step into, could he?"

"How do you know he didn't follow her down?" demanded Beale quickly.

"Oh—well, if it comes to that, I don't. I only know what she told me later, that he wouldn't be coming for a bit, and if he didn't buck up she'd give him the go-by and take me on again."

"So you still wanted her to resume your former—well, partnership?"

"That's right. We wouldn't ever have split up if she hadn't got herself shopped, only—"

"Six months is a long time," Beale finished. "Now Ellis, just answer this question, and don't fly off the handle. Do you know anything at all about Alice West's death apart from what's in the papers?"

"Nothing," said the other emphatically. "Strike me dead if I do."

"All right: and now another. Are you willing to give me what help you can in finding the person responsible?"

The reply was equally prompt, and equally definite.

"Yes—I'd like to see him strung up, curse him."

"Well, I can't promise that much, but I intend to get somebody for it. Oh, not just anyone,"—as Ellis looked for a moment rather apprehensive. "The right person, I mean. Now, as a beginning tell me everything you know about this husband of hers. Unless you can suggest a better line of enquiry?"

"No fear—I reckon he did it all right. You see, Alice wasn't everyone's cup of tea. For one thing, she'd a pretty sharp tongue when she cared to use it—we used to quarrel like monkeys, only somehow we always made it up. Till the row about Flo, that is," he added, "and that was my fault, I reckon.

"Honest, Chief, I wish I could tell you more about her blasted husband, only I can't—not even his name. What she always called him was 'The Angel'. 'When I was living with the Angel,' she'd say, or 'That's what the Angel used to tell me.' She didn't talk about him much, though—for one thing, I never wanted to listen."

"No, that's understandable. Did you ever see a photo of him?"

"Never, and I don't know where he worked, or what at, or if. Honest, I don't know a thing about the ——. He was better-looking than me, she said once, but that ain't much to go by."

"All right, we'll leave him for a bit. How did you come to follow Alice down south?"

"Like I told horse-face. I was sick about losing her, and anyway I hadn't been doing so well in town. A fellow told me Tilgate was turning out pretty good pools, so I thought I'd give it a try. I was reckoning if I could show her I was making a tenner a week, that might get her back. She was fond of a bit of money to spend. When I saw her the day before she went off she promised to send me a card with her address on, and she did. The minute I got it I bought a motor-bike and cleared out after her—about a week later, that was."

"And how did she receive you?"

"Not bad—better'n I'd hoped. You see, I didn't know till I called round at Weatherall Road that the Angel had never turned up. After that I spent my time trying to talk her into coming back to me before he did."

"And what did she say?"

"She told me she'd wait a bit and see how I got on at Tilgate. Her half-stretch hadn't done her any good—she wanted to feel safe, I reckon."

"Were you giving her money while she was at Mrs. Topley's?"

Ellis looked at him in some surprise.

"No fear—what d'you take me for? If she could have got what she wanted without coming back she needn't have come, would she? I gave her ten bob twice, to keep her sweet, but no more, and I never took her out much. She could have what she wanted in reason if she'd pair up with me again, but not else. Hell, that was only fair, wasn't it?"

"Oh yes, yes, it sounds perfectly all right to me. It was because you wouldn't take her out that you spent so much time in the bed-sitting-room?"

"Yes, but we went to the pictures now and again."

"I see. Now, tell me about last Thursday. Did you call by arrangement?"

"Oh yes—I always did. Well, I got there soon after 2.00 and found her still in her dressing-gown. She said she hadn't been feeling well, and she wasn't in a very good temper, so I didn't stay long. I left by about quarter to four."

"Why so early—because of her temper?"

"Yes—mostly. And because she told me to go, too—said she still felt groggy, and was going back to bed."

"Anything serious?"

"I don't think so—indigestion, probably. What do you expect if you drink tea all day long?"

Beale smiled.

"I don't get the chance to," he remarked. "Now think carefully: looking back on things, does it strike you that she may have been trying to get rid of you?"

Ellis puckered his face at the question.

"I wouldn't be surprised," he said slowly at last. "Not that I got the idea then, mind you, or I'd never have gone."

"And that's the last time you ever saw the girl?"

"Yes—around quarter to four on Thursday."

"Did you arrange any future meeting?"

"Today—I was to have called there at 3.00."

"And what about the previous Tuesday? Was your visit then by arrangement?"

"Yes—we went to the pictures."

"I see. By the way, which were your dog-nights?"

"Tuesday and Friday at Tilgate, and Wednesday over near Brighton."

"Thank you. Now, Mrs. Topley says that when you called at her place you never stayed after about six o'clock. Was there any reason for that?"

Ellis became very earnest.

"Yes—though you mayn't believe it," he said. "The fact is, I can't bear riding about at night. It always gives me a splitting head."

"Ah. Ever go to a pawnbroker in Craybourne?"

"Me? What on earth for?"

"To be precise, a trunk."

"Oh, the one in the paper. No, it wasn't me, Chief, on my oath."

"What time did you go to the pictures on Tuesday?"

"I don't know exactly. I should think we went in about half past three, or maybe a bit later."

"So you couldn't have been anywhere near the railway station at half past four?"

"Certainly not. What's that, something fresh?"

"Well, something you apparently don't know about."

Beale gave him a searching glance as he spoke, but the man seemed genuinely ignorant. He then returned to the statement.

"You'd no inkling that anything was wrong till the following afternoon, Friday," he said, "when you happened to catch sight of a paragraph in a local evening paper headed *Suicide Disappears From Craybourne—Weatherall Road Mystery.* The word Weatherall took your eye, and you were flabbergasted to read that it was Alice Carter who'd vanished. Why was she calling herself Carter, by the way?"

"Can't say. I've been figuring to myself it must be her husband's name."

"Possibly. You became frightened, especially at the direct mention of your own name, and certain peculiarities, and decided you'd had enough of the south coast. Not to put too fine a point upon it, you immediately ran away, whether the night ride gave you a headache or whether it didn't. First you went to London, and then to Woking, where you have a brother. It was there that you were located yesterday by Detective-sergeant Matthews. You agreed to make a full statement of your recent movements and so on, and place yourself at his disposal until it could be checked. It appears that for Thursday evening from six o'clock onwards you have an alibi, which I understand is now being examined."

He leant back, steadily staring at Ellis.

"Two obvious questions spring to mind," he said quietly. "First, why did you industriously spend Sunday afternoon pumice-stoning your finger-tips smooth? The answer you give here is that after reading the papers you fancied you came under suspicion: possibly of murder, possibly only of possessing information the police would like to share. Whichever it was, you preferred to take what precautions you could against being traced. You were pretty certain that there must be plenty of your prints in the room at No. 14, and you didn't know how much the landlady had been told about you. It seemed on the cards that Alice had mentioned Tilgate and greyhound-racing, which would make it easier for us to pick you up. In addition, there was the motor-cycle: someone might have noticed the registration number while it was standing outside the house. Anything else to say?"

"No. At least, I'm not sure. If there's anything you want to know, I'll tell you if I can."

"That's better—that's decidedly better: because it doesn't strike me as being by any means a complete explanation. Innocent people haven't anything to be afraid of, Ellis. It's the guilty ones who decamp."

"And so because anyone skips, that means he did it? Hell, what *can* you do but run away from blokes that think like that? And if you want more, here it is. What about Oscar Slater? Eh, what

about him? Eighteen years he did for a murder he never committed, poor devil, and on just about as good evidence as you could
have raked up against me. Blazes, you don't think I'm going to sit
quiet and wait for eight o'clock on a winter's morning, do you? Or
a lifer."

"It's nine o'clock these days," corrected Beale. "Yes, that
sounds like a point to you. All the same, I think you could have
chosen a better instance of what you mean. I've always believed
he was innocent myself, but his eventual pardon didn't settle the
question officially. He received it on the ground that the jury had
been misdirected, not because the Court of Appeal considered
their verdict wrong. Still, for the time being I'll accept your story
that you rubbed your fingers smooth because you were frightened
of our stupidity. It was an action which couldn't fail to arouse suspicion, though, and anyway the impressions grow again."

"Everybody knows that. But not for a while—not till you'd
have had time to collar the bloke who really did it."

"Very well: and now for the second question, and this time I
shall want a really convincing answer. I certainly don't think much
of the one mentioned here. You say that when you visited 14
Weatherall Road you wore dark glasses and a long blue coat, and
kept your cap on, because Alice Carter told you to, but you don't
know why. I'm sorry to be a nuisance, but we'll have to have
something a bit less feeble than that, please."

He spoke briskly, almost jocularly, and was disappointed to see
Ellis scowl again.

"I tell you, I *don't* know why. She just said flat I couldn't go to
the place unless I did myself up like that."

"Did she inform you of that by letter?"

"No—yes."

"Or both. Still got it?"

"No—I don't keep letters."

"That's a pity. And what do you mean by 'like that'? Did she
specifically mention dark glasses and a long coat all buttoned up?"

"No, she didn't. She just said I wasn't to come as myself, I had
to put on a false moustache or something. I chose glasses—they
don't tickle so much. And I don't know why there's all the fuss
about the coat: it's the one I generally wear. You can see it if you
like—it's outside."

"Thanks, I don't think I'll bother."

He pondered for a moment, not at all satisfied with the repeated
explanation.

"And do you generally keep your hat on indoors?" he asked. "You were always wearing it when Mrs. Topley saw you. I'm sorry you won't come clean—and just as we were getting on so well, too. I'm afraid I shall have to alter my plans unless you change your mind. Look here, I'll be as fair as possible. Did your reason for wearing the glasses have anything to do with Alice Carter? If not, if you were really hiding your face for some reason of your own, I won't press for details provided you can make me believe you're telling the truth."

It was Ellis's turn to think.

"All right," he said at last, with a twisted smile and an air of reluctant relief. "All right, I may as well tell you. The truth is I've got my troubles same as other people. I'm married too, and I used to live in Craybourne for three years, and for all I know my old woman still does, and I wouldn't let her get a sight of my mug for a thousand quid."

"Ah, that sounds more probable. Which three years?"

"Christmas 1930 to November 1933."

"Where did you live?"

"Lime Street."

Beale turned to the colonel.

"Your go, sir," he said. "Will you please find out if he knows the place?"

"Rather!" agreed Bagshaw, glad to break his inaction. For five minutes he fired questions at Ellis, and at the end of that time declared himself satisfied.

"And what was your job while you lived there?" enquired Beale. "Or is that a silly question? All right, I can see it is. You were working, but doubtless not at any recognized trade. I suspect the nimble fingers in the alien pocket myself, but I won't voice my suspicions.

"All right, Ellis: you wrapped your face up because you were afraid your wife might tap you on the shoulder and claim her own. If you'd said as much to begin with you'd have saved me a lot of breath: I'm interested in runaway murderers, not in runaway husbands. Now, about four more questions and I've done with you for the present. First, did Alice Carter know your address in Tilgate?"

"Yes."

"Next, when you went out of Mrs. Topley's on Thursday did you pick up a note with your name on the envelope on the hall table?"

"Oh yes—about her not paying her rent, and would I please do something. I took it up to show her, and she got crosser still, so I hopped it. Sorry I forgot that."

"What happened to the note?"

"Don't know—I left it with her."

"I see. Thirdly, where in the world did Alice get all her kit from, if she only came out of gaol on August 9th? Had you been keeping it for her?"

"Some of it."

"Including the china ornament that was a present from the Angel?"

"Yes."

"Very well: describe it."

Ellis frankly grinned at the request.

"You won't catch me out like that," he declared. "It was seven or eight inches high, and it was a girl with no clothes on standing on a sundial."

"Valuable?"

"I don't know. She always said it was—the Angel had paid four pound ten for it or something daft."

"Thanks: and the rest of her clothes and things?"

"Well, that ought to be easy: what did she go to clink for?"

"Yes, of course, shoplifting—you know all the answers. Finally, do you recognize these?"

As he spoke he undid the parcel containing the green underclothes, the footless stockings, and the variegated garters. As they came into view Ellis turned pale.

"Yes," he said, "yes, they're hers. She had 'em on Thursday, and a pink dressing-gown. Has one of the stockings got a hole in the back? Yes, that's it all right. No, I don't want to touch—that's blood, isn't it? Curse the devil, whoever he is."

# XXII

D URING LUNCH Beale faithfully related to the others the gist of his conversation with Ellis. Then he turned to Dickie.

"I'm going to take you into Craybourne and let you loose," he said. "You'll have a couple of hours to find out if a Mrs. Ellis ever lived in Lime Street, or still does, or anywhere else. Do it in less time if you can."

"And me, sir?" asked Matthews. "Look after the so-and-so? I thought as much. The next time I open my trap too wide I hope an elephant flies in. Will I be settling down till his fingerprints grow again? Because if so I'm going to join the local library, or learn to knit, or something."

"Ah, and talking about waiting," put in Bagshaw, "I've a bit of news, too. The hospital rang up earlier about Oakes; he's still unconscious, a little delirious but not intelligibly so. They're afraid he's in for a nervous breakdown, and won't be fit to talk to for days, or maybe weeks."

"Confound the man!" said Beale. "That may prove awkward."

When they had dropped Dickie in Craybourne, and were alone, Tony faced his friend firmly.

"I won't budge till I've had a drink," he declared: "We've got twenty minutes. Also, I want a spot of consideration for my theory: in the new circumstances I feel entitled to ask for it."

Beale shook his head.

"You won't get anywhere much with the husband idea," he said.

"You mean Ellis isn't telling the truth?"

"Not necessarily: in fact, I'm inclined to believe him, and if Dickie finds out there was a wife I'll be more inclined still. No, I mean that I think you're starting the wrong end. In my opinion this is a case where you've got to work on actions and not on motives. The second body didn't die of CO poisoning; therefore it isn't Alice Carter; therefore the first one is; therefore we know what time the first one died, within a few minutes; therefore we know its head was cut off not later than 9.15. That effectually does the same for your theory, I think—unless you prefer to consider it still-born. Take my advice, and try sticking to the facts for a change. And drink up: I'm going to show Mrs. Topley those snapshots I got from Harrington. If she says they look anything like her lodger, then I'll be satisfied that Oakes made a mistake in thinking the head he found in his car was Philippa's."

Tony contorted his face into a sneer.

"Facts!" he jibed. "The stains are full of CO; so is the bungalow body: why piffle about with snapshots?"

"As a precaution: in case Mrs. Topley says nobody in or out of his senses could mistake one for the other, however dark and dead they were."

"And if she does?"

"Then I'll know my facts aren't facts."

"How stimulating! And what will that turn them into—anamorphoses?"

"I dare say, if that means errors of judgment on my part."

"And then what will you do?"

"It depends: try axinomancy, probably."

Tony groaned.

"What's that?" he asked. "Something to do with choppers, by the sound of it."

"Exactly—divination by a balanced hatchet."

"Well, try another drink first, because you're not leaving this pub till I get satisfaction. Kindly prove to me, by the use of facts or any other means, that Best couldn't have had time to do the necessary on Thursday. You left it a bit sketchy before, and this husband business interests me in spite of what you say."

Beale sighed.

"All right," he agreed. "I suppose persistence is some sort of a virtue, however misapplied. You'll pay for the drink, though—I'm hanged if I'm going to spend good money as well as disprove a bad theory. You admit that Best couldn't have left Craybourne in the van before 7.15 at the very earliest?" he went on. "Mrs. Topley didn't go for the police till 7.12, remember, and the trunk had to be carried out of the house."

"Yes, I'll accept 7.15."

"Good: and how long to do the five and three-quarter miles to the bungalow? Don't overlook the drive through the town, the wet state of the roads, nor the character of the vehicle."

"Well, say he took twelve minutes. That's only averaging about 29 m.p.h., but I don't expect he'd manage more."

"If as much. Very well, he arrives there at 7.27. He then removes the trunk from the van, tips the body out because the combined weight would be too much for him, and carries them indoors separately. The distance is about forty yards each way, and both journeys would take him six or seven minutes from start to finish: till 7.33, say. Agree?"

"Yes, I suppose so: things begin to look murky. But then he could nip back as quick as he knew how, couldn't he?"

"By no means. I keep telling you that the head *must* be removed within two hours of death, which means then and there as far as Best's concerned. He didn't go on duty till 10.00, and that'd be far too late."

"Oh curse! All right, another five minutes—not a second more."

"Which in itself is impossible, I think. If he didn't take his clothes off before he started chopping he'd have been in a bit of a mess when he met Harrington later, I don't doubt. Still, for the sake of another drink say five minutes, by which time it's at least 7.38. Next he leaves the bungalow, gets into the van, and drives it back three-quarters of a mile to Smuggler's Lane, where he carefully parks it in the place usually reserved for Deacon: another three minutes, by the time he's ready to clear off home.

"And there the poor wretch is, a mile and three-quarters from the place where he meets Harrington nine minutes later. Kindly note I'm giving him an extra five in case Harrington was that much out. What's more, he wouldn't dare risk cycling, even if he had a bike hidden in the hedge, in case somebody saw him and remembered it afterwards.

"I repeat—may I have another free beer, please?—he finds himself with one and three-quarter miles to cover in a maximum of nine minutes, and he'd have to walk the last quarter, again in case he were seen. Well, what is it now?"—as Tony opened his mouth.

"A fresh possibility that occurred to me. If Harrington's all right, then I agree we can't time their meeting—his and Best's—later than 7.50: but suppose he isn't all right? Suppose he and Best are conspiring together?"

Beale tapped his half-empty tankard significantly.

"It'll cost you something before you decide to shut up, by the look of it," he observed. "Not that I mind—I'm rather enjoying it.

You expect an answer to that last brilliance? Then have the obvious one—subtlety would be wasted. If they were in league together, as you cretinously suggest, do you imagine they wouldn't put themselves right in baulk by saying they met at half past seven? Especially as it's Harrington's business to think of things like that. The time was quarter to eight, to which has been added five minutes' extension in honour of Purdon's Patent Tankard-filling Process.

"For the last time I survey the facts of the matter. Best has nine minutes to cover a mile and three-quarters in, one quarter of a mile of which must be walked. All right, Landlord, you needn't worry —I'm a policeman in private life. The quarter would take him two and a half minutes at 6 m.p.h., which is good going if you don't want to be stared at. As for the first mile and a half in six and a half minutes, at night and in ordinary clothes, I can only suggest you publish it as an all-time world's record."

Tony nodded.

"It's a pity," he said. "We've squeezed things till you can practically see through them, and only managed to turn him into a streak of lightning. There'd have to be at least another five minutes available."

"And you certainly can't get that at the bungalow—your only hope is to prove the van can do eighty. Why don't you ask Deacon if you can borrow the thing, while I'm seeing Mrs. Topley?"

At half past three they reported to one another.

"Then van does exactly forty-four and a bit, flat out and fit to bust," said Tony. "I tried the actual journey to the bungalow—it took me twelve minutes one way and twelve and a half the other. Deacon came with me, and I dare say he's still shivering. How did you get on?"

Beale smiled mysteriously.

"The snapshots are very like, according to Mrs. Topley. I also got some other very interesting information out of her—or rather, I verified some we already possess, and obtained three fresh items which we might easily have suspected—or two of them. No, I shan't tell you what, but I don't mind saying that I really think I may have solved it all, or be on the way to solving it."

"Marvellous," said his friend light-heartedly, not realizing that Beale was serious. "You've done it once now, and I've done it at least twice: it's a shame the others are so slow."

"Don't you worry about them—they haven't woken up yet."

"Woken up? To what? Here, what're you talking about?"

He stared at his companion's face intently.

"Hang it, I believe I've been left in the lurch again—whatever a lurch is. Am I asleep too?"

"I wouldn't wonder. Your anamorphosis has come true: we've all been labouring—literally—under a misapprehension. Far too late for me to be pleased with myself, I've spotted that, but I'm pretty sure you haven't."

"Well, don't gloat. A misapprehension about what in particular?"

"Nothing in particular: the business as a whole. The case, in fact, is just beginning."

"But if you know all the ways and wherefores, it ought to be ending, not beginning."

"Well, then, ending: when a circle's complete it doesn't matter. I shan't be long now, and if you want to catch up you'd better hurry, and you won't do it unless you give why and wherefore a rest. For once, as I told you earlier, motive isn't the thing to go for: it's what we know happened, and what we can deduce must have happened, that counts."

"But there *was* a motive?"

"I dare say. It's simply that I don't need to know one way or the other in order to identify the person or persons responsible for the crime or crimes, if any. Could I be less ambiguous?"

Later at Craybourne police-station they encountered Dickie, and were told that Mrs. Ellis not only existed, but still lived in Lime Street.

"I got a description of the runaway husband," said the reporter: "pretended I was looking for someone of that name who'd been left a diamond-mine. It's the chap Matthews brought down, all right. Moreover, Mrs. Ellis is the sort of woman nobody in his wits would marry on any consideration, and if he did have a day off and go mad he'd certainly clear out the day after."

"Yet he lasted at least three years."

"Well, I understand she had money—once. But it wouldn't have been enough for me, not if she put a tenner into my hand every time the clock struck."

Further confirmation of Ellis's story was received later at Belling, Tilgate reporting by telephone that his alibi held good for the period between 6.00 P.M. and 11.00 P.M. the previous Thursday. Matthews looked unexpectedly glum at the news, but Beale seemed not to mind.

"And now I'm going out for a walk," he announced. "And alone, what's more. I hope that when I come back I shall be able to tell you all about everything. Good-bye."

There was a chorus of expostulation.

"You mean you know who did it?" demanded Bagshaw incredulously.

"More than that, Colonel—I believe I also know what and how. The last is the only thing I'm not feeling certain about, but I have my suspicions, and I shall call in at the bungalow to test them."

And with a cheerful wave of the hand he was gone.

# INTERLUDE

*Those who have reached this point in the story, and who care to, can now formally pass an opinion upon each of the following questions:*

*(1) Who murdered Alice Carter and Philippa Saunderson?*

*(2) How were these murders respectively carried out?*

*(3) For what specific purpose has Chief-inspector Beale visited the bungalow again?*

*The general answer to (3), as he has just said, is to test his theory with regard to (part of) (2). This opportunity is unfortunately not open to readers, who may perhaps be consoled with the assurance that no information in Beale's possession has been concealed from them.*

# XXIII

I T WAS SEVEN O'CLOCK when Beale sat down in Colonel Bagshaw's study to explain. His audience consisted of the colonel himself, Tony, Matthews, Dickie Donovan, and Inspector Creevy.

"Now, where had I better start?" he asked. "Perhaps by clearing up the misapprehension I told Tony about this afternoon. I'm afraid there's been a lot of eye-trouble in this case: we had a strong lead to the solution under our noses from the beginning, and we did everything but recognize it.

"First of all, let me deal with Mrs. Topley. She informed Inspector Creevy—and he remembered to mention it in his excellent report—that from a chink in the dining-room door on Thursday afternoon she watched Alice Carter walk across the hall to admit Ellis. In addition to her dressing-gown the girl was then wearing the clothes found on the first body, including the torn stocking. Now, you've all been inside 14 Weatherall Road except Matthews, and you know that as you enter the front door the dining-room is on the left and the stairs are on the right.[2] That means that when Mrs. Topley saw the hole in the stocking she was behind and to the right of Alice Carter; which in turn means that since the girl had her dressing-gown on, the hole simply *must* have been in the right leg. However much the gown gaped, the back of the left leg wouldn't have been visible, and it's made clear in the Inspector's report that the hole was seen when the girl moved *towards* the door.

"Very well: yet Mrs. Topley also says that the body she saw through the glass partition was lying on its right side, and had the hole in the stocking of the upper leg,[3] the left one, and that of course corresponds with what was found in the bungalow.

By now the others were frowning, which made Beale smile.

---

[2] Chapter XI

[3] See Chap. I: Mrs. Topley's story never varied in essentials.

"That's my first point," he went on, "and the second is this. Simulating the conditions in the bedroom as far as they were known, Sergeant Turner learnt that it took 8½ minutes for the smell of gas to reach the landing, by which time the room was naturally full. In those circumstances it would plainly be impossible for anyone to remain alive inside, or for anyone to open the door subsequently without greatly increasing the smell outside. How can these facts be reconciled with Mrs. Topley's assertion that when she returned with the police it was scarcely any stronger? I raised the point with her myself this afternoon,[4] and if you think that's cheating, I can only say that anybody else could have done the same had it occurred to him.

"Excluding gas-masks issued during the crisis, which are useless against coal-gas, I could find only three possible answers to the problem. First, that Mrs. Topley's sense of smell was defective—but Sergeant Turner's report about his test proves otherwise. Next, that the door was never opened during her absence between 7.12 and 7.21: but that's ridiculous if we accept her evidence at all, and no reason has been suggested why we shouldn't. Finally, that the smell on the landing noticed by her before 7.04 *did not originate from the bedroom.*"

"Corks!" exclaimed Tony. "But that means—"

"Only one thing, especially in conjunction with my first point: it means that there never was a dead body in the first-floor front room at 14 Weatherall Road."

A general murmuring ensued, during which Dickie and the colonel were understood to mention their own previous doubts on the matter. Creevy said nothing, but it seemed likely from his expression that he would be speaking later. It was Tony who asked a question.

"All this since the beer this afternoon?" he enquired.

"And plenty more," Beale assured him. "It wasn't till after I saw Mrs. Topley today that I woke up. Incidentally, the no-body idea was surely the natural corollary of your suspicion—guess—that the one in the bungalow was Alice Carter, wasn't it? If you'd gone just that one step further, simplicity would certainly have triumphed.

"And now comes another question: what can possibly be the point of rigging up a body if no one sees it?"

---

[4] But the reader knows from Chapter I.

"Ah, I've been waiting for that!" broke in Creevy instantly. "Giving you the benefit of the doubt, as it were—there seemed just a chance you meant that Mrs. Topley's been telling lies."

He cleared his throat ominously.

"May I remind you that last night on the telephone you wouldn't hear of a dummy?" he said. "That you even produced a convincing psychological reason for ridiculing the suggestion?"

Beale smiled, and shook his head.

"I'm sorry to contradict, but you're piling it on too thick," he answered. "All I ridiculed was the use of a draper's dummy. I admit that at the time I wasn't considering any other kind, but I'm still quite sure I didn't lay down hard and fast rules to exclude all dummies."

"No, that's true. I can't think of any other sort that has recognizable legs, though. They weren't just any old thing, you know: breakfast sausages in stockings, say. And what happens to your psychology?"

"It remains valid. I asked what trickster could resist the temptation to show more than legs. But suppose there were no temptation—suppose legs were the only human resemblances he had available for showing? You must all have seen the things I mean scores of times: in Woolworths', or the window of almost any shop that sells stockings. They're separate, and hollow, and flesh-coloured, and they finish about four inches above the knee. A pair of them was what the murderer used: the rest consisted of bedclothes under a blanket. And please don't let anyone tell me I'm merely speculating, because I shan't agree. There *must* have been a dummy, and it couldn't have been a full-length draper's dummy. If you suggest that only the lower half of one was used I won't quarrel about it, but I shall still think my own idea the more likely.

"In passing, I confess I don't know how or where the legs were procured. At a guess, they were stolen by Alice Carter, who from Matthews's account of her seems to have been quite good at the shop-lifting game.

"And now to repeat my third question: what was the sense in rigging up a dummy that no one saw? Answer, no sense: in other words, it was meant to be seen. That conclusion leads to more psychology, this time on the murderer's part. Allow him Alice as a source of information—I'll deal with that again later—and you give him access to the following facts about Mrs. Topley. First, she always goes out on Thursday afternoons about 3.30, and returns just about 7.00. Second, her late husband's best friend was

Station-sergeant Turner, on duty only two hundred yards away. How did Alice Carter know that? Because she'd been told—that was another of my questions this afternoon.[5] Third, Mrs. Topley is an inquisitive woman—witness the way she stared at us while we were in the builders' yard on Saturday, Tony. It occurred to me to wonder if she'd ever tried spying on Ellis and the girl through the glass partition previously. After some hesitation she admitted that she had, and said she wasn't at all sure she hadn't been spotted once.[6]

"Very well: now for the psychology. Mrs. Topley returns to 14 Weatherall Road soon after 7.00, and the moment she gets inside she hears her wireless set going full blast in one of the rooms above. That she'll immediately investigate can be taken for granted, as also that before she's been upstairs many seconds she'll smell gas. The source, of course, was the fixture on the landing: if you didn't notice it for yourselves you could have read about it in the Inspector's report. The thought that then leaps into her mind would occur to the proverbial ninety-nine people out of a hundred in similar conditions: suicide.

"And now comes the critical point: what will she do next? For the fulfillment of the murderer's plan she must behave exactly as she in fact does: climb on a chair and look through the partition *before* going for help. In view of her character and previous like activities, the chances in favour of that are about five in six, I should say. It's worth emphasizing that should she fail to do what was expected of her, however, the murderer suffers no serious inconvenience—none threatening his safety. The reason is simple: at that time he was not a murderer except in intention. No one has yet died.

"All right: the hoax worked. Mrs. Topley dashed out of the house at 7.12, confident it contained a body not long dead of coal-gas poisoning. The question which then arises is, how long can the murderer rely on being safe from interruption? My own answer is that he could reasonably count on five minutes. As you mention in your report, Inspector, the street is badly lit, and you told us yesterday that at that time the nearest policeman would be at the station two hundred yards away. Also, the person Mrs. Topley wanted to see was undoubtedly Sergeant Turner: it was most unlikely that she'd tell her news to any casual stranger, and almost

---

[5] But the reader knows from Chapter I.
[6] Chapter I.

equally unlikely that in so short a distance she'd meet anyone she knew. I think five minutes would be a fair minimum period for her to arrive, get her breath back, tell a coherent story, and return with help. In actual fact nine minutes elapsed, but that's by the way: three would be enough for the murderer.

"Before going on I must deal with his earlier actions, though. Where he hid between 7.04 and 7.12 I can't say: probably in the bedroom itself. He'd know the old woman couldn't break in by herself, though she says she was going to try if necessary, so that even if she failed to look through the glass he'd still have time to escape. I'm inclined to believe he *was* in there, out of sight on or under the bed. The trunk certainly was, already packed except for the china ornament still in its usual place on the mantelpiece and perhaps the things on the dressing-table, in case she looked.

"The moment she'd gone he undid his dummy, bundled the legs into the trunk together with the rubber tubing and the statuette, put the blankets back on the bed with the wireless set, got the trunk outside on to the landing, turned the gas-fire full on, and locked the door. Then he ran down and signalled to the man Prince."

"One moment," interrupted the colonel. "The bedroom key was found on the mantelpiece: what did he lock the door with?"

"Either a duplicate he'd made previously," answered Beale, "or the one from the spare room, which the Inspector reported as fitting Alice Carter's."

Bagshaw nodded, and turned to Creevy.

"I take back all I ever said or thought about details," he declared gruffly. "You seem to have produced an absolute blue-book of information."

"And a question for me," interposed Dickie. "It's all plain sailing now till Prince has had his five bob, except for one thing. What was in the trunk to make it the right weight?"

"Lor, even I can guess that," said Matthews. "There was a yard full of bricks next door, wasn't there?"

"Well, I propose to leave that side of the story for a bit," continued Beale. "We have the deception satisfactorily accomplished, and the police—once they're convinced that Mrs. Topley believes her tale—looking wildly for a missing body which died from CO poisoning at or about 7.00. The van and the trunk and Prince hardly need explaining. They were the result of careful reconnaissance, all designed to assist the illusion and all incidentally serving to show that the murderer was someone with local knowledge, or opportunities for acquiring it.

"And now let's turn to the murder of Philippa Saunderson, dealing first with the telegrams. There were three, one for Oakes and two for Dennison; all despatched in her name and all handed in at Craybourne post-office on Thursday at 5.49 P.M. Their contents you know: the question is, did Philippa really send them?

"My answer is that she didn't, and I can give two reasons for it, both originating from the account of her movements on Thursday made out by Colonel Bagshaw. To begin with, consider the times of her two journeys, from Belling to Craybourne to meet Best, and from Craybourne home again to Belling. The first, to keep an appointment, took her seventeen minutes, from 4.45 to 5.02. Best wouldn't lie about when she arrived, in case somebody happened to notice and contradict him later. Similarly he'd tell the truth about the time their talk ended. Her second journey, then, provided she set off at quarter to six, took fifteen minutes, two less than the first. That difference isn't big enough to be unconvincing: but if it was she who handed in the telegrams, then she couldn't have been outside the post-office and in motion before 5.50. This would mean that although there was no special hurry she covered the seven miles between the two places at an average speed of 42 m.p.h., whereas previously it had been only about 25 m.p.h. Frankly, I don't believe that, especially as Mary Adams gives the top speed of the car as only 60 m.p.h. on a good road.

"My second reason for saying that Philippa didn't send the telegrams is this. According to the post-office girl the person who handed them in was very wet; but a study of the Colonel's timetable shows that Philippa had no opportunity for getting wet after 3.30.

"If you find that part acceptable, I can get on with the next step—the assumption that the telegrams originated from the murderer. The description of the sender—a fair-haired girl in a fawn raincoat—makes it obvious that she was meant to be taken for Philippa. That not only rules out the possibility that they were authentic, but handed to someone else for despatch, but gives us a second definite link between the two dead girls: the first, of course, is what was done to both of them after death. In short, the wet young woman in the post-office was Alice Carter, an idea that's borne out by what Mrs. Topley said when I showed her some snapshots of Philippa."

"But why?" demanded Bagshaw.

"Oh, that isn't difficult: Oakes and Dennison were to be lured down here so that we'd have someone to suspect for Philippa's murder. I'll mention that again presently, but first let's deal with the question of the murderer's identity. You all know it by now, of course, and Tony was so upset that he bet me an incredible amount of free beer I couldn't prove I didn't guess it. I shall do my best to satisfy him—no pun intended.

"From what I've said so far it follows that before I could be satisfied I'd got the right man I had to see that three conditions were fulfilled, *(a):* He must be aware of Philippa's relations with Oakes, or there's no point in throwing suspicion on the man. *(b):* He must also know about her relations with Dennison. Finally, *(c),* he must be in a position to count absolutely on being able to murder Philippa that night; or, in other words, be the person she went out to see 'on business'.

"Leaving out Ellis because his alibi was proved, five people seemed to me to be possible suspects: Oakes, Dennison, Harrington, Mary Adams, Best. The first two can be excluded because of the telegrams. Each of the others either did definitely know about *(a)* and *(b),* or in Mary's case could be suspected of knowing: Best told me himself on Sunday that he understood Philippa and Dennison were practically engaged. As for *(c),* the girl's availability, they all seemed to have an equal chance there too, and the problem was how to choose between them. This is how I did it, Tony, and where—I hope—I quench a lifetime's thirst.

"Since—we've decided—the telegrams were sent without Philippa's knowledge, then her 'business' that night wasn't to meet either Oakes or Dennison. Yet it appeared probable—virtually certain—that she had some kind of appointment, as I said just now. Or put it this way. The telegrams indicate that by 5.49 a settled intention to murder her existed: hence the person holding that intention must obviously know where to find her. Therefore if she weren't meeting him by appointment she was going somewhere—without doubt the bungalow—where he could be sure of locating her: *and had been sure since before* 5.49. Yet until she'd seen Best how could the girl possibly know what her future plans would be? And how could she inform Harrington or Mary Adams between 5.45 and 5.49, when Colonel Bagshaw reports that no telephone calls were received at *Cairngorm* after midday on Thursday? Finally, if the appointment—the 'business'—*were* with either of them, why go out and leave them behind?

"From consideration of the telegrams, Best was clearly indicated as the murderer: not only of Philippa, but also of Alice, in view of the description of the girl in the post-office and the treatment of the bodies. Accordingly I looked for confirmation of the idea. He fitted as far as local knowledge went, and he was in Craybourne on Thursday. Also, he wouldn't have had much trouble in getting hold of Philippa's key to the bungalow—you'll remember I did agree over that, Tony, when you first pointed your finger at him.

"There were two further considerations which clinched the matter in my mind, though. First, the dates respectively of his holiday and Alice Carter's arrival in Craybourne. That doesn't need much elaboration: he went to London on August 27th, as he informed us on Friday morning, saw Oakes the following Tuesday, and Alice turned up at Mrs. Topley's on the Wednesday, the 31st. Please note that nothing there clashes with what Ellis told me earlier today.

"The second point is a little subtler, but none the worse for that. Last Saturday evening, while Tony and I were waiting for Oakes to come back from viewing the body, Best told us that after he left Philippa outside the post-office he walked down to the beach and ran home. Yet even before he specifically mentioned running along the beach you tumbled to it, Tony, and I suggest you did so because you were brighter than I was. You'd just heard Harrington say he met Best at 7.45, and you knew Best left Philippa at 5.45. The moment he filled in the two hours' interval by talking of running, part of your mind jibbed at the idea: it wouldn't take a young fellow like him that long to walk a few hundred yards and then run seven miles, especially as he's in training. But your mind didn't jib hard enough to make you call him a liar: only enough to make you remember something you once heard about performing on shingle. That *would* explain the time taken: therefore it must be what he meant, and he was quick to agree with you."

"Smart fellow!" remarked his friend. "I won't quarrel about it, though I can't say I was aware of all that."

"Of course not: you were reasoning subconsciously. Before I go on, here's something else about Best's suitability for the part of murderer. He possessed samples of Philippa's handwriting to help him forge the telegrams, and you'll remember they weren't written in the post-office: the fair-haired girl went straight to the counter and stood behind an old man of ninety-something. In passing, nobody expects writing on telegraph forms to be wholly characteristic: most people make it consciously rather more legible than usual.

"And now a brief word about motive. With regard to Alice Carter's murder, Tony, I'm prepared to accept your suggestions practically *en bloc,* now they've been backed up by Ellis. Best wanted his freedom from a regrettable marriage incurred while he was living in London, so that he could make a fresh start with Mary Adams. Alice wouldn't do what he asked, so he decided to murder her. But even though I accept that much, I still maintain that the correct procedure for solving this case was to argue from murderer to motive, and not the other way round. If I couldn't think of a single reason why Best wished to get rid of Alice, I should still believe he did.

"As for Philippa Saunderson, the most obvious incentive was the £1000 taken from Mr. Harrington's biscuit tin, yet I fancy it wasn't the main one. I rather think what chiefly prompted him to kill her was that she knew too much for his safety, but that comes in a minute. All the same, I've no doubt that Best induced her to keep their appointment with a full purse. He may have done that by blackmail, which might account for his possession of the photographs he got from Oakes: but more probably he pitched her some yarn about Oakes's servant bringing the negatives to the bungalow that night without his master's knowledge, in return for hard cash. He'd put some such suggestion as 'How much money could you produce by midnight tonight?' in with the bundle at the bank: which would mean that his plans were complete by September 25th, the date mentioned in Colonel Bagshaw's time-table. I think something like that probably happened: it was *before* she went into Craybourne that Philippa spoke to her uncle about money. When she was in the car with Best he'd tell her to bring the photos so that she could check up on the genuineness of the negatives. I dare say he also had some plausible story about handing the cash over, and then regaining it by trickery or force. The whole yarn would give an adequate reason for her going out late: the note in the biscuit tin was in case Harrington discovered the loss before she was able to replace it. The reason she didn't take him into her confidence was doubtless because Best made her promise not to.

"Also worth mentioning is the fact that she left *Cairngorm* on foot, and not as one might have expected by car. Best would suggest that ostensibly as a precaution on her behalf—in case she were seen by Sergeant Tukes, for instance: but actually of course he was looking after his own interests. The time she set out wouldn't quite fit in with the supposed reason for her excursion, to keep a midnight appointment at the Martello Tower, because she needn't have started for there until 11.30 at the earliest. That couldn't be helped, though: it was essential that she didn't run into Dennison by accident, or the game was up. Incidentally, the whole point of making the Tower the meeting-place was lost because of Dennison's dullness. It was there that he first met Philippa, as he told me yesterday. Best would have learnt that from Mary, and obtained the necessary addresses for the telegrams while he was in London—he'd only have to look in the Telephone Directory.

"And now I'll go on to another most important question: was the body found in the bungalow Philippa's or Alice's? Our reason for thinking it couldn't be Philippa's was the cause of death. My own reasons for being sure it *was* hers are these. First, the only sensible point of the hoax at Weatherall Road was to establish the presence there long before midnight of a girl in green underclothes dead of coal-gas poisoning. One look at the corpse in the bungalow ought then to be enough to convince people that it came from Mrs. Topley's."

"Especially as Philippa never wore green," said Tony.

"Yes, he may have taken that into account, but it's not of much consequence. My second reason is the absence of the feet, combined with, third, the presence of the racket-covers. Sir Douglas Henderson told us what *they* were for: to retain the gas in the lungs, and so enable its source to be determined. Those on the arms were merely blinds, of course: only the one on the neck was really necessary, but to use that by itself might have made us suspicious. Your theory about the feet is undoubtedly correct, Tony. Philippa's were too clean and well cared-for to be mistaken for Alice's, so they had to come off. Best hadn't bargained for that, though, and hence had nothing for the ends of the legs."

"But would a chap like him know about keeping the gas in the lungs?" asked Dickie dubiously.

"Not from books, perhaps, but I think he could have worked it out. People who die that way obviously inhale gas into their lungs. If you intend to cut their heads off, but want the origin of the gas to be discoverable, you've got to make sure it can't escape through the windpipe. He probably didn't know about the blood-clot, of course. I dare say that what he expected was a noticeable smell of coal-gas the moment the bag on the neck was removed.

"There's one more thing to mention about the two bodies, their similarity of height and shape and colouring as recorded by Dr. Duncan. Unlike anyone else we've heard about but Oakes, Best knew what Philippa looked like naked because he'd seen the photographs, and he could probably manage to find out that Alice hadn't altered since they last met.

"And now I must get on. For how long Best had been trying to trace his wife it's impossible to say: but last February—I suspect—he read something in the papers about her conviction for shoplifting. Quite probably West was what he called himself when he married her. To a man without a real name—you told me his father was never finally decided, Tony—one's almost as good as another, and anyway it wouldn't be a big change from what he was used to.

"Knowing she'd be out of gaol by the end of August, he plans to spend his holidays in London searching for her. Quite unexpectedly he then receives his commission from Philippa with regard to Oakes and the letters. Also unexpectedly, as soon as he arrives in town he achieves minor notoriety to the extent of getting his name and photograph in the papers. And as well, as you told us and him on Saturday morning, Dickie, your paper noted his address in London. In my opinion what subsequently happened wasn't so much that he found Alice as that she found him. Not long out of prison, and having quarrelled with Ellis, she was looking for someone to support her, read all about her brave husband, and thought she'd give him a trial again.

"Nobody knows where they met or what occurred between them, but one may follow Tony's version. Best let out something about Mary Adams, and after that Alice knew she was on to a good thing. In desperation he told her he was on the way to earning £200, and she could have it if she'd agree to a divorce. She did so, but insisted on coming down south so that she could expose him if he tried to let her down. The moment she stuck out for that, I don't doubt, was the moment that Best first considered murder. In any event, he probably didn't put much faith in her promises.

"Very well: Alice sets out on Wednesday in possession of Philippa's name as a future provider of £200. Her first action the next day is to verify what she'd been told, which explains the girl in the red sports-car seen by Mrs. Amos. It also explains what I meant by saying that Philippa knew too much for Best's safety, or at least that he could never be sure she didn't. Somehow he got to hear about the meeting, and couldn't trust Alice far enough to be sure she hadn't given away the fact of his marriage.

"Yes,"—as Matthews shuffled, "I know what you're going to say. Why didn't Best divorce Alice whether she liked it or whether she didn't? I think the answer is that he was genuinely in love with Mary Adams, who I'm sure had no part whatever in the affair. She's a fine type of girl, as everyone seems to agree, and he didn't want her even to know he'd been married in case she was upset. For that reason the divorce must be carried through quietly in his guise as West, and Alice's help was essential. He didn't feel he could rely on her, but was confident enough about himself to believe he could settle his problems by murder.

"It really seems to be for once a case of evil originating from good: two people had to die because Mary deserved something cleaner than Alice Carter's ex-husband. Best could never give her that in fact, of course, but he did think he could spare her any knowledge of the past. She's the person I'm sorriest for, because she'll suffer most. Dennison still has his career and Harrington his books, but there won't be much for her but bitter memories.

"Well, there Best is in London on August 31st, having seen Oakes and Alice and contemplating murder. He writes to Philippa as agreed, but it strikes me as significant that he didn't give her time to answer before she went to Scotland, or even to run up to town to see him. He undoubtedly knew about the trip: Harrington told us it had been arranged for weeks. It may also be significant that he didn't produce Philippa's first letter to him with the other stuff on Saturday, perhaps because it contained some reference to her meeting with Alice. That's unimportant, though: his destruction of it would fit his role as honest young ambassador. Incidentally, he played the part very well: I feel it was an especially nice touch to return the £200 cheque.

"Back down here, he starts planning in earnest, taking advantage of every fact that allowed him to. In particular, he made use of Ellis's presence and disguise, and all the information he could get from Alice: about Mrs. Topley's habits, that she knew Sergeant Turner, had spied on the girl through the partition, and so on. He wouldn't risk calling at Weatherall Road when the old woman was about because he was taller than Ellis, but I dare say he paid a visit or two on Thursday afternoons.

"Over the actual commission of the crimes I needn't be long. Matters were coming to a climax with Philippa's return from Scotland on October 20th. On Tuesday the 18th he bought the trunk and made his arrangements with Prince, and it's possible that he made sure Ellis would be in the town that day so that he could be duly suspected later. One small point needs mention. Haines, the pawnbroker, said that the purchaser of the trunk carried a suitcase. When Best was dressed as himself, that case would contain his disguise—trench coat, cap, and tinted glasses: when he was appearing as an imitation Ellis, it would contain his own things. The exchange he doubtless effected in the most obvious place, a public lavatory.

"As I say, on Thursday came the climax, and to help him Best employed the unsuspecting Alice. He probably told her he was due to receive the £200 outside the post-office, and invited her to be standing about to see there was no deception. Or perhaps she didn't need an invitation."

"But how could he know Philippa would pay up?" asked the colonel.

"By taking steps to ensure that she did, I expect: by not including *all* the photographs in the bundle at the bank, but a note instead saying 'Other three on presentation of this demand and a cheque' or something like that. The other ways he made use of Alice, I believe, were first by persuading her to steal a pair of legs for him, and by arranging that she should receive a visit from Ellis that Thursday, but get rid of him early. I may be wrong there, though, because I can't think of any reason he could offer why she should do that. Anyway his attempts to throw subsequent suspicion on Ellis were quite the weakest part of his plot, but I'll give my opinion of that later.

"Finally, I suspect, he told Alice that he didn't see any sense in paying the back rent she owed, and suggested that she cleared out instead. He'd arrange all that for her: all he wanted was her door-key. He may even have found out what she'd been wearing in the house that day by some talk of playing a practical joke on Mrs. Topley with the help of the legs: it would provide an explanation why he wanted them. No harm would be done if he didn't succeed, though. We know from Inspector Creevy's report that Alice was untidy: Best could safely assume that any clothes lying about in the room were the ones he wanted, and when all's said and done the important thing was for the dummy to be displaying garments which Mrs. Topley couldn't fail to recognize.

"As soon as Philippa had paid him and set off home at 5.45 he turned to Alice—watching nearby and incidentally getting very wet—and handed her three telegraph forms and a ten-shilling note.

'Send these off for Miss Saunderson,' he says. 'She's in a hurry, and I've got to go and fix up your room. Then we'll celebrate.'

The fact that by leaving Weatherall Road Alice would be letting Ellis down needn't worry her, of course. She knew the man's Tilgate address, as he told us, she knew too that he was keen to get her back, and once she had her share of the £200 she probably intended to leave him flat till next time she was short. His final injunction to her was to meet him on the outskirts of the town at 7.15, when he'd pick her up in the van. I expect he called it a car, though. If she talked about returning to Mrs. Topley's to help he'd turn surly, and threaten that if she didn't do what she was told she wouldn't get a penny. Once he could wave the cheque in her face she wouldn't give much trouble till she got it.

"What happened at 14 Weatherall Road you can guess. It goes without saying that he spent part of the time removing fingerprints from the room. Why? Because that was what Ellis would have done if he'd been guilty. Another task was to turn on the gas-jet on the landing for half a minute or so at seven o'clock, and still another had to do with something I haven't yet dealt with: Best's plan for killing Philippa Saunderson at the bungalow that night."

"Ah, that's what I've been waiting for," said Matthews. "I s'pose it's possible, or you wouldn't be talking so much, but I'm blamed if I can see how."

"Yet it's not so very difficult. He obviously needed a portable supply of coal-gas, but I couldn't think of anything suitable myself till I remembered that pile of flat pneumatic cushions in the cupboard at the bungalow.[7] Best probably saw them when he was looking round to make sure the place would meet his requirements, and realized his weapon was all ready for him. Empty and folded, one would easily go into his suitcase, and when he'd filled it at Mrs. Topley's he'd put it in the cabin trunk. When I went for my walk this afternoon my chief object was to examine those cushions, and the fifth one down distinctly smelt of gas."

"But why anything as large as that?" asked Dickie. "Why not an ordinary penny balloon?"

"Because—so I understand—there isn't enough pressure from household gas-fittings to fill it full enough. Therefore he needed something bigger, and also something that would itself stand pressure when it was ready for use. The procedure with regard to Philippa's death was roughly this, so Dr. Duncan tells me. First

[7] Chapter IX.

Best stunned her and put her on the floor. Then he fitted one end of a thin rubber tube to the outlet valve of the cushion, and inserted the other in one of the girl's nostrils. While she lay unconscious he saw to it that she breathed *in* through the nostril plugged with the tube and *out* through the free one. Apparently that could be managed without much trouble by the correct use of his fingers on her nose and the tubing. Also, every time she breathed in he'd apply pressure to the cushion, to make sure she got a good dose of gas; use the thing as a bellows between his knees, probably. It's pretty horrible and cold-blooded, I know, but then so is premeditated murder of any kind, and at least it was a painless death. Any questions?"

"Why did he put the cushion back?" queried the detective-sergeant.

"Because he didn't dare not to, in case Oakes or the servant ever missed it. To leave the thing smelling of gas was carelessness, of course, but lucky for us. And now is it clear till he picks up Alice in the van?"

"Except how he got to know about the thing," suggested Tony.

"As I said, by reconnaissance. The one he'd seen Deacon and his girl in was just what he wanted, and he made it his business to find out where the thing was kept. As a matter of fact, I shouldn't be at all surprised if he didn't spot it accidentally one day when he was visiting Alice. That the van happened to be garaged next door to where she was living obviously wasn't his doing. But while I remember I'll tell you something else that I think was: the burglaries at the bathing chalets, Colonel. The owners' complaints would almost certainly result in stricter patrolling along the coast road, and give him opportunities for helping his plans along.

"In some ways he went to work very thoroughly, but it mustn't be forgotten that he could take his time. He had several weeks for his preparations, while Philippa was in Scotland, and he wasn't able to get going till she returned. Probably his hardest job during that period was keeping Alice quiet. And, again before I forget, the reason she didn't mention Best to Ellis was because she intended going back to him, especially if his racing system produced better results down south. She told him she was in communication with her husband, of course, but vaguely enough to make him all the keener on reestablishing their former partnership. If he'd ever dreamt that she was really married to a policeman, he'd probably have been off like a bullet however much he liked her. Alice kept quiet, though: she was out for all she could grab.

"Soon after 7.15, then, Best meets her as arranged, and drives towards the bungalow. Only, he never gets there. Instead he turns up Smuggler's Lane, lands Alice one on the jaw that stuns her, and hastily completes the foul business. I imagine he first covered her head with something, possibly his blue trench coat that he wouldn't need again, and then killed her with the chopper he used again later. If so, he doubtless had it in readiness nearby: if not, perhaps he strangled her. Anyway, once she's dead he locks the body in the trunk out of harm's way, together with his disguise and the weapon if there was one. First, of course, he takes out his normal outdoor clothes from his suitcase, which he put into the trunk at Weatherall Road.

"He wouldn't have time to do any more, so he just leaves things like that and clears off home: he wants to be as far away as possible as soon as possible, and every minute counts. Very probably, too, he was feeling a bit upset: remember it was his first murder. It may sound as if he deliberately ran an enormous risk of discovery, but actually it was quite small. The lane's unfrequented and Deacon never went there on Thursdays, as he told the Colonel.

"I suggest that Best's time-table was as follows. He left Mrs. Topley's at 7.15, picked up Alice at 7.17 or 7.18 and was stunning her in Smuggler's Lane at 7.29. That allows eleven minutes for five miles, not quite so good a performance as your own worse effort this afternoon, Tony. Give him four minutes to finish her off and deal with the body, the trunk, and his clothes, and he's ready to start for home by 7.33. That makes him cover the mile and three-quarters till he meets Harrington in twelve minutes: a good show but by no means a world's record.

"In detail, he walks quarter of a mile in 2½ minutes at 6 m.p.h., and sprints the first mile and a half in 9½ minutes, which oughtn't to be beyond the powers of someone who admits he does a bit of running. He couldn't know he'd see Harrington, naturally, but the chance encounter doubtless pleased him.

"We now pass to later that night. By soon after 11.00 he's completed the double journey with the van from Smuggler's Lane to the bungalow and back, and is waiting for Philippa. When she turns up he uses the gas-filled cushion in the way I explained just now, and then sets about the beheading, for which he doubtless undresses. He has until about one o'clock or a bit later until he need start away: in that time he does the dismemberment and afterwards disposes of the trunk and Alice's remains in the sea. As Colonel Bagshaw told us, high water was at 10.32 that night, which means that the tide would do most of his work for him. The bricks from the trunk went into the water too, and the chopper: also one of Oakes's logs, I dare say. The tell-tale legs, being hollow, wouldn't be difficult to break up. The bits either go in his pocket, to be got rid of at leisure, or else he scatters them about the beach. He certainly takes charge of Philippa's £1000, which even in small notes wouldn't need much room.

"What happens to her body we know, of course. Before the mutilation he strips it and puts on instead the green underclothes from the trunk, but leaves the dressing-gown and slippers to establish a further connection between what will be found and what Mrs. Topley saw. He also repeats his mistake with the torn stocking, not knowing which leg Alice had worn it on earlier. Fortunately, Inspector Creevy's report gave me the clue to that.

"By about quarter to one, I expect, he'd finished clearing up some of the mess and was in uniform again. He still has several items to deal with, though: in detail, Philippa's head and hands and feet, her clothes, which go into his suitcase, and the things he wore when impersonating Ellis. Everything but them he's saving for Oakes, and temporarily hides the lot near the bungalow. Then it's time to start for his meeting with Tukes, and a brief word on the way with Dennison if he's still by the Tower.

"He's free again about quarter to two, but naturally goes nowhere near *Cairngorm* as he said. Instead he hurries back to wait for Oakes. The minute the man's arrived and gone indoors he produces Philippa's head and so on from wherever he's hidden them, and puts them inside the car, probably wrapped up in her vest or something thin enough for the blood to soak through. He also gets rid of his suitcase full of her other clothes in the same way, I believe."

"But why?" demanded Dickie. "Isn't it about the daftest thing he can do?"

"Not in my opinion: I think it was the cleverest stroke in the whole business. He knows just how Oakes stands as a blackmailer and taker of rude photographs, and he also knows that the man's got a career to look after. There's a big difference between having a bad reputation for seducing girls, and admitting possession of all the clothes and the severed head of one of them. Especially one he'd been treating as he treated Philippa, too, and he knew that Best at least had heard about that. If he turned up at a police-station with an accurate account of what had happened, what chance was there he'd be believed when the blackmail story came out, as it was bound to? Precious little.

"What he did with the things he found in the Daimler I don't yet know. I expect he stopped on the way back to town and buried the human parts at least, and the suitcase may be in a cloak-room somewhere. I hope we shall find out when he recovers from his breakdown. I should have tackled him the moment we received Atkins's report, of course, only he cracked up first.

"By half past two, then, Best has accomplished everything but the disposal of one trench coat, one check cap, and one pair of spectacles. They'd be easy, but it's difficult to say what happened to the first two things. In all probability he concealed them for the time being, and made adequate arrangements for getting rid of them on Friday. How? Heaven knows—use your imagination. What's the matter with making himself up as a black man and posting them to Australia?[8]

"And now there's not much more to tell. Best's subsequent actions were all designed to make him seem entirely innocent: especially the tentative theory he gave me on Sunday about the man he was supposed to have heard on the beach. That was quite clever, and also the way he refrained from openly implicating Oakes or Dennison.

"The principal intentions of the plot as a whole were first to mislead us about the bodies, and second to prevent the identification of Alice Carter as Alice West, in case anything came out about his marriage. My chief criticism is that he tried to complicate things too much, particularly in the matter of providing suspects. Just think: for Alice's murder there was to be Ellis, primarily, with the mysterious husband in the background if Ellis talked. He doubtless knew enough about the man to be certain he wouldn't talk unless he had to, though. For Philippa's murder there were again to be two scapegoats available, Oakes and Dennison. Neither might have turned up, of course, but since the body in the bungalow was apparently the one from Weatherall Road, Best needn't be unduly upset. It would have meant disposing of the head and clothes elsewhere, and he might have found that troublesome, but there was always the sea again as a last resort.

"What he obviously didn't know about—and I was in the same boat—was the effect of carbon-monoxide poisoning on the colour of blood and brain-substance. He didn't realize that whenever and

---

[8] But Best had not thought of that: they were among his personal effects.

in whatever condition we found a head, we should always be able
to say whether it belonged to the body in the bungalow or not. The
other obvious fault in his plot was the weakness of his attempts to
throw suspicion on Ellis—he simply couldn't stop the man from
having an alibi. The brightest thing, apart from his disposal of the
head and his use of the racket-covers, was the way he overcame
the difference in height between himself and Ellis. At least, I
credit him with having purposely picked out Haines and Prince to
deal with because one was half blind and the other a dwarf: but
that may have been accidental in both cases.

"A curious point was that no one could say positively if the first
body was Philippa's or not: but Best's knowledge from the photographs of what she looked like nude would reassure him that she
hadn't any distinguishing marks such as moles or scars. It was
probably the sight of them which originally gave him the idea of
interchanging the corpses.

"Well, there you are, and if anyone's disappointed all I can say
is that he shouldn't be. As far as you're concerned, Tony, it ought
to prove a genuine surprise ending. Do you remember G.K. Ches-
terton's axiom for detective stories, that the real criminal must be
suspected at least once, and then apparently cleared, whereupon he
becomes theoretically unsuspectable? At one stage you were
nearer to the truth than any of us. All you had to do to make your
idea work—to provide those extra few minutes you needed—was
to realize that no one died at Mrs. Topley's. Once that fact is
grasped there's no question of beheading till midnight or later, and
everything's plain sailing.

"As regards future proceedings, I doubt if any attempt will be
made to convict him for the murder of Alice Carter. They'll concentrate on Philippa's, and there ought to be plenty of evidence
about if somebody looks hard enough. I expect you'll get roped in
for that, Colonel: to find the £1000, I mean, and when and where
he bought the coat and cap and glasses. He must have done that
fairly locally, because he wouldn't know he needed them till after
Ellis came this way in September. Then there's the racket-covers
as well, which may be traceable, and the missing weapon, and
some draper's shop may remember losing a pair of legs. I doubt if
the fingerprints on the bedpost will be his, though: more probably
they were some of Ellis's he missed.

"In respect of this explanation, although I came in at the end I
really seem to have done less than anyone here. The Colonel found
the body and the van—and must have disappointed Best consid-

erably. He probably expected a delay of some days before the bungalow was searched, which would have made the time of death far more vague. As it was, Duncan said right away that if he'd known nothing of the Craybourne affair he'd have gone for somewhere about midnight. However, that bit went wrong, but I understand that Best did his unrehearsed part on Friday night very well. In any case, he could hardly have welcomed another sight of the body.

"To go on with all the things other people did, Matthews supplied the link to Alice Carter's true identity by recognizing the china ornament, and incidentally finding Ellis. Dickie located the second body, Harrington suggested the idea of a dummy, Inspector Creevy's report was invaluable, and Tony excelled himself. He not only spotted the murderer, however dubious his means, but provided the almost certain motive too. I shall hardly feel entitled to what little money I get for joining all those bits together."

"Rot," said Dickie. "None of us could have done it. One point for query, and I'm entirely satisfied. Every time Best went to Craybourne pretending to be Ellis dodging his wife he had to have his disguise with him, and therefore his suitcase. Where did he keep it on other days?"

Beale nodded.

"It's a brute, isn't it?" he agreed. "I've thought and thought, and all I can conclude is that he took the risk of arranging to park it—locked, of course—somewhere in Craybourne: for instance, at a small tobacconist's or newsagent's. If so, he'd collect it and change between the time he left Alice just going to despatch the telegrams and his arrival at Mrs. Topley's. The one fairly sure thing is that he wouldn't dare keep it at Tukes's cottage."[9]

"And one obvious question from me," said Bagshaw. "You included Harrington in your list of possible suspects, but did you ever seriously consider him?"

Beale looked a little guilty.

"As a matter of fact, yes," he answered. "He was the outsider I mentioned to Tony on Sunday afternoon—the one I thought might

---

[9] Beale's surmise was afterwards found to be correct: as also the further fact that Best had been thoughtful enough to provide himself with a second waistcoat-pocket disguise, consisting of a beret and a false moustache, to avoid being recognized by the owner of the sweet-shop he employed.

be better than Best. Quite why I suspected him I can't say: probably because he was so clearly an adept at inventing complications,
and equally clearly aware of his adeptness. However, I'm hoping
you won't press the point too hard: especially as it was his attitude
towards the bungalow body which did so much to defeat the plot."

He turned to the Craybourne Inspector, but no questions were
forthcoming there: only manifest respect and one comment.

"What I can't get over is using those legs for a dummy," declared Creevy. "Why, I must have seen thousands of the things in
my time, but I'd never have thought of that if I were Methuselah."

Beale smiled.

"When you look at stockings in drapers' shop-windows," he
said courteously, "perhaps your mind is actually on higher things."


THE END

# RAMBLE HOUSE's

## HARRY STEPHEN KEELER WEBWORK MYSTERIES

(RH) indicates the title is available ONLY in the RAMBLE HOUSE edition

The Ace of Spades Murder
The Affair of the Bottled Deuce (RH)
The Amazing Web
The Barking Clock
Behind That Mask
The Book with the Orange Leaves
The Bottle with the Green Wax Seal
The Box from Japan
The Case of the Canny Killer
The Case of the Crazy Corpse (RH)
The Case of the Flying Hands (RH)
The Case of the Ivory Arrow
The Case of the Jeweled Ragpicker
The Case of the Lavender Gripsack
The Case of the Mysterious Moll
The Case of the 16 Beans
The Case of the Transparent Nude (RH)
The Case of the Transposed Legs
The Case of the Two-Headed Idiot (RH)
The Case of the Two Strange Ladies
The Circus Stealers (RH)
Cleopatra's Tears
A Copy of Beowulf (RH)
The Crimson Cube (RH)
The Face of the Man From Saturn
Find the Clock
The Five Silver Buddhas
The 4th King
The Gallows Waits, My Lord! (RH)
The Green Jade Hand
Finger! Finger!
Hangman's Nights (RH)
I, Chameleon (RH)
I Killed Lincoln at 10:13! (RH)
The Iron Ring
The Man Who Changed His Skin (RH)
The Man with the Crimson Box
The Man with the Magic Eardrums
The Man with the Wooden Spectacles
The Marceau Case
The Matilda Hunter Murder
The Monocled Monster

The Murder of London Lew
The Murdered Mathematician
The Mysterious Card (RH)
The Mysterious Ivory Ball of Wong Shing
  Li (RH)
The Mystery of the Fiddling Cracksman
The Peacock Fan
The Photo of Lady X (RH)
The Portrait of Jirjohn Cobb
Report on Vanessa Hewstone (RH)
Riddle of the Travelling Skull
Riddle of the Wooden Parrakeet (RH)
The Scarlet Mummy (RH)
The Search for X-Y-Z
The Sharkskin Book
Sing Sing Nights
The Six From Nowhere (RH)
The Skull of the Waltzing Clown
The Spectacles of Mr. Cagliostro
Stand By—London Calling!
The Steeltown Strangler
The Stolen Gravestone (RH)
Strange Journey (RH)
The Strange Will
The Straw Hat Murders (RH)
The Street of 1000 Eyes (RH)
Thieves' Nights
Three Novellos (RH)
The Tiger Snake
The Trap (RH)
Vagabond Nights (Defrauded Yeggman)
Vagabond Nights 2 (10 Hours)
The Vanishing Gold Truck
The Voice of the Seven Sparrows
The Washington Square Enigma
When Thief Meets Thief
The White Circle (RH)
The Wonderful Scheme of Mr. Christopher
  Thorne
X. Jones—of Scotland Yard
Y. Cheung, Business Detective

## Keeler Related Works

**A To Izzard: A Harry Stephen Keeler Companion** by Fender Tucker — Articles and stories about Harry, by Harry, and in his style. Included is a compleat bibliography.

**Wild About Harry: Reviews of Keeler Novels** — Edited by Richard Polt & Fender Tucker — 22 reviews of works by Harry Stephen Keeler from *Keeler News*. A perfect introduction to the author.

**The Keeler Keyhole Collection:** Annotated newsletter rants from Harry Stephen Keeler, edited by Francis M. Nevins. Over 400 pages of incredibly personal Keeleriana.

**Fakealoo** — Pastiches of the style of Harry Stephen Keeler by selected demented members of the HSK Society. Updated every year with the new winner.

# RAMBLE HOUSE's OTHER LOONS

**Strands of the Web: Short Stories of Harry Stephen Keeler** — Edited and Introduced by Fred Cleaver

**The Sam McCain Novels** — Ed Gorman's terrific series includes *The Day the Music Died, Wake Up Little Susie* and *Will You Still Love Me Tomorrow?*

**A Shot Rang Out** — Three decades of reviews from Jon Breen

**Blood Moon** — The first of the Robert Payne series by Ed Gorman

**The Time Armada** — Fox B. Holden's 1953 SF gem.

**Black River Falls** — Suspense from the master, Ed Gorman

**Sideslip** — 1968 SF masterpiece by Ted White and Dave Van Arnam

**The Triune Man** — Mindscrambling science fiction from Richard A. Lupoff

**Detective Duff Unravels It** — Episodic mysteries by Harvey O'Higgins

**Mysterious Martin, the Master of Murder** — Two versions of a strange 1912 novel by Tod Robbins about a man who writes books that can kill.

**The Master of Mysteries** — 1912 novel of supernatural sleuthing by Gelett Burgess

**Dago Red** — 22 tales of dark suspense by Bill Pronzini

**The Night Remembers** — A 1991 Jack Walsh mystery from Ed Gorman

**Rough Cut & New, Improved Murder** — Ed Gorman's first two novels

**Hollywood Dreams** — A novel of the Depression by Richard O'Brien

**Six Gelett Burgess Novels** — *The Master of Mysteries, The White Cat, Two O'Clock Courage, Ladies in Boxes, Find the Woman, The Heart Line*

**The Organ Reader** — A huge compilation of just about everything published in the 1971-1972 radical bay-area newspaper, THE ORGAN.

**A Clear Path to Cross** — Sharon Knowles short mystery stories by Ed Lynskey

**Old Times' Sake** — Short stories by James Reasoner from Mike Shayne Magazine

**Freaks and Fantasies** — Eerie tales by Tod Robbins, collaborator of Tod Browning on the film FREAKS.

**Five Jim Harmon Sleaze Double Novels** — *Vixen Hollow/Celluloid Scandal, The Man Who Made Maniacs/Silent Siren, Ape Rape/Wanton Witch, Sex Burns Like Fire/Twist Session*, and *Sudden Lust/Passion Strip*. More doubles to come!

**Marblehead: A Novel of H.P. Lovecraft** — A long-lost masterpiece from Richard A. Lupoff. Published for the first time!

**The Compleat Ova Hamlet** — Parodies of SF authors by Richard A. Lupoff – New edition!

**The Secret Adventures of Sherlock Holmes** — Three Sherlockian pastiches by the Brooklyn author/publisher, Gary Lovisi.

**The Universal Holmes** — Richard A. Lupoff's 2007 collection of five Holmesian pastiches and a recipe for giant rat stew.

**Four Joel Townsley Rogers Novels** — By the author of *The Red Right Hand: Once In a Red Moon, Lady With the Dice, The Stopped Clock, Never Leave My Bed*

**Two Joel Townsley Rogers Story Collections** — Night of Horror and Killing Time

**Twenty Norman Berrow Novels** — *The Bishop's Sword, Ghost House, Don't Go Out After Dark, Claws of the Cougar, The Smokers of Hashish, The Secret Dancer, Don't Jump Mr. Boland!, The Footprints of Satan, Fingers for Ransom, The Three Tiers of Fantasy, The Spaniard's Thumb, The Eleventh Plague, Words Have Wings, One Thrilling Night, The Lady's in Danger, It Howls at Night, The Terror in the Fog, Oil Under the Window, Murder in the Melody, The Singing Room*

**The N. R. De Mexico Novels** — Robert Bragg presents *Marijuana Girl, Madman on a Drum, Private Chauffeur* in one volume.

**Four Chelsea Quinn Yarbro Novels featuring Charlie Moon** — *Ogilvie, Tallant and Moon, Music When the Sweet Voice Dies, Poisonous Fruit* and *Dead Mice*

**Four Walter S. Masterman Mysteries** — *The Green Toad, The Flying Beast, The Yellow Mistletoe* and *The Wrong Verdict*, fantastic impossible plots. More to come.

**Two Hake Talbot Novels** — *Rim of the Pit, The Hangman's Handyman*. Classic locked room mysteries.

**Two Alexander Laing Novels** — *The Motives of Nicholas Holtz* and *Dr. Scarlett*, stories of medical mayhem and intrigue from the 30s.

**Four David Hume Novels** — *Corpses Never Argue, Cemetery First Stop, Make Way for the Mourners, Eternity Here I Come*, and more to come.

**Three Wade Wright Novels** — *Echo of Fear, Death At Nostalgia Street* and *It Leads to Murder*, with more to come!

**Five Rupert Penny Novels** — *Policeman's Holiday, Policeman's Evidence, Lucky Policeman, Sealed Room Murder* and *Sweet Poison*, classic impossible mysteries.

**Five Jack Mann Novels** — Strange murder in the English countryside. *Gees' First Case, Nightmare Farm, Grey Shapes, The Ninth Life, The Glass Too Many.*

**Seven Max Afford Novels** — *Owl of Darkness, Death's Mannikins, Blood on His Hands, The Dead Are Blind, The Sheep and the Wolves, Sinners in Paradise* and *Two Locked Room Mysteries and a Ripping Yarn* by one of Australia's finest novelists.

**Five Joseph Shallit Novels** — *The Case of the Billion Dollar Body, Lady Don't Die on My Doorstep, Kiss the Killer, Yell Bloody Murder, Take Your Last Look.* One of America's best 50's authors.

**Two Crimson Clown Novels** — By Johnston McCulley, author of the Zorro novels, *The Crimson Clown* and *The Crimson Clown Again.*

**The Best of 10-Story Book** — edited by Chris Mikul, over 35 stories from the literary magazine Harry Stephen Keeler edited.

**A Young Man's Heart** — A forgotten early classic by Cornell Woolrich

**The Anthony Boucher Chronicles** — edited by Francis M. Nevins
Book reviews by Anthony Boucher written for the *San Francisco Chronicle,* 1942 – 1947. Essential and fascinating reading.

**Muddled Mind:** Complete Works of Ed Wood, Jr. — David Hayes and Hayden Davis deconstruct the life and works of a mad genius.

**Gadsby** — A lipogram (a novel without the letter E). Ernest Vincent Wright's last work, published in 1939 right before his death.

**My First Time:** The One Experience You Never Forget — Michael Birchwood — 64 true first-person narratives of how they lost it.

**Automaton** — Brilliant treatise on robotics: 1928-style! By H. Stafford Hatfield

**The Incredible Adventures of Rowland Hern** — Rousing 1928 impossible crimes by Nicholas Olde.

**Slammer Days** — Two full-length prison memoirs: *Men into Beasts* (1952) by George Sylvester Viereck and *Home Away From Home* (1962) by Jack Woodford

**Murder in Black and White** — 1931 classic tennis whodunit by Evelyn Elder

**Killer's Caress** — Cary Moran's 1936 hardboiled thriller

**The Golden Dagger** — 1951 Scotland Yard yarn by E. R. Punshon

**Beat Books #1** — Two beatnik classics, *A Sea of Thighs* by Ray Kainen and *Village Hipster* by J.X. Williams

**A Smell of Smoke** — 1951 English countryside thriller by Miles Burton

**Ruled By Radio** — 1925 futuristic novel by Robert L. Hadfield & Frank E. Farncombe

**Murder in Silk** — A 1937 Yellow Peril novel of the silk trade by Ralph Trevor

**The Case of the Withered Hand** — 1936 potboiler by John G. Brandon

**Finger-prints Never Lie** — A 1939 classic detective novel by John G. Brandon

**Inclination to Murder** — 1966 thriller by New Zealand's Harriet Hunter

**Invaders from the Dark** — Classic werewolf tale from Greye La Spina

**Fatal Accident** — Murder by automobile, a 1936 mystery by Cecil M. Wills

**The Devil Drives** — A prison and lost treasure novel by Virgil Markham

**Dr. Odin** — Douglas Newton's 1933 potboiler comes back to life.

**The Chinese Jar Mystery** — Murder in the manor by John Stephen Strange, 1934

**The Julius Caesar Murder Case** — A classic 1935 re-telling of the assassination by Wallace Irwin that's much more fun than the Shakespeare version

**West Texas War and Other Western Stories** — by Gary Lovisi

**The Contested Earth and Other SF Stories** — A never-before published space opera and seven short stories by Jim Harmon.

**Tales of the Macabre and Ordinary** — Modern twisted horror by Chris Mikul, author of the *Bizarrism* series.

**The Gold Star Line** — Seaboard adventure from L.T. Reade and Robert Eustace.

**The Werewolf vs the Vampire Woman** — Hard to believe ultraviolence by either Arthur M. Scarm or Arthur M. Scram.

**Black Hogan Strikes Again** — Australia's Peter Renwick pens a tale of the outback.

**Don Diablo: Book of a Lost Film** — Two-volume treatment of a western by Paul Landres, with diagrams. Intro by Francis M. Nevins.

**The Charlie Chaplin Murder Mystery** — Movie hijinks by Wes D. Gehring

**The Koky Comics** — A collection of all of the 1978-1981 Sunday and daily comic strips by Richard O'Brien and Mort Gerberg, in two volumes.

**Suzy** — Another collection of comic strips from Richard O'Brien and Bob Vojtko

**Dime Novels: Ramble House's 10-Cent Books** — *Knife in the Dark* by Robert Leslie Bellem, *Hot Lead* and *Song of Death* by Ed Earl Repp, *A Hashish House in New York* by H.H. Kane, and five more.

**Blood in a Snap** — The *Finnegan's Wake* of the 21$^{st}$ century, by Jim Weiler and Al Gorithm

**Stakeout on Millennium Drive** — Award-winning Indianapolis Noir — Ian Woollen.

**Dope Tales #1** — Two dope-riddled classics; *Dope Runners* by Gerald Grantham and *Death Takes the Joystick* by Phillip Condé.

**Dope Tales #2** — Two more narco-classics; *The Invisible Hand* by Rex Dark and *The Smokers of Hashish* by Norman Berrow.

**Dope Tales #3** — Two enchanting novels of opium by the master, Sax Rohmer. *Dope* and *The Yellow Claw.*

**Tenebrae** — Ernest G. Henham's 1898 horror tale brought back.

**The Singular Problem of the Stygian House-Boat** — Two classic tales by John Kendrick Bangs about the denizens of Hades.

**Tiresias** — Psychotic modern horror novel by Jonathan M. Sweet.

**The One After Snelling** — Kickass modern noir from Richard O'Brien.

**The Sign of the Scorpion** — 1935 Edmund Snell tale of oriental evil.

**The House of the Vampire** — 1907 poetic thriller by George S. Viereck.

**An Angel in the Street** — Modern hardboiled noir by Peter Genovese.

**The Devil's Mistress** — Scottish gothic tale by J. W. Brodie-Innes.

**The Lord of Terror** — 1925 mystery with master-criminal, Fantômas.

**The Lady of the Terraces** — 1925 adventure by E. Charles Vivian.

**My Deadly Angel** — 1955 Cold War drama by John Chelton.

**Prose Bowl** — Futuristic satire — Bill Pronzini & Barry N. Malzberg .

**Satan's Den Exposed** — True crime in Truth or Consequences New Mexico — Award-winning journalism by the *Desert Journal*.

**The Amorous Intrigues & Adventures of Aaron Burr** — by Anonymous — Hot historical action.

**I Stole $16,000,000** — A true story by cracksman Herbert E. Wilson.

**The Black Dark Murders** — Vintage 50s college murder yarn by Milt Ozaki, writing as Robert O. Saber.

**Sex Slave** — Potboiler of lust in the days of Cleopatra — Dion Leclerq.

**You'll Die Laughing** — Bruce Elliott's 1945 novel of murder at a practical joker's English countryside manor.

**The Private Journal & Diary of John H. Surratt** — The memoirs of the man who conspired to assassinate President Lincoln.

**Dead Man Talks Too Much** — Hollywood boozer by Weed Dickenson

**Red Light** — History of legal prostitution in Shreveport Louisiana by Eric Brock. Includes wonderful photos of the houses and the ladies.

**A Snark Selection** — Lewis Carroll's *The Hunting of the Snark* with two Snarkian chapters by Harry Stephen Keeler — Illustrated by Gavin L. O'Keefe.

**Ripped from the Headlines!** — The Jack the Ripper story as told in the newspaper articles in the *New York* and *London Times.*

**Geronimo** — S. M. Barrett's 1905 autobiography of a noble American.

**The White Peril in the Far East** — Sidney Lewis Gulick's 1905 indictment of the West and assurance that Japan would never attack the U.S.

**The Compleat Calhoon** — All of Fender Tucker's works: Includes *The Totah Trilogy, Weed, Women and Song* and *Tales from the Tower*, plus a CD of all of his songs.

# RAMBLE HOUSE
Fender Tucker, Prop.
www.ramblehouse.com    fender@ramblehouse.com
228-826-1783   10329 Sheephead Drive, Vancleave MS 39565